Grimm's Fairy Tales

By

Jacob Grimm and Wilhelm Grimm

Edited By

FRANCES JENKINS OLCOTT

Illustrations by

RIE CRAMER

HE SAID, "LITTLE TABLE SET THYSELF!"

GRIMM'S FAIRY TALES

EDITED BY

FRANCES JENKINS OLCOTT

Illustrated By

Rie Cramer

THE PENN PUBLISHING
COMPANY PHILADELPHIA
1927

Grimm's Fairy Tales
Printed in the U. S. A.

FOREWORD

To our American boys and girls is offered this volume which is really Grimm's *Fairy Tales*, not an abridgment superficial and colorless, nor an insipid retelling of the stories.

This edition is based on the Hunt version, with an introduction by the folk-lorist, Andrew Lang. The Hunt version is considered a most accurate English translation.

From the full collection, fifty-one stories suitable for children have been selected. Among these are famous tales as well as many delightful ones not usually included in children's volumes.

Where the Hunt wording is too stilted, the text of the *Hausmärchen* itself has been followed. The very long sentences have been subdivided. While that quaint old-fashioned translation, illustrated with woodcuts by Wehnert, has contributed its bit of folk phraseology. The Editor's desire is to restore to the children as large a collection as possible of Grimm's *Fairy Tales* unmutilated in their literary perfection.

The illustrations are by the well-known Dutch artist, Mrs. Rie Cramer. Some of Rie Cramer's other fairy tale pictures published in England, are said by admiring critics there, to be very charming, of exceptional merit, and to have high artistic merit of their own.

Her illustrations for Grimm are particularly harmonious in color, while their quaint charm grows on one more and more as one lives with them. They are fanciful or humorous. They have the quality, rare in fairy tales, of actually illustrating their text. This will mean added pleasure to the children. Rie Cramer's little black and white headings are particularly pretty and graceful in outline.

The tales are presented here in their original form, with nothing left out of child-heartedness, humor, poetic feeling, and delicate sentiment and fancy. Indeed, it is all here—the poesy and purity which those profound and child-loving scholars, the

Brothers Grimm, retained in the old folk-tales which, with so much pains, they gathered largely from among the peasant-folk themselves.

And the Brothers explained, in their preface, that they had planned the volume as an educational book as well as one for scholars; for which reason they had eliminated everything which they feared might harm the children. But since the Brothers issued their book, about a hundred years ago, educational requirements of what is ethically best for children have materially advanced. Therefore, in this book, a few other parts unsuitable for children have been omitted.

So now this volume of Grimm's *Fairy Tales* is offered to our American boys and girls; and may they have continued delight in the beautiful old folk-fictions, which have come down to us from the fresh and sparkling meadows and woods of ancient days.

Fathers and mothers, too, will enjoy reading the tales aloud and sharing with the children the humor and the deep but simple ethical truths so tenderly and poetically set forth therein.

Teachers and story-tellers, also, may find in this sincere version, rich material for kindling the imagination and feeding the poetic fancy of their pupils.

The Editor,
Frances Jenkins Olcott.

ACKNOWLEDGMENTS

The Editor's acknowledgments are due to the following texts:

Kinder und Hausmärchen, following the last edition authorized by William Grimm with the Grimm Introduction on the origin and educational use of the tales.

Household Stories, illustrated by Wehnert, first published in London, 1853.

But most especially to *Household Tales*, with the Author's notes, translated by Margaret Hunt, introduction by Andrew Lang, Bohn Library.

For the use of the Hunt text the Editor gratefully acknowledges the gracious permission of Messrs. Harcourt, Brace and Company, American Publishers of the Bohn Library.

CONTENTS

ILLUSTRATIONS

GRIMM'S FAIRY TALES

THE FROG-KING; OR, IRON HENRY

In old times, when wishing was having, there lived a King whose daughters were all beautiful, but the youngest was so beautiful that the sun itself, which has seen so much, was astonished whenever it shone in her face.

Close by the King's castle lay a great dark forest, and under an old lime-tree in the forest, was a fountain. When the day was very warm, the King's Child went out into the forest and sat down by the side of the cool fountain, and when she was dull she took a golden ball, and threw it up in the air and caught it. And this ball was her favorite plaything.

Now, it so happened one day, the King's Daughter's golden ball did not fall into the little hand which she was holding up for it, but on to the ground, and rolled straight into the water. The King's Daughter followed it with her eyes; but it vanished, and the well was deep, so deep that the bottom could not be seen. On this she began to cry, and cried louder and louder, and could not be comforted.

And as she thus lamented, some one said to her, "What ails you, King's Daughter? You weep so that even a stone would show pity."

She looked round to the side from whence the voice came, and saw a Frog stretching its thick, ugly head from the water. "Ah! old water-splasher, is it you?" said she; "I am weeping for my golden ball, which has fallen into the fountain."

"Be quiet, and do not weep," answered the Frog, "I can help you. But what will you give me if I bring your plaything up again?"

"Whatever you will have, dear Frog," said she—"my clothes, my pearls and jewels, and even the golden crown which I am wearing."

The Frog answered, "I do not care for your clothes, your pearls and jewels, or your golden crown, but if you will love me and let me be your companion and playfellow, and sit by you at your little table, and eat off your little golden plate, and drink out of your little cup, and sleep in your little bed—if you will promise me this, I will go down below, and bring your golden ball up again."

"Oh, yes," said she, "I promise you all you wish, if you will but bring my ball back again." She, however, thought, "How the silly Frog does talk! He lives in the water with the other frogs and croaks, and can be no companion to any human being!"

But the Frog, when he had received this promise, put his head into the water and sank down. In a short time he came swimming up again with the ball in his mouth, and threw it on the grass. The King's Daughter was delighted to see her pretty plaything once more, and picked it up, and ran away with it.

"Wait, wait," said the Frog. "Take me with you. I can't run as you can." But what did it avail him to scream his *croak, croak,* after her, as loudly as he could? She did not listen to it, but ran home and soon forgot the poor Frog, who was forced to go back into his fountain again.

The next day, when she had seated herself at table with the King and all the courtiers, and was eating from her little golden plate, something came creeping *splish splash, splish splash,* up the marble staircase. When it got to the top, it knocked at the door, and cried:

"*King's Daughter, youngest.*
Open the door!"

She ran to see who was outside, but when she opened the door, there sat the Frog in front of it. Then she slammed the door in great haste, sat down to dinner again, and was quite frightened.

The King saw plainly that her heart was beating violently, and said, "My Child, what are you so afraid of? Is there a Giant outside who wants to carry you away?"

"Ah, no," replied she, "it is no Giant, but a disgusting Frog."

"What does the Frog want with you?"

"Ah, dear Father, yesterday when I was in the forest sitting by the fountain, playing, my golden ball fell into the water. And because I cried so, the Frog brought it out again for me. And because he insisted so on it, I promised him he should be my companion; but I never thought he would be able to come out of the water! And now he is here, and wants to come in."

In the meantime, it knocked a second time, and cried:

"*King's Daughter, youngest!*
Open to me!
Don't you remember yesterday,
And all that you to me did say,
Beside the cooling fountain's spray?
King's Daughter, youngest!
Open to me!"

Then said the King, "That which you have promised you must perform. Go and let him in."

She went and opened the door, and the Frog hopped in and followed her, step by step, to her chair. There he sat still and cried, "Lift me up beside you."

She delayed, until at last the King commanded her to do it. When the Frog was once on the chair, he wanted to be on the table, and when he was on the table, he said, "Now, push your little golden plate nearer to me that we may eat together."

She did this, but it was easy to see that she did not do it willingly. The Frog enjoyed what he ate, but almost every mouthful she took, choked her.

At length he said, "I have eaten and am satisfied. Now I am tired, carry me into your little room and make your little silken bed ready; and we will both lie down and go to sleep."

The King's Daughter began to cry, for she was afraid of the cold Frog, which she did not like to touch, and which was now to sleep in her pretty, clean little bed.

But the King grew angry and said, "He who helped you when you were in trouble, ought not afterward to be despised."

So she took hold of the Frog with two fingers, carried him upstairs, and put him in a corner. But when she was in bed, he crept to her and said, "I am tired, I want to sleep as well as you; lift me up or I will tell your father."

Then she was terribly angry, and took him up and threw him with all her might against the wall.

"Now, you will be quiet, odious Frog," said she.

But when he fell down, he was no Frog but a King's Son with beautiful kind eyes!

He, by her father's will, was now her dear companion and husband. Then he told her how he had been bewitched by a wicked Witch, and how no one could have delivered him from the fountain but herself, and that to-morrow they would go together into his kingdom.

Then they went to sleep, and next morning when the sun awoke them, a coach came rolling up drawn by eight white horses, with white ostrich feathers on their heads. They were harnessed with golden chains, and behind stood the young King's servant, Faithful Henry. Faithful Henry had been so unhappy when his master was changed into a Frog, that he had three iron bands laid round his heart, lest it should burst with grief and sadness.

The coach was to conduct the young King into his kingdom. Faithful Henry helped them both in, and placed himself behind again, and was full of joy because of this deliverance.

And when they had driven a part of the way, the King's Son heard a cracking behind him as if something had broken. So he turned round and cried:

"Henry, the coach does break!"
"No, no, my lord, you do mistake!
It is the band around my heart,
That felt such great and bitter smart,
When you were in the fountain strange,
When you into a Frog were changed!"

Again and once again, while they were on their way, something cracked; and each time the King's Son thought the carriage was breaking. But it was only the bands which were springing from the heart of Faithful Henry because his master was set free and was happy.

THE WOLF AND THE SEVEN LITTLE KIDS

There was once on a time, an old Goat who had seven little Kids, and loved them with all the love of a mother for her children.

One day, she wanted to go into the forest and fetch some food. So she called all seven to her and said, "Dear Children, I have to go into the forest. Be on your guard against the Wolf. If he come in, he will devour you all—skin, hair, and all. The wretch often disguises himself; but you will know him at once by his rough voice and his black feet."

The Kids said, "Dear Mother, we will take good care of ourselves. You may go away without any anxiety."

Then the old one bleated, and went on her way with an easy mind.

It was not long before some one knocked at the house-door, and cried, "Open the door, dear Children! Your mother is here, and has brought something back with her for each of you."

But the little Kids knew that it was the Wolf, by his rough voice. "We will not open the door," cried they; "you are not our mother. She has a soft, pleasant voice, but your voice is rough. You are the Wolf!"

Then the Wolf went away to a shopkeeper, and bought a great lump of chalk, ate this and made his voice soft with it. Then he came back, knocked at the door of the house, and cried, "Open the door, dear Children! Your mother is here and has brought something back with her for each of you."

But the Wolf had laid his black paws against the window, and the children saw them, and cried, "We will not open the door, our mother has not black feet like you. You are the Wolf!"

Then the Wolf ran to a baker, and said, "I have hurt my feet, rub some dough over them for me."

And when the baker had rubbed his feet over, he ran to the miller and said, "Strew some white meal over my feet for me." The miller thought to himself, "The Wolf wants to deceive some one," and refused. But the Wolf said, "If you will not do it, I will devour you." Then the miller was afraid, and made his paws white for him. Yes! so are men!

Now, the wretch went for the third time to the house-door, knocked at it, and said, "Open the door for me, Children! Your dear little mother has come home, and has brought every one of you something from the forest with her."

The little Kids cried, "First show us your paws that we may know if you are our dear little mother."

Then he put his paws in through the window. And when the Kids saw that they were white, they believed all that he said, and opened the door. But who should come in but *the Wolf*!

They were terrified and wanted to hide themselves. One sprang under the table, the second into the bed, the third into the stove, the fourth into the kitchen, the fifth into the cupboard, the sixth under the washing-bowl, and the seventh into the clock-casc. But thc Wolf found them all and made no delay, but swallowed one after the other down his throat. The youngest in the clock-case was the only one he did not find.

THE LITTLE KIDS CRIED, "FIRST SHOW US YOUR PAWS"

When the Wolf had satisfied his appetite, he took himself off, laid himself down under a tree in the green meadow outside, and began to sleep.

Soon afterward, the old Goat came home again from the forest. Ah! what a sight she saw there! The house-door stood wide open. The table, chairs, and benches were thrown down, the washing-bowl lay broken to pieces, and the quilts and pillows were pulled off the bed.

She sought her children, but they were nowhere to be found. She called them one after another by name, but no one answered. At last, when she called the youngest, a soft voice cried, "Dear Mother, I am in the clock-case."

She took the Kid out, and it told her that the Wolf had come and had eaten all the others. Then you may imagine how she wept over her poor children!

At length, in her grief she went out, and the youngest Kid ran with her. When they came to the meadow, there lay the Wolf by the tree and he was snoring so loud that the branches shook. She looked at him on every side and saw that something was moving and struggling in his stomach. "Ah!" said she, "is it possible that my poor children, whom he has swallowed down for his supper, can be still alive?"

Then the Kid had to run home and fetch scissors, and a needle and thread, and the Goat cut open the monster's stomach. Hardly had she made one cut, than a little Kid thrust its head out, and when she had cut farther, all six sprang out one after another, and were all still alive, and had suffered no hurt whatever, for in his greediness the monster had swallowed them whole.

What rejoicing there was! They embraced their dear mother, and jumped like a tailor at his wedding. The mother, however, said, "Now go and look for some big stones. We will fill the wicked beast's stomach with them, while he is asleep."

Then the seven Kids dragged the stones thither with all speed, and put as many of them into his stomach as they could get in. And the mother sewed him up again in the greatest haste; so that he was not aware of anything and never once stirred.

When the Wolf had had his sleep out, he got on his legs, and as the stones in his stomach made him very thirsty, he wanted to go to a well to drink. But when he began to walk and to move about, the stones in his stomach knocked against each other and rattled. Then cried he:

"*What rumbles and tumbles*
Against my poor bones?
I thought 'twas six Kids,
But it's only big stones!"

And when he got to the well and stooped over the water and was just about to drink, the heavy stones made him fall in. There was no help for it, but he had to drown miserably!

When the seven Kids saw that, they came running to the spot and cried aloud, "The Wolf is dead! The Wolf is dead!" and danced for joy round about the well with their mother.

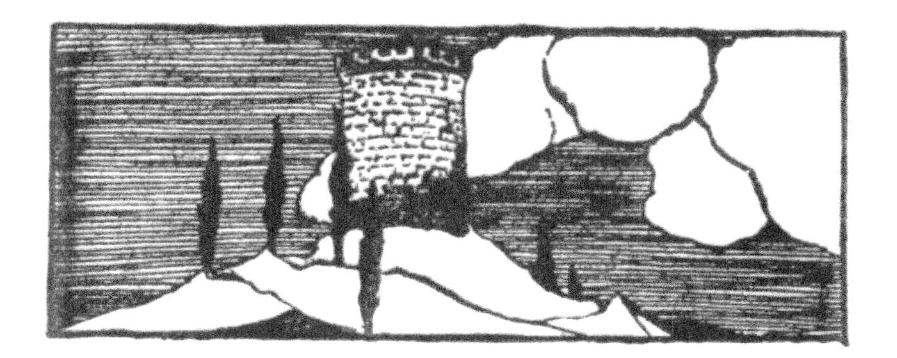

RAPUNZEL

There was once a man and a woman, who had long in vain wished for a child. At length, the woman hoped that God was about to grant her desire.

These people had a little window at the back of their house from which a splendid garden could be seen. It was full of the most beautiful flowers and herbs. It was, however, surrounded by a high wall, and no one dared to go into it because it belonged to a Witch, who had great power and was dreaded by all the world.

One day, the woman was standing by this window and looking down into the garden, when she saw a bed which was planted with the most beautiful rampion (rapunzel), and it looked so fresh and green that she longed for it, and had the greatest desire to eat some.

This desire increased every day, and as she knew that she could not get any of it, she quite pined away, and looked pale and miserable.

Then her husband was alarmed, and asked, "What ails you, dear Wife?"

"Ah," she replied, "if I can't get some of the rampion to eat, which is in the garden behind our house, I shall die."

The man, who loved her, thought, "Sooner than let your wife die, bring her some of the rampion yourself, let it cost you what it will!"

In the twilight of evening, he clambered over the wall into the garden of the Witch, hastily clutched a handful of rampion, and took it to his wife. She at once made herself a salad of it, and ate it with much relish.

She, however, liked it so much—so very much—that the next day she longed for it three times as much as before. If he was to have any rest, her husband must once more descend into the garden. In the gloom of evening, therefore, he let himself down again. But when he had clambered down the wall he was terribly afraid, for he saw the Witch standing before him.

"How dare you," said she with angry look, "descend into my garden and steal my rampion like a thief? You shall suffer for it!"

"Ah," answered he, "let mercy take the place of justice! I had to do it out of necessity. My wife saw your rampion from the window, and felt such a longing for it that she would have died, if she had not got some to eat."

Then the Witch let her anger be softened, and said to him, "If the case be as you say, I will allow you to take away with you as much rampion as you will, only I make one condition, you must give me the child which your wife will bring into the world. It shall be well treated, and I will care for it like a mother."

The man in his terror consented to everything, and when the woman at last had a little daughter, the Witch appeared at once, gave the child the name of Rapunzel, and took it away with her.

Rapunzel grew into the most beautiful child beneath the sun. When she was twelve years old, the Witch shut her into a tower, which lay in a forest, and had neither stairs nor door. But quite at the top was a little window. When the Witch wanted to go in, she placed herself beneath this, and cried:

"*Rapunzel, Rapunzel,*
Let down thy hair."

Rapunzel had magnificent long hair, fine as spun gold, and when she heard the voice of the Witch, she unfastened her braided tresses and wound them round one of the hooks of the window above. And then the hair fell twenty ells down, and the Witch climbed up by it.

After a year or two, it came to pass that the King's Son rode through the forest and went by the tower. Then he heard a song, which was so charming that he stood still and listened. This was Rapunzel, who in her solitude passed her time in letting her sweet voice resound.

The King's Son wanted to climb up to her, and looked for the door of the tower, but none was to be found. He rode home, but the singing had so deeply touched his heart, that every day he went out into the forest and listened to it.

Once when he was thus standing behind a tree, he saw that a Witch came there, and he heard how she cried:

"*Rapunzel, Rapunzel,*
Let down thy hair."

Then Rapunzel let down the braids of her hair, and the Witch climbed up to her.

"If that is the ladder by which one mounts, I will for once try my fortune," said he.

The next day when it began to grow dark, he went to the tower and cried:

"*Rapunzel, Rapunzel,*
Let down thy hair."

Immediately the hair fell down, and the King's Son climbed up.

At first Rapunzel was terribly frightened when a man, such as her eyes had never yet beheld, came to her. But the King's Son began to talk to her quite like a friend, and told her that his heart had been so stirred, that it had let him have no rest, so he had been forced to see her.

Then Rapunzel lost her fear, and when he asked her if she would take him for her husband, and she saw that he was young and handsome, she thought, "He will love me more than old Dame Gothel does;" and she said yes, and laid her hand in his.

She said also, "I will willingly go away with you, but I do not know how to get down. Bring with you a skein of silk every time that you come, and I will weave a ladder with it. When that is ready I will descend, and you will take me on your horse."

They agreed that until that time, he should come to her every evening, for the old woman came by day. The Witch remarked nothing of this, until once Rapunzel said to her, "Tell me, Dame Gothel, how it happens that you are so much heavier for me to draw up, than the young King's Son—he is with me in a moment."

"Ah! you wicked Child!" cried the Witch. "What do I hear you say! I thought I had separated you from all the world, and yet you have deceived me!"

In her anger she clutched Rapunzel's beautiful tresses, wrapped them twice round her left hand, seized a pair of scissors with the right, and *snip, snap,* they were cut off, and the lovely braids lay on the ground. And she was so pitiless that she took poor Rapunzel into a desert, where she had to live in great grief and misery.

On the same day, however, that she cast out Rapunzel, the Witch, in the evening, fastened the braids of hair which she had cut off, to the hook of the window; and when the King's Son came and cried:

"Rapunzel, Rapunzel,
Let down thy hair,"

she let the hair down.

The King's Son ascended. He did not find his dearest Rapunzel above, but the Witch, who gazed at him with wicked and venomous looks.

"Aha!" she cried mockingly, "you would fetch your dearest! But the beautiful bird sits no longer singing in the nest. The cat has got it, and will scratch out your eyes as well. Rapunzel is lost to you! You will never see her more!"

The King's Son was beside himself with grief and in his despair he leapt down from the tower. He escaped with his life, but the thorns into which he fell, pierced his eyes. Then he wandered quite blind about the forest, ate nothing but roots and berries, and did nothing but lament and weep over the loss of his dearest wife.

Thus he roamed about in misery for some years, and at length came to the desert where Rapunzel lived in wretchedness. He heard a voice, and it seemed so familiar to him that he went toward it. When he approached, Rapunzel knew him, and fell on his neck and wept. Two of her tears wetted his eyes and they grew clear again, and he could see with them as before.

He led her to his Kingdom where he was joyfully received, and they lived for a long time, happy and contented.

LITTLE BROTHER AND LITTLE SISTER

Little brother took his little sister by the hand and said, "Since our mother died, we have had no happiness; our stepmother beats us every day, and if we come near her, she kicks us away with her foot. Our meals are the hard crusts of bread that are left over. The little dog under the table is better off, for she often throws it a nice bit. May Heaven pity us! If our mother only knew! Come, we will go forth together into the wide world."

They walked the whole day over meadows, fields, and stony places; and when it rained the little sister said, "Heaven and our hearts are weeping together."

In the evening they came to a large forest, and they were so weary with sorrow and hunger and the long walk, that they lay down in a hollow tree and fell asleep.

The next day when they awoke, the sun was already high and shone down hot into the tree. Then the little brother said, "Little Sister, I am thirsty. If I knew of a little brook I would go and take a drink. I think I hear one running." The little brother got up and took the little sister by the hand, and they set off to find the brook.

But the wicked stepmother was a Witch, and had seen how the two children had gone away. She had crept after them, as Witches do creep, and had bewitched all the brooks in the forest.

Now, when they found a little brook leaping brightly over the stones, the little brother was going to drink out of it, but the little sister heard how it said as it ran:

"Who drinks of me, a Tiger be!
Who drinks of me, a Tiger be!"

Then the little sister cried, "Pray, dear little Brother, do not drink, or you will become a wild beast, and tear me to pieces."

The little brother did not drink, although he was so thirsty, but said, "I will wait for the next spring."

When they came to the next brook, the little sister heard this say:

"Who drinks of me, a wild Wolf be!
Who drinks of me, a wild Wolf be!"

Then the little sister cried out, "Pray, dear little Brother, do not drink, or you will become a Wolf, and devour me."

The little brother did not drink, and said, "I will wait until we come to the next spring, but then I must drink, say what you like; for my thirst is too great."

And when they came to the third brook, the little sister heard how it said as it ran:

"Who drinks of me, a Roebuck be!
Who drinks of me, a Roebuck be!"

The little sister said, "Oh, I pray you, dear little Brother, do not drink, or you will become a Roe, and run away from me."

But the little brother had knelt by the brook, and had bent down and drunk some of the water. And as soon as the first drops touched his lips, he lay there a young Roe.

And now the little sister wept over her poor bewitched little brother, and the little Roe wept also, and sat sorrowfully near to her. But at last the girl said, "Be quiet, dear little Roe, I will never, never leave you."

Then she untied her golden garter and put it round the Roe's neck, and she plucked rushes and wove them into a soft cord. With this she tied the little animal and led it on; and she walked deeper and deeper into the forest.

And when they had gone a very long way, they came to a little house. The girl looked in; and as it was empty, she thought, "We can stay here and live."

Then she sought for leaves and moss to make a soft bed for the Roe. Every morning she went out and gathered roots and berries and nuts for herself, and brought tender grass for the Roe, who ate out of her hand, and was content and played round about her. In the evening, when the little sister was tired, and had said her prayer, she laid her head upon the Roe's back: that was her pillow, and she slept softly on it. And if only the little brother had had his human form, it would have been a delightful life.

For some time, they were alone like this in the wilderness. But it happened that the King of the country held a great hunt in the forest. Then the blasts of the horns, the barking of dogs, and the merry shouts of the huntsmen rang through the trees, and the Roe heard all, and was only too anxious to be there.

"Oh," said he to his little sister, "let me be off to the hunt, I cannot bear it any longer;" and he begged so much that at last she agreed.

"But," said she to him, "come back to me in the evening. I must shut my door for fear of the rough huntsmen, so knock and say, 'My little Sister, let me in!' that I may know you. And if you do not say that, I shall not open the door."

Then the young Roe sprang away; so happy was he and so merry in the open air.

The King and the huntsmen saw the pretty creature, and started after him. But they could not catch him, and when they thought that they surely had him, away he sprang through the bushes and was gone.

When it was dark he ran to the cottage, knocked, and said, "My little Sister, let me in." Then the door was opened for him, and he jumped in, and rested himself the whole night through upon his soft bed.

The next day, the hunt went on afresh, and when the Roe again heard the bugle-horn, and the *ho! ho!* of the huntsmen, he had no peace, but said, "Sister, let me out, I must be off."

His sister opened the door for him, and said, "But you must be here again in the evening and say your password."

When the King and his huntsmen again saw the young Roe with the golden collar, they all chased him, but he was too quick and nimble for them. This went on for the whole day, but by evening the huntsmen had surrounded him, and one of them wounded him a little in the foot, so that he limped and ran slowly. Then a hunter crept after him to the cottage and heard how he said, "My little Sister, let me in," and saw that the door was opened for him, and was shut again at once.

The huntsman took notice of it all, and went to the King and told him what he had seen and heard. Then the King said, "To-morrow we will hunt once more."

The little sister, however, was dreadfully frightened when she saw that her little Roe was hurt. She washed the blood off him, laid herbs on the wound, and said, "Go to your bed, dear Roe, that you may get well again."

But the wound was so slight that the Roe, next morning, did not feel it any more. And when he again heard the sport outside, he said, "I cannot bear it, I must be there. They shall not find it so easy to catch me!"

The little sister cried, and said, "This time they will kill you, and here am I alone in the forest, and forsaken by all the world. I will not let you out."

"Then you will have me die of grief," answered the Roe. "When I hear the bugle-horns I feel as if I must jump out of my skin."

Then the little sister could not do otherwise, but opened the door for him with a heavy heart, and the Roe, full of health and joy, bounded away into the forest.

When the King saw him, he said to his huntsman, "Now chase him all day long till nightfall, but take care that no one does him any harm."

As soon as the sun had set, the King said to the huntsmen, "Now come and show me the cottage in the wood;" and when he was at the door, he knocked and called out, "Dear little Sister, let me in."

Then the door opened, and the King walked in, and there stood a maiden more lovely than any he had ever seen. The maiden was frightened when she saw, not her little Roe, but a man with a golden crown upon his head. But the King looked kindly at her, stretched out his hand, and said:

"Will you go with me to my palace and be my dear wife?"

"Yes, indeed," answered the maiden, "but the little Roe must go with me. I cannot leave him."

The King said, "He shall stay with you as long as you live, and shall want nothing."

Just then he came running in, and the little sister again tied him with the cord of rushes, took it in her own hand, and went away with the King from the cottage.

The King took the lovely maiden upon his horse and carried her to his palace, where the wedding was held with great pomp. She was now the Queen, and they lived for a long time happily together. The Roe was tended and cherished, and ran about in the palace-garden.

But the wicked Witch, because of whom the children had gone out into the world, thought all the time that the little sister had been torn to pieces by the wild beasts in the wood, and that the little brother had been shot for a Roe by the huntsmen. Now when she heard that they were so happy, and so well off, envy and hatred rose in her heart and left her no peace, and she thought of nothing but how she could bring them again to misfortune.

THE KING SAID, "WILL YOU BE MY DEAR WIFE?"

Her own daughter, who was as ugly as night, and had only one eye, grumbled at her and said, "A Queen! that ought to have been my luck."

"Only be quiet," answered the old woman, and comforted her by saying, "when the time comes I shall be ready."

As time went on, the Queen had a pretty little boy. It happened that the King was out hunting; so the old Witch took the form of the chambermaid, went into the room where the Queen lay, and said to her, "Come, the bath is ready. It will do you good, and give you fresh strength. Make haste before it gets cold."

The daughter also was close by; so they carried the weak Queen into the bathroom, and put her into the bath. Then they shut the door and ran away. But in the bathroom they had made a fire of such deadly heat, that the beautiful young Queen was soon suffocated.

When this was done, the old woman took her daughter, put a nightcap on her head, and laid her in bed in place of the Queen. She gave her too the shape and the look of the Queen, only she could not make good the lost eye. But, in order that the King might not see it, she was to lie on the side on which she had no eye.

In the evening, when he came home and heard that he had a son, he was heartily glad, and was going to the bed of his dear wife to see how she was. But the old woman quickly called out, "For your life leave the curtains closed. The Queen ought not to see the light yet, and must have rest."

The King went away, and did not find out that a false Queen was lying in the bed.

But at midnight, when all slept, the nurse, who was sitting in the nursery by the cradle, and who was the only person awake, saw the door open and the true Queen walk in. She took the child out of the cradle, laid it on her arm and nursed it. Then she shook up its pillow, laid the child down again, and covered it with the little quilt. And she did not forget the Roe, but went into the corner where he lay, and stroked his back. Then she went quite silently out of the door again.

The next morning, the nurse asked the guards whether any one had come into the palace during the night, but they answered, "No, we have seen no one."

She came thus many nights and never spoke a word. The nurse always saw her, but she did not dare to tell any one about it.

When some time had passed in this manner, the Queen began to speak in the night, and said:

"How fares my child, how fares my Roe?
Twice shall I come, then never moe!"

The nurse did not answer, but when the Queen had gone again, went to the King and told him all.

The King said, "Ah, heavens! what is this? To-morrow night I will watch by the child."

In the evening he went into the nursery, and at midnight the Queen again appeared, and said:

"How fares my child, how fares my Roe?
Once shall I come, then never moe!"

And she nursed the child as she was wont to do before she disappeared. The King dared not speak to her, but on the next night he watched again. Then she said:

"How fares my child, How fares my Roe?
This time I come, then never moe!"

At that the King could not restrain himself. He sprang toward her, and said, "You can be none other than my dear wife."

She answered, "Yes, I am your dear wife," and at the same moment she received life again, and by God's grace became fresh, rosy, and full of health.

Then she told the King the evil deed which the wicked Witch and her daughter had been guilty of toward her. The King ordered both to be led before the judge, and judgment was delivered against them. The daughter was taken into the forest where she was torn to pieces by wild beasts, but the Witch was cast into the fire and miserably burnt.

And as soon as she was burnt the Roe changed his shape, and received his human form again. So the little sister and little brother lived happily together all their lives.

THE STAR-MONEY

There was once on a time, a little girl whose father and mother were dead. She was so poor that she no longer had any little room to live in, or bed to sleep in. At last, she had nothing else but the clothes she was wearing and a little bit of bread in her hand which some charitable soul had given her. She was, however, good and pious.

And as she was thus forsaken by all the world, she went forth into the open country, trusting in the good God.

Then a poor man met her, who said, "Ah, give me something to eat, I am so hungry!"

She reached him the whole of her piece of bread, and said, "May God bless it to your use," and went onward.

Then came a child who moaned and said, "My head is so cold, give me something to cover it with."

So she took off her hood and gave it to him.

And when she had walked a little farther, she met another child who had no jacket and was frozen with cold. Then she gave it her own.

A little farther on one begged for a frock, and she gave away that also.

At length, she got into a forest and it had already become dark, and there came yet another child, and asked for a little shirt.

The good little girl thought to herself, “It is a dark night and no one sees me. I can very well give my little shirt away,” and took it off, and gave away that also.

And she so stood, and had not one single thing left. Then suddenly some Stars from heaven fell down, and they were nothing else but hard smooth pieces of money! And although she had just given her little shirt away, lo! she had a new one which was of the very finest linen.

Then she gathered together the money into this, and was rich all the days of her life.

THE FISHERMAN AND HIS WIFE

There was once on a time, a Fisherman who lived with his wife in a miserable hovel close by the sea, and every day he went out fishing. And once, as he was sitting with his rod, looking at the clear water, his line suddenly went down, far down below, and when he drew it up again, he brought out a large Flounder.

Then the Flounder said to him: "Hark, you Fisherman, I pray you, let me live. I am no Flounder really, but an enchanted Prince. What good will it do you to kill me? I should not be good to eat. Put me in the water again, and let me go."

"Come," said the Fisherman, "there is no need for so many words about it—a fish that can talk I should certainly let go, anyhow."

With that he put him back again into the clear water, and the Flounder went to the bottom, leaving a long streak of blood behind him. Then the Fisherman got up and went home to his wife in the hovel.

"Husband," said the woman, "have you caught nothing to-day?"

"No," said the man, "I did catch a Flounder, who said he was an enchanted Prince, so I let him go again."

"Did you not wish for anything first?" said the woman.

"No," said the man; "what should I wish for?"

"Ah," said the woman, "it is surely hard to have to live always in this dirty hovel. You might have wished for a small cottage for us. Go back and call him. Tell him we want to have a small cottage. He will certainly give us that."

"Ah," said the man, "why should I go there again?"

"Why," said the woman, "you did catch him, and you let him go again. He is sure to do it. Go at once."

The man still did not quite like to go, but did not want to oppose his wife, and went to the sea.

When he got there the sea was all green and yellow, and no longer smooth. So he stood and said:

"*Flounder, Flounder in the sea,*
Come, I pray thee, here to me;
For my wife, Dame Ilsabil,
Wills not as I'd have her will."

Then the Flounder came swimming to him and said, "Well, what does she want, then?"

"Ah," said the man, "I did catch you, and my wife says I really ought to have wished for something. She does not like to live in a wretched hovel any longer. She would like to have a cottage."

"Go, then," said the Flounder, "she has it already."

When the man got home, his wife was no longer in the hovel. But instead of it, there stood a small cottage, and she was sitting on a bench before the door. Then she took him by the hand and said to him, "Just come inside, look. Now isn't this a great deal better?"

So they went in, and there was a small porch, and a pretty little parlor and bedroom, and a kitchen and pantry, with the best of furniture, and fitted up with the most beautiful things made of tin and brass, whatsoever was wanted. And behind the cottage, there was a small yard, with hens and ducks, and a little garden with flowers and fruit.

"Look," said the wife, "is not that nice!"

"Yes," said the husband, "and so we must always think it,—now we will live quite contented."

"We will think about that," said the wife.

With that they ate something and went to bed.

Everything went well for a week or a fortnight, and then the woman said, "Hark you, Husband, this cottage is far too small for us, and the garden and yard are little. The Flounder might just as well have given us a larger house. I should like to live in a great stone castle. Go to the Flounder, and tell him to give us a castle."

"Ah, Wife," said the man, "the cottage is quite good enough. Why should we live in a castle?"

"What!" said the woman; "go at once, the Flounder can always do that."

"No, Wife," said the man, "the Flounder has just given us the cottage. I do not like to go back so soon, it might make him angry."

"Go," said the woman, "he can do it quite easily, and will be glad to do it. Just you go to him."

The man's heart grew heavy, and he did not wish to go. He said to himself, "It is not right," and yet he went.

And when he came to the sea, the water was quite purple and dark-blue, and gray and thick, and no longer green and yellow, but it was still quiet. And he stood there and said:

"Flounder, Flounder in the sea,
Come, I pray thee, here to me;
For my wife, Dame Ilsabil,
Wills not as I'd have her will."

"Well, what does she want, now?" said the Flounder.

"Alas," said the man, half scared, "she wants to live in a great stone castle."

"Go to it, then, she is standing before the door," said the Flounder.

Then the man went home, and when he got there, he found a great stone palace, and his wife was just standing on the steps going in. She took him by the hand and said, "Come in."

So he went with her, and in the castle was a great hall paved with marble, and many servants, who flung wide the doors. The walls were all bright with beautiful hangings, and in the rooms were chairs and tables of pure gold. Crystal chandeliers hung from the ceiling, and all the rooms and bedrooms had carpets. Food and wine of the very best were standing on all the tables, so that they nearly broke down beneath it.

Behind the house, too, there was a great courtyard, with stables for horses and cows, and the very best of carriages. There was a magnificent large garden, too, with the most beautiful flowers and fruit-trees, and a park quite half a mile long, in which were stags, deer, and hares, and everything that could be desired.

"Come," said the woman, "isn't that beautiful?"

"Yes, indeed," said the man, "now let it be; and we will live in this beautiful castle and be content."

"We will consider about that," said the woman, "and sleep upon it;" thereupon they went to bed.

Next morning, the wife awoke first. It was just daybreak, and from her bed she saw the beautiful country lying before her. Her husband was still stretching himself, so she poked him in the side with her elbow, and said, "Get up, Husband, and just peep out of the window. Look you, couldn't we be the King over all that land? Go to the Flounder, we will be the King."

"Ah, Wife," said the man, "why should we be King? I do not want to be King."

"Well," said the wife, "if you won't be King, I will. Go to the Flounder, for I will be King."

"Ah, Wife," said the man, "why do you want to be King? I do not like to say that to him."

"Why not?" said the woman; "go to him at once. I must be King!"

So the man went, and was quite unhappy because his wife wished to be King. "It is not right; it is not right," thought he. He did not wish to go, but yet he went.

And when he came to the sea, it was quite dark-gray, and the water heaved up from below, and smelt putrid. Then he went and stood by it, and said:

"Flounder, Flounder in the sea,
Come, I pray thee, here to me;
For my wife, Dame Ilsabil,
Wills not as I'd have her will."

"Well, what does she want, now?" said the Flounder.

"Alas," said the man, "she wants to be King."

"Go to her; she is King already."

So the man went, and when he came to the palace, the castle had become much larger, and had a great tower and magnificent ornaments. The sentinel was standing before the door, and there were numbers of soldiers with kettledrums and trumpets. And when he went inside the house, everything was of real marble and gold, with velvet covers and great golden tassels. Then the doors of the hall were opened, and there was the Court in all its splendor, and his wife was sitting on a high throne of gold and diamonds, with a great crown of gold on her head, and a sceptre of pure gold and jewels in her hand. On both sides of her, stood her maids-in-waiting in a row, each of them always one head shorter than the last.

Then he went and stood before her, and said, "Ah, Wife, and now you are King."

"Yes," said the woman, "now I am King."

So he stood and looked at her, and when he had looked at her thus for some time, he said, "And now that you are King, let all else be, we will wish for nothing more."

"Nay, Husband," said the woman, quite anxiously, "I find time pass very heavily, I can bear it no longer. Go to the Flounder—I am King, but I must be Emperor, too."

"Alas, Wife, why do you wish to be Emperor?"

"Husband," said she, "go to the Flounder. I will be Emperor."

"Alas, Wife," said the man, "he cannot make you Emperor. I may not say that to the fish. There is only one Emperor in the land. An Emperor, the Flounder cannot make you! I assure you he cannot."

"What!" said the woman, "I am the King, and you are nothing but my husband. Will you go this moment? go at once! If he can make a King, he can make an Emperor. I will be Emperor. Go instantly."

So he was forced to go. As the man went, however, he was troubled in mind, and thought to himself, "It will not end well! It will not end well! Emperor is too shameless! The Flounder will at last be tired out."

With that, he reached the sea, and the sea was quite black and thick, and began to boil up from below, so that it threw up bubbles. And such a sharp wind blew over it that it curdled, and the man was afraid. Then he went and stood by it, and said:

"Flounder, Flounder in the sea,
Come, I pray thee, here to me;
For my wife, Dame Ilsabil,
Wills not as I'd have her will."

"Well, what does she want, now?" said the Flounder.

"Alas, Flounder," said he, "my wife wants to be Emperor."

"Go to her," said the Flounder; "she is Emperor already."

So the man went, and when he got there the whole palace was made of polished marble with alabaster figures and golden ornaments. And soldiers were marching before the door blowing trumpets, and beating cymbals and drums. In the house, barons, and counts, and dukes were going about as servants. Then they opened the doors to him, which were of pure gold. And when he entered, there sat his wife on a throne, which was made of one piece of gold, and was quite two miles high; and she wore a great golden crown that was three yards high, and set with diamonds and carbuncles. In one hand she had the sceptre, and in the other the imperial orb. And on both sides of her stood the yeomen of the guard in two rows, each being smaller than the one before him, from the biggest Giant, who was two miles high, to the very smallest Dwarf, just as big as my little finger. And before it stood a number of princes and dukes.

Then the man went and stood among than, and said, "Wife, are you Emperor now?"

"Yes," said she, "now I am Emperor."

Then he stood and looked at her well, and when he had looked at her thus for some time, he said, "Ah, Wife, be content, now that you are Emperor."

"Husband," said she, "why are you standing there? Now, I am Emperor, but I will be Pope too. Go to the Flounder."

"Alas, Wife," said the man, "what will you not wish for? You cannot be Pope. There is but one in Christendom. He cannot make you Pope."

"Husband," said she, "I will be Pope. Go immediately. I must be Pope this very day."

"No, Wife," said the man, "I do not like to say that to him; that would not do, it is too much. The Flounder can't make you Pope."

"Husband," said she, "what nonsense! if he can make an Emperor he can make a Pope. Go to him directly. I am Emperor, and you are nothing but my husband. Will you go at once?"

“YES,” SAID SHE “NOW I AM EMPEROR”

Then he was afraid and went. But he was quite faint, and shivered and shook, and his knees and legs trembled. And a high wind blew over the land, and the clouds flew, and toward evening all grew dark, and the leaves fell from the trees, and the water rose and roared as if it were boiling, and splashed upon the shore. In the distance he saw ships which were firing guns in their sore need, pitching and tossing on the waves. And yet in the midst of the sky, there was still a small bit of blue, though on every side it was as red as in a heavy storm. So, full of despair, he went and stood in much fear, and said:

"Flounder, Flounder in the sea,
Come, I pray thee, here to me;
For my wife, Dame Ilsabil,
Wills not as I'd have her will."

"Well, what does she want, now?" said the Flounder.

"Alas," said the man, "she wants to be Pope."

"Go to her then," said the Flounder; "she is Pope already."

So he went, and when he got there, he saw what seemed to be a large church surrounded by palaces. He pushed his way through the crowd. Inside, however, everything was lighted with thousands and thousands of candles, and his wife was clad in gold, and she was sitting on a much higher throne, and had three great golden crowns on, and round about her there was much churchly splendor. And on both sides of her was a row of candles, the largest of which was as tall as the very tallest tower, down to the very smallest kitchen candle; and all the emperors and kings were on their knees before her, kissing her shoe.

"Wife," said the man, and looked attentively at her, "are you now Pope?"

"Yes," said she, "I am Pope."

So he stood and looked at her, and it was just as if he was looking at the bright sun. When he had stood looking at her thus for a short time, he said, "Ah, Wife, if you are Pope, do let well alone!"

But she looked as stiff as a post, and did not move or show any signs of life. Then said he, "Wife, now that you are Pope, be satisfied, you cannot become anything greater."

"I will consider about that," said the woman.

Thereupon they both went to bed. But she was not satisfied, and greediness let her have no sleep, for she was continually thinking what there was left for her to be.

The man slept well and soundly, for he had run about a great deal during the day. But the woman could not fall asleep at all, and flung herself from one side to the other the whole night through, thinking what more was left for her to be, but unable to call to mind anything else.

At length the sun began to rise, and when the woman saw the red of dawn, she sat up in bed and looked at it. And when, through the window, she saw the sun thus rising, she said, "Cannot I, too, order the sun and moon to rise?"

"Husband," said she, poking him in the ribs with her elbows, "wake up! go to the Flounder, for I wish to be even as God is."

The man was still half asleep, but he was so horrified that he fell out of bed. He thought he must have heard amiss, and rubbed his eyes, and said, "Alas, Wife, what are you saying?"

"Husband," said she, "if I can't order the sun and moon to rise, and have to look on and see the sun and moon rising, I can't bear it. I shall not know what it is to have another happy hour, unless I can make them rise myself." Then she looked at him so terribly that a shudder ran over him, and said, "Go at once. I wish to be like unto God."

"Alas, Wife," said the man, falling on his knees before her, "the Flounder cannot do that. He can make an Emperor and a Pope. I beseech you, go on as you are, and be Pope."

Then she fell into a rage, and her hair flew wildly about her head, and she cried, "I will not endure this, I'll not bear it any longer. Will you go?" Then he put on his trousers and ran away like a madman.

But outside a great storm was raging, and blowing so hard that he could scarcely keep his feet. Houses and trees toppled over, mountains trembled, rocks rolled into the sea, the sky was pitch black, and it thundered and lightened. And the sea came in with black waves as high as church-towers and mountains, and all with crests of white foam at the top. Then he cried, but could not hear his own words:

"*Flounder, Flounder in the sea,*
Come, I pray thee, here to me;
For my wife, Dame Ilsabil,
Wills not as I'd have her will."

"Well; what does she want, now?" said the Flounder.

"Alas," said he, "she wants to be like unto God."

"Go to her, and you will find her back again in the dirty hovel."

And there they are living at this very time.

THE WHITE SNAKE

Along time ago, there lived a King who was famed for his wisdom through all the land. Nothing was hidden from him, and it seemed as if news of the most secret things was brought to him through the air.

But he had a strange custom. Every day after dinner, when the table was cleared, and no one else was present, a trusty servant had to bring him one more dish. It was covered and even the servant did not know what was in it. Neither did any one know, for the King never took off the cover to eat of it, until he was quite alone.

This had gone on for a long time, when one day the servant, who took away the dish, was overcome with such curiosity that he could not help carrying the dish into his room. When he had carefully locked the door, he lifted up the cover, and saw a White Snake lying on the dish. But when he saw it, he could not deny himself the pleasure of tasting it, so he cut off a little bit and put it into his mouth.

No sooner had it touched his tongue than he heard a strange whispering of little voices outside his window. He went and listened, and then noticed that it was the sparrows who were chattering together, and telling one another of all kinds of things which they had seen in the fields and woods. Eating the Snake had given him power to understand the language of animals!

Now, it so happened, that on this very day the Queen lost her most beautiful ring, and suspicion of having stolen it fell upon this trusty servant, who was allowed to go everywhere. The King ordered the man to be brought before him, and threatened with angry words that unless he could, before the morrow, point out the thief, he himself should be looked upon as guilty and should be executed. In vain, he declared his innocence. He was dismissed with no better answer.

In his trouble and fear, he went down into the courtyard, and took thought how to help himself out of his trouble. Now some ducks were sitting together quietly by a brook and taking their rest. And, whilst they were making their feathers smooth with their bills, they were having a confidential conversation. The servant stood by and listened.

They were telling one another of all the places where they had been waddling about all the morning, and what good food they had found. And one said in a pitiful tone, "Something lies heavy on my stomach; as I was eating in haste I swallowed a ring which lay under the Queen's window."

The servant at once seized her by the neck, carried her to the kitchen, and said to the cook, "Here is a fine duck. Pray kill her."

"Yes," said the cook, and weighed her in his hand; "she has spared no trouble to fatten herself, and has been waiting long enough to be roasted."

So he cut off her head; and as she was being dressed for the spit, the Queen's ring was found inside her.

The servant could now easily prove his innocence. The King, to make amends for the wrong, allowed him to ask a favor, and promised him the best place in the Court. The servant refused everything, and asked only for a horse and some money for traveling, as he had a mind to see the world and go about a little. When his request was granted, he set out on his way.

One day he came to a pond, where he saw three fishes caught in the reeds and gasping for water. Now, though it is said that fishes are dumb, he heard them lamenting that they must perish so miserably. As he had a kind heart, he got off his horse and put the three prisoners back into the water.

They quivered with delight, put out their heads, and cried to him, "We will remember you, and repay you for saving us!"

He rode on, and after a while it seemed to him that he heard a voice in the sand at his feet. He listened, and heard an Ant-King complain, "Why cannot folk, with their clumsy beasts, keep off our bodies? That stupid horse, with his heavy hoofs, has been treading down my people without mercy!"

So he turned on to a side path and the Ant-King cried out to him, "We will remember you—-one good turn deserves another!"

The path led him into a wood, and there he saw two old ravens standing by their nest, and throwing out their young ones. "Out with you, you idle, good-for-nothing creatures!" cried they; "we cannot find food for you any longer. You are big enough, and can provide for yourselves."

But the poor young ravens lay upon the ground flapping their wings, and crying, "Oh, what helpless chicks we are! We must shift for ourselves, and yet we cannot fly! What can we do, but lie here and starve?"

So the good young fellow alighted and killed his horse with his sword, and gave it to them for food. Then they came hopping up to it, satisfied their hunger, and cried, "We will remember you —one good turn deserves another!"

And now he had to use his own legs, and when he had walked a long way, he came to a large city. There was a great noise and crowd in the streets, and a man rode up on horseback, crying aloud, "The King's Daughter wants a husband. But whoever sues for her hand must perform a hard task. If he does not succeed he will forfeit his life."

Many had already made the attempt, but in vain. Nevertheless, when the youth saw the King's Daughter he was so overcome by her great beauty, that he forgot all danger, went before the King, and declared himself a suitor.

So he was led out to the sea, and a gold ring was cast into it. Then the King ordered him to fetch this ring up from the bottom of the sea, and added, "If you come up without it, you will be thrown in again and again until you perish amid the waves."

All the people grieved for the handsome youth; then they went away; leaving him alone by the sea.

THERE LAY THE GOLD RING IN THE SHELL

He stood on the shore and considered what he should do, when suddenly he saw three fishes come swimming toward him.

They were the very fishes whose lives he had saved. The one in the middle held a mussel in its mouth, which it laid on the shore at the youth's feet. When he had taken it up and opened it, there lay the gold ring in the shell. Full of joy he took it to the King, and expected that he would grant him the promised reward.

But when the proud Princess perceived that he was not her equal in birth, she scorned him, and required him first to perform another task. She went down into the garden and strewed with her own hands ten sacksful of millet-seed on the grass.

Then she said, "To-morrow morning before sunrise these must be picked up, and not a single grain be wanting."

The youth sat down in the garden and considered how he might perform this task. But he could think of nothing, and there he sat sorrowfully awaiting the break of day, when he should be led to death. But as soon as the first rays of the sun shone into the garden, he saw all the ten sacks standing side by side, quite full, and not a single grain was missing. The Ant-King had come in the night with thousands and thousands of ants, and the grateful creatures had, by great industry, picked up all the millet-seeds and gathered them into the sacks.

Presently, the King's Daughter herself came down into the garden, and was amazed to see that the young man had done the task she had given him.

But she could not yet conquer her proud heart, and said, "Although he has performed both the tasks, he shall not be my husband, until he has brought me an apple from the Tree of Life."

The youth did not know where the Tree of Life stood, but he set out, and would have gone on forever, as long as his legs would carry him, though he had no hope of finding it. After he had wandered through three kingdoms, he came one evening to a wood, and lay down under a tree to sleep.

But he heard a rustling in the branches, and a Golden Apple fell into his hand. At the same time three ravens flew down to him, perched themselves upon his knee, and said, "We are the three young ravens whom you saved from starving. When we had grown big, and heard that you were seeking the Golden Apple, we flew over the sea to the end of the world, where the Tree of Life stands, and have brought you the apple."

The youth, full of joy, set out homeward, and took the Golden Apple to the King's beautiful Daughter, who had now no more excuses left to make. They cut the Apple of Life in two and ate it together; and then her heart became full of love for him, and they lived to a great age in undisturbed happiness.

HAENSEL AND GRETHEL

Hard by a great forest, dwelt a poor woodcutter with his wife and his two children. The boy was called Haensel and the girl, Grethel. He had little to bite and to break; and once when great scarcity fell on the land, he could no longer procure daily bread.

Now, when he thought over this by night in his bed, and tossed about in his anxiety, he groaned and said to his wife, "What is to become of us? How are we to feed our poor children, when we no longer have anything even for ourselves?"

"I'll tell you what, Husband," answered the woman, "early to-morrow morning we will take the children out into the forest to where it is the thickest; there we will light a fire for them, and give each of them one piece of bread more. Then we will go to our work and leave them alone. They will not find the way home again, and we shall be rid of them."

"No, Wife," said the man, "I will not do that. How can I bear to leave my children alone in the forest?—the wild animals would soon come and tear them to pieces."

"Oh, you fool!" said she. "Then we must all four die of hunger. You may as well plane the planks for our coffins."

And she left him no peace until he consented. "But I feel very sorry for the poor children, all the same," said the man.

The two children had also not been able to sleep for hunger, and had heard what the woman had said to their father.

Grethel wept bitter tears, and said to Haensel, "Now all is over with us."

"Be quiet, Grethel," said Haensel, "do not distress yourself, I will soon find a way to help us."

And when the old folk had fallen asleep, he got up, put on his little coat, opened the door below, and crept outside. The moon shone brightly, and the white pebbles, which lay in front of the house, glittered like real silver pennies. Haensel stooped and put as many of them in the little pocket of his coat as he could possibly get in.

Then he went back and said to Grethel, "Be comforted, dear little Sister, and sleep in peace. God will not forsake us," and he lay down again in his bed.

When day dawned, but before the sun had risen, the woman came and awoke the two children, saying, "Get up, you sluggards! we are going into the forest to fetch wood." She gave each a little piece of bread, and said, "There is something for your dinner, but do not eat it up before then, for you will get nothing else."

Grethel took the bread under her apron, as Haensel had the stones in his pocket. Then they all set out together on the way to the forest. When they had walked a short time, Haensel stood still and peeped back, and did so again and again while he was throwing the white pebble-stones one by one out of his pocket onto the road.

When they had reached the middle of the forest, the father said, "Now, Children, pile up some wood, and I will light a fire that you may not be cold."

Haensel and Grethel gathered brushwood together, as high as a little hill. The brushwood was lighted, and when the flames were burning very high, the woman said, "Now, Children, lay yourselves down by the fire and rest. We will go into the forest and cut some wood. When we have done, we will come back and fetch you away."

Haensel and Grethel sat by the fire, and when noon came, each ate a little piece of bread; and, as they heard the strokes of the wood-axe, they believed that their father was near. It was, however, not the axe, it was a branch which he had fastened to a withered tree which the wind was blowing backward and forward. And as they had been sitting such a long time, their eyes shut with fatigue, and they fell fast asleep.

When at last they awoke, it was already dark night. Grethel began to cry and said, "How are we to get out of the forest now?"

But Haensel comforted her, and said, "Just wait a little, until the moon has risen, and then we shall soon find the way."

And when the full moon had risen, Haensel took his little sister by the hand, and followed the pebbles which shone like newly-coined silver pieces, and showed them the way.

They walked the whole night long, and, by break of day, came once more to their father's house. They knocked at the door; and when the woman opened it and saw that it was Haensel and Grethel, she said, "You naughty children, why have you slept so long in the forest?—we thought you were never coming back at all!"

The father, however, rejoiced, for it had cut him to the heart to leave them behind alone.

Not long afterward, there was another famine in all parts, and the children heard their mother saying at night to their father, "Everything is eaten again, we have one-half loaf left, and after that there is an end. The children must go, we will take them farther into the wood, so that they will not find their way out again. There is no other means of saving ourselves!"

The man's heart was heavy, and he thought "it would be better for you to share the last mouthful with your children!" The woman, however, would listen to nothing that he had to say, but scolded and reproached him. He who says A must say B, likewise, and as he had yielded the first time, he had to do so a second time also.

The children were, however, still awake and had heard the conversation. When the old folk were asleep, Haensel again got up to go out and pick up pebbles. But the woman had locked the door, and Haensel could not get out. Nevertheless he comforted his little sister, and said, "Do not cry, Grethel, go to sleep quietly, the good God will help us."

Early in the morning, came the woman, and took the children out of their beds. Their bit of bread was given to them, but it was still smaller than the time before. On the way into the forest, Haensel crumbled his in his pocket, and often stood still and threw a morsel on the ground, and little by little, threw all the crumbs on the path.

The woman led the children still deeper into the forest, where they had never in their lives been before. Then a great fire was again made, and the mother said, "Just sit there, you Children, and when you are tired you may sleep a little. We are going into the forest to cut wood. In the evening, when we are done, we will come and fetch you away."

When it was noon, Grethel shared her piece of bread with Haensel, who had scattered his by the way. Then they fell asleep, and evening passed, but no one came to the poor children.

They did not awake until it was dark night, and Haensel comforted his little sister and said, "Just wait, Grethel, until the moon rises, and then we shall see the crumbs of bread which I have strewn. They will show us our way home again."

When the moon came, they set out, but they found no crumbs, for the many thousands of birds, which fly about in the woods and fields, had picked them all up. Haensel said to Grethel, "We shall soon find the way," but they did not find it.

They walked the whole night and all the next day, from morning till evening, but they did not get out of the forest, and were very hungry, for they had nothing to eat but two or three berries, which grew on the ground. And as they were so weary that their legs would carry them no longer, they lay down beneath a tree and fell asleep.

It was now three mornings since they had left their father's house. They began to walk again, but they always got deeper into the forest. If help did not come soon, they must die of hunger and weariness!

When it was midday, they saw a beautiful Snow-White Bird sitting on a bough, which sang so delightfully that they stood still and listened to it. And when it had finished its song, it spread its wings and flew away before them. They followed it until they reached a little house, on the roof of which it alighted.

When they came quite up to the little House they saw that it was built of bread and covered with cakes, but that the windows were of clear sugar.

"We will set to work on that," said Haensel, "and have a good meal. I will eat a bit of the roof, and you, Grethel, can eat some of the window; it will taste sweet."

Haensel reached up and broke off a little of the roof to try how it tasted. Grethel leant against the window and nibbled at the panes. Then a soft voice cried from the room:

"*Nibble, nibble, gnaw!*

Who nibbles at my door?"

but the children went on eating without disturbing themselves. Haensel, who thought the roof tasted very nice, tore down a great piece of it. Grethel pushed out the whole of one round window-pane, sat down, and enjoyed herself with it.

Suddenly the door opened, and a very, very old woman, leaning on crutches, came creeping out. Haensel and Grethel were so terribly frightened that they let fall what they had in their hands.

The Old Woman, however, nodded her head, and said, "Oh, you dear Children, who has brought you here? Do come in, and stay with me. No harm shall happen to you."

She took them both by the hand, and led them into her little house. Then she set good food before them, milk and pancakes, with sugar, apples, and nuts. Afterward she covered two pretty little beds with clean white linen, and Haensel and Grethel lay down in them, and thought they were in Heaven.

The Old Woman had only pretended to be so kind. She was really a wicked Witch, who lay in wait for children, and who had built the little bread house in order to entice them there. When a child fell into her power, she killed it, cooked, and ate it; and that was a feast-day with her.

Witches have red eyes, and cannot see far, but they have a keen scent like the beasts', and are aware when human beings draw near. When Haensel and Grethel came into her neighborhood, she laughed maliciously, and said mockingly, "I have them, they shall not escape me again!"

Early in the morning before the children were awake, she was up. And when she saw both of them sleeping and looking so pretty, with their plump red cheeks, she muttered to herself, "That will be a dainty mouthful!"

Then she seized Haensel with her shrivelled hand, carried him into a little stable, and shut him in with a grated door. He might scream as he liked, that was of no use!

Then she went to Grethel, shook her till she awoke, and cried, "Get up, lazy thing, fetch some water, and cook something good for your brother. He is in the stable outside, and is to be made fat. When he is fat, I will eat him."

Grethel began to weep bitterly. But it was all in vain, she was forced to do what the wicked Witch ordered her.

And now the best food was cooked for poor Haensel, while Grethel got nothing but crab-shells. Every morning the woman crept to the little stable, and cried, "Haensel, stretch out your finger that I may feel if you will soon be fat."

When four weeks had gone by she was seized with impatience and would not wait any longer. "Ho, there! Grethel," she cried to the girl, "be active, and bring some water. Let Haensel be fat or lean, to-morrow I will kill him, and cook him."

Ah! how the poor little sister did lament when she had to fetch the water, and how her tears did flow down over her cheeks! "Dear God, do help us," she cried. "If the wild beasts in the forest had but devoured us, we should at any rate have died together!"

"Just keep your noise to yourself," said the Old Woman, "all that won't help you at all."

Early in the morning, Grethel had to go out and hang up the cauldron, full of water, and light the fire.

"We will bake first," said the Old Woman, "I have already heated the oven, and kneaded the dough." She pushed poor Grethel out to the oven, from which flames of fire were darting.

"Creep in," said the Witch, "and see if it is properly heated, so that we can shut the bread in." And when once Grethel was inside, she intended to shut the oven and let her bake in it, and then eat her, too.

But Grethel saw what she had in her mind, and would not creep in. "Silly Goose," said the Old Woman; "the door is big enough. Just look, I can get in myself!" and she crept up and thrust her head in. Then she fell over into the oven and was miserably burnt to death.

Grethel, however, ran as quick as lightning to Haensel, opened his little stable, and cried, "Haensel, we are saved! The old Witch is dead!"

Then Haensel sprang out like a bird from its cage, when the door is opened for it. How they did rejoice and embrace each other, and dance about and kiss each other! And as they had no longer any need to fear her, they went into the Witch's house, and in every corner there stood chests full of pearls and jewels.

"These are far better than pebbles!" said Haensel, and thrust into his pockets whatever could be got in.

And Grethel said, "I, too, will take something home with me," and filled her pinafore full.

"But now we will go away," said Haensel, "that we may get out of the Witch's forest."

When they had walked for two hours, they came to a great piece of water. "We cannot get over," said Haensel, "I see no foot-plank, and no bridge."

"And no boat crosses either," answered Grethel, "but a white duck is swimming there. If I ask her, she will help us over." Then she cried:

"Little Duck, little Duck, dost thou see,
Haensel and Grethel are waiting for thee?
There's never a plank, nor a bridge in sight,
Take us across on thy back so white."

The duck came to them, and Haensel seated himself on her back, and told his sister to sit by him. "No," replied Grethel, "that will be too heavy for the little duck. She shall take us across, one after the other."

The good little duck did so, and when they were once safely across and had walked for a short time, the forest seemed to be more and more familiar to them. At length, they saw from afar their father's house. Then they began to run, rushed into the parlor, and threw themselves into their father's arms. The man had not known one happy hour since he had left the children in the forest. The woman, however, was dead.

Grethel emptied her pinafore until pearls and precious stones ran about the room, and Haensel threw one handful after another out of his pocket to add to them. Then all trouble was at an end, and they lived together in perfect happiness.

My tale is done, there runs a mouse, whosoever catches it, may make himself a big, big fur cap out of it!

THE SEVEN RAVENS

There was once a man who had seven sons, but never a daughter no matter how much he wished for one.

At length, his wife had a child, and it was a daughter. The joy was great. But the child was sickly and small, and so weak that it had to be baptized at once.

The father sent one of the boys in a hurry to the spring, to fetch water for the baptism. The other six boys ran along with him. And as each strove to be the first to fill the jug, it fell into the spring. There they stood, and did not know what to do. None of them dared to go home.

When they did not come back, the father grew impatient, and said, "They have forgotten all about it in a game of play, the wicked boys!"

Soon he grew afraid lest the child should die without being baptized, and he cried out in anger, "I wish the boys were all turned into Ravens!"

Hardly was the word spoken, before he heard a whirring of wings in the air above his head. He looked up, and saw seven coal-black Ravens flying high and away.

The parents could not recall the curse. And though they grieved over the loss of their seven sons, yet they comforted themselves somewhat with their dear little daughter, who soon grew strong and every day more beautiful.

For a long time, she did not know that she had had brothers. Her parents were careful not to mention them before her. But one day, she chanced to overhear some people talking about her, and saying, "that the maiden is certainly beautiful, but really to blame for the misfortune of her seven brothers."

Then she was much troubled, and went to her father and mother, and asked if it was true that she had had brothers, and what was become of them.

The parents did not dare to keep the secret longer, and said that her birth was only the innocent cause of what had happened to her brothers. But the maiden laid it daily to heart, and thought that she must deliver her brothers.

She had no peace and rest until she set out secretly, and went forth into the wide world to seek them out, and set them free, let it cost what it might. She took nothing with her but a little ring belonging to her parents as a keepsake, a loaf of bread against hunger, a little pitcher of water against thirst, and a little chair as a provision against weariness.

And now, she went continually onward, far, far, to the very end of the world. Then she came to the Sun, but it was too hot and terrible, and devoured little children. Hastily she ran away, and ran to the Moon, but it was far too cold, and also awful and malicious. And when it saw the child, it said:

"I smell, I smell
The flesh of men!"

On this she ran swiftly away, and came to the Stars, which were kind and good to her, and each of them sat on its own little chair. But the Morning Star arose, and gave her the drumstick of a chicken, and said, "If you have not that drumstick you cannot open the Glass Mountain, and in the Glass Mountain are your brothers."

EACH STAR SAT ON ITS OWN LITTLE CHAIR

The maiden took the drumstick, wrapped it carefully in a cloth, and went onward again until she came to the Glass Mountain. The door was shut, and she thought she would take out the drumstick. But when she undid the cloth, it was empty, and she had lost the good Star's present. What was she now to do? She wished to rescue her brothers, and had no key to the Glass Mountain. The good little sister took a knife, cut off one of her little fingers, put it in the door, and succeeded in opening it.

When she had got inside, a little Dwarf came to meet her, who said, "My Child, what are you looking for?"

"I am looking for my brothers, the Seven Ravens," she replied.

The Dwarf said, "The Lord Ravens are not at home, but if you wish to wait here until they come, step in."

Thereupon the little Dwarf carried the Ravens' dinner in, on seven little plates, and in seven little glasses. The little sister ate a morsel from each plate, and from each little glass she took a sip. But in the last little glass she dropped the ring which she had brought away with her.

Suddenly, she heard a whirring of wings and a rushing through the air, and then the little Dwarf said, "Now the Lord Ravens are flying home."

Then they came, and wanted to eat and drink, and looked for their little plates and glasses. Then said one after the other, "Who has eaten something from my plate? Who has drunk out of my little glass? It was a human mouth."

And when the seventh came to the bottom of the glass, the ring rolled against his mouth. Then he looked at it, and saw that it was a ring belonging to his father and mother, and said, "God grant that our little sister may be here, and then we shall be free."

When the maiden, who was standing behind the door watching, heard that wish, she came forth, and on this all the Ravens were restored to their human form again. And they embraced and kissed each other, and went joyfully home.

ASH-MAIDEN

The wife of a rich man fell sick, and as she felt that her end was drawing near, she called her only daughter to her bedside and said, "Dear Child, be good and pious, and then the dear God will always protect you, and I will look down on you from Heaven and be near you." Thereupon she closed her eyes and departed.

Every day, the maiden went out to her mother's grave and wept, and she remained pious and good. When winter came the snow spread a white sheet over the grave, and when the spring-sun had drawn it off again, the man had taken another wife.

The woman had brought two daughters into the house with her, who were beautiful and fair of face, but vile and black of heart. Now began a bad time for the poor child. "Is the stupid goose to sit in the parlor with us?" said they. "He who wants to eat bread, must earn it. Out with the kitchen-wench!"

They took her pretty clothes away from her, put an old gray bedgown on her and gave her wooden shoes. "Just look at the proud Princess, how decked out she is!" they cried, and laughed, and led her into the kitchen.

There she had to do hard work from morning till night, get up before daybreak, carry water, light fires, cook and wash. Besides this, the sisters did her every imaginable injury—they mocked her and emptied her peas and lentils into the ashes, so that she was forced to sit and pick them out again.

In the evening, when she had worked till she was weary, she had no bed to go to, but had to sleep by the fireside in the ashes. And as on that account she always looked dusty and dirty, they called her Ash-Maiden.

It happened once that the father was going to the Fair, and he asked the two daughters what he should bring back for them.

"Beautiful dresses," said one. "Pearls and jewels," said the second.

"And you, Ash-Maiden," said he, "what will you have?"

"Father, break off for me the first branch which knocks against your hat on your way home."

So he bought beautiful dresses, pearls and jewels for the two daughters, and on his way home, as he was riding through a green thicket, a hazel twig brushed against him and knocked off his hat. Then he broke off the branch and took it with him.

When he reached home he gave the two daughters the things which they had wished for, and to Ash-Maiden he gave the branch from the hazel-bush. Ash-Maiden thanked him, went to her mother's grave and planted the branch on it, and wept so much that the tears fell down on it and watered it.

It grew, however, and became a handsome tree. Thrice a day Ash-Maiden went and sat beneath it, and wept and prayed, and a little White Bird always came on the tree. And if Ash-Maiden expressed a wish, the bird threw down to her what she had wished for.

It happened that the King gave a feast, which was to last three days. To it all the beautiful young girls in the country were invited, in order that his son might choose himself a Bride. When the two sisters heard that they too were to appear among the number, they were delighted.

They called Ash-Maiden and said, "Comb our hair, brush our shoes, and fasten our buckles, for we are going to the feast at the King's palace."

Ash-Maiden obeyed, but wept, because she too would have liked to go with them to the dance, and she begged her mother to allow her to do so.

"You go, Ash-Maiden!" said she; "you are dusty and dirty, and would go to the feast? You have no clothes and shoes, and yet would dance!"

As, however, Ash-Maiden went on asking, the mother at last said, "I have emptied a dish of lentils into the ashes for you. If you have picked them out again in two hours, you shall go with us."

The maiden went through the back-door into the garden, and called, "You tame Pigeons, you Turtledoves, and all you birds beneath the sky, come and help me to pick

"The good into the pot,
The bad into the crop!"

Then two white pigeons came in by the kitchen-window, and afterward the turtledoves. And at last all the birds beneath the sky came whirring and crowding in, and alighted amongst the ashes. And the pigeons nodded with their heads and began *pick, pick, pick, pick,* and the rest began also *pick, pick, pick, pick,* and gathered all the good grains into the dish. Hardly had one hour passed before they had finished, and all flew out again.

Then the girl took the dish to the mother, and was glad, and believed that now she would be allowed to go with them to the feast.

But the mother said, "No, Ash-Maiden, you have no clothes and you cannot dance. You would only be laughed at."

And as Ash-Maiden wept at this, the mother said, "If you can pick two dishes of lentils out of the ashes for me in one hour, you shall go with us." And she thought to herself, "That she most certainly cannot do."

When the mother had emptied the two dishes of lentils amongst the ashes, the maiden went through the back-door into the garden and cried, "You tame Pigeons, you Turtledoves, and all you birds under heaven, come and help me to pick

"The good into the pot,
The bad into the crop!"

Then two white pigeons came in by the kitchen-window, and afterward the turtledoves. And at last all the birds beneath the sky came whirring and crowding in, and alighted amongst the ashes. And the doves nodded with their heads and began *pick, pick, pick, pick,* and the others began also *pick, pick, pick, pick,* and gathered all the good seeds into the dishes.

And before half an hour was over they had already finished, and all flew out again.

Then the maiden carried the dishes to the mother and was delighted, and believed that she might now go with them to the feast.

But the mother said, "All this will not help you. You go not with us, for you have no clothes and cannot dance. We should be ashamed of you!"

Then she turned her back on Ash-Maiden, and hurried away with her two proud daughters.

As no one was now at home, Ash-Maiden went to her mother's grave beneath the hazel-tree, and cried:

"Shiver and quiver, Little Tree,
Silver and gold throw over me!"

Then the bird threw a gold and silver dress down to her, and slippers embroidered with silk and silver. She put on the dress with all speed, and went to the feast.

Her sisters and the mother, however, did not know her, and thought she must be a foreign Princess, for she looked so beautiful in the golden dress. They never once thought of Ash-Maiden, and believed that she was sitting at home in the dirt, picking lentils out of the ashes.

The Prince went to meet her, took her by the hand, and he danced with her. He would dance with no other maiden, and never let go of her hand. And if any one else came to invite her, he said, "This is my partner."

She danced till it was evening, and then she wanted to go home. But the King's Son said, "I will go with you and bear you company," for he wished to see to whom the beautiful maiden belonged.

She escaped from him, however, and sprang into the pigeon-house. The King's Son waited until her father came, and then he told him that the stranger maiden had leapt into the pigeon-house. The old man thought, "Can it be Ash-Maiden?" and they had to bring him an axe and a pickaxe that he might hew the pigeon-house to pieces, but no one was inside it.

And when they got home, Ash-Maiden lay in her dirty clothes among the ashes, and a dim little oil-lamp was burning on the mantelpiece. For Ash-Maiden had jumped quickly down from the back of the pigeon-house, and had run to the little hazel-tree. There she had taken off her beautiful clothes and laid them on the grave, and the bird had taken them away again. Then she had placed herself in the kitchen amongst the ashes, in her gray gown.

Next day, when the feast began afresh, and her parents and the sisters had gone once more, Ash-Maiden went to the hazel-tree, and said:

"Shiver and quiver, Little Tree,
Silver and gold throw over me!"

Then the bird threw down a much more beautiful dress than on the preceding day. And when Ash-Maiden appeared at the feast in this dress, every one was astonished at her beauty.

The King's Son had waited until she came, and instantly took her by the hand and danced with no one but her. When others came and invited her, he said, "She is my partner."

When evening arrived, she wished to leave, and the King's Son followed her, and wanted to see into which house she went. But she sprang away from him, and into the garden behind the house. Therein stood a beautiful tall tree on which hung the most magnificent pears. She clambered, like a squirrel, so nimbly between the branches, that the King's Son did not know where she was gone.

He waited until her father came, and said to him, "The stranger-maiden has escaped from me, and I believe she has climbed up the pear-tree."

The father thought, "Can it be Ash-Maiden?" and had an axe brought and cut the tree down, but no one was on it.

And when they got into the kitchen, Ash-Maiden lay there amongst the ashes, as usual, for she had jumped down on the other side of the tree, had taken the beautiful dress to the bird on the little hazel-tree, and had put on her gray gown.

On the third day, when the parents and sisters had gone away, Ash-Maiden went once more to her mother's grave, and said to the little tree:

"Shiver and quiver, Little Tree,
Silver and gold throw over me!"

And now the bird threw down to her a dress which was more splendid and magnificent than any she had yet had, and the slippers were golden.

And when she went to the feast in the dress, no one knew how to speak for astonishment. The King's Son danced with her only, and if any one invited her to dance, he said, "She is my partner."

When evening came, Ash-Maiden wished to leave, and the King's Son was anxious to go with her; but she escaped from him so quickly that he could not follow her. The King's Son, however, had caused the whole staircase to be smeared with pitch, and there, when she ran down, had the maiden's left slipper remained sticking. The King's Son picked it up, and it was small and dainty, and all golden.

Next morning, he went with it to the father, and said to him, "No one shall be my wife, but she whose foot this golden slipper fits."

Then were the two sisters glad, for they had pretty feet. The eldest went with the shoe into her room and wanted to try it on, and her mother stood by. But she could not get her big toe into it, for the shoe was too small for her.

Then her mother gave her a knife, and said, "Cut the toe off. When you are Queen you will have no more need to go on foot."

The maiden cut the toe off, forced the foot into the shoe, swallowed the pain, and went out to the King's Son. Then he took her on his horse as his Bride, and rode away with her. They were, however, obliged to pass the grave, and there, on the hazel-tree, sat the two pigeons and cried:

"Turn and peep, turn and peep,
There's blood within the shoe!
The shoe it is too small for her,
The true Bride waits for you!"

Then he looked at her foot, and saw how the blood was streaming from it. He turned his horse round and took the false Bride home again, and said she was not the true one, and that the other sister was to put the shoe on.

Then this one went into her chamber and got her toes safely into the shoe, but her heel was too large.

So her mother gave her a knife, and said, "Cut a bit off your heel. When you are Queen you will have no more need to go on foot."

The maiden cut a bit off her heel, forced her foot into the shoe, swallowed the pain, and went out to the King's Son. He took her on his horse as his Bride, and rode away with her. But when they passed by the hazel-tree, two little pigeons sat on it, and cried:

"Turn and peep, turn and peep,
There's blood within the shoe!
The shoe it is too small for her,
The true Bride waits for you!"

He looked down at her foot, and saw how the blood was running out of her shoe, and how it had stained her white stocking. Then he turned his horse and took the false Bride home again. "This also is not the right one," said he. "Have you no other daughter?"

"No," said the man; "there is only a little stunted kitchen-girl which my late wife left behind her, but she cannot possibly be the Bride."

The King's Son said he was to send her up to him; but the mother answered, "Oh, no, she is much too dirty, she cannot show herself!"

He insisted on it, and Ash-Maiden had to be called. She first washed her hands and face clean, and then went and bowed down before the King's Son, who gave her the golden shoe.

Then she seated herself on a stool, drew her foot out of the heavy wooden shoe, and put it into the slipper, which fitted like a glove.

And when she rose up and the King's Son looked at her face he recognized the beautiful maiden who had danced with him, and cried, "That is the true Bride!"

The mother and the two sisters were terrified and became pale with rage. He, however, took Ash-Maiden on his horse and rode away with her. As they passed by the hazel-tree, the two white doves cried:

"Turn and peep, turn and peep,
No blood is in the shoe!
The shoe is not too small for her,
The true Bride rides with you!"

and when they had cried that, the two came flying down and placed themselves on Ash-Maiden's shoulders, one on the right, the other on the left, and remained sitting there.

When the wedding with the King's Son had to be celebrated, the two false sisters came and wanted to get into favor with Ash-Maiden and share her good fortune. When the betrothed couple went to church, the elder was at the right side and the younger at the left, and the pigeons pecked out one eye of each of them. Afterward as they came back, the elder was at the left, and the younger at the right, and then the pigeons pecked out the other eye of each. And thus, for their wickedness and falsehood, they were punished with blindness as long as they lived.

THE ELVES AND THE SHOEMAKER

A shoemaker, by no fault of his own, had become so poor that at last he had nothing left but leather for one pair of shoes. So in the evening, he cut out the shoes which he wished to make the next morning. And as he had a good conscience, he lay down quietly in his bed, commended himself to God, and fell asleep.

In the morning, after he had said his prayers, and was just going to sit down to work, lo! both shoes stood all finished on his table. He was astounded, and did not know what to say. He took the shoes in his hands to examine them closer, and they were so neatly made that there was not one bad stitch in them, just as if they were meant for a masterpiece.

Soon after, a buyer came in, and as the shoes pleased him well, he paid more for them than was customary. And, with the money, the shoemaker was able to purchase leather for two pairs of shoes.

He cut them out at night, and next morning was about to set to work with fresh courage; but he had no need to do so, for, when he got up, they were already made. And buyers also were not wanting, who gave him money enough to buy leather for four pairs of shoes.

The following morning, too, he found the four pairs made. And so it went on constantly, what he cut out in the evening was finished by morning, so that he soon had his honest living again, and at last became a wealthy man.

Now it befell that, one evening not long before Christmas, when the man had been cutting out, he said to his wife, before going to bed, "What think you, if we were to stay up to-night to see who it is that lends us this helping hand?"

The woman liked the idea, and lighted a candle, and then they hid themselves in a corner of the room, behind some clothes which were hanging there, and watched.

When it was midnight, two pretty tiny naked Little Men came, sat down by the shoemaker's table, took all the work which was cut out before them and began to stitch, sew, and hammer so skilfully and so quickly with their little fingers, that the shoemaker could not turn away his eyes for astonishment. They did not stop until all was done, and stood finished on the table, and then they ran quickly away.

Next morning, the woman said, "The Little Men have made us rich, and we really must show that we are grateful for it. They run about so much, and have nothing on, and must be cold. I'll tell you what I'll do. I will make them little shirts, coats, vests, and trousers, and knit both of them a pair of stockings. Do you make them two little pairs of shoes."

The man said, "I shall be very glad to do it."

And one night, when everything was ready, they laid their presents, instead of the cut-out work, all together on the table, and then concealed themselves to see how the Little Men would behave.

At midnight they came bounding in, and wanted to get to work at once. But as they did not find any leather cut out, only the pretty little articles of clothing, they were at first astonished, and then they showed intense delight. They dressed themselves with the greatest rapidity, putting the pretty clothes on, and singing:

THE ELVES BEGAN TO STITCH, SEW, AND HAMMER

"Now we are boys so fine to see,
Why should we longer cobblers be?"

Then they danced and skipped and leapt over chairs and benches. At last, they danced out of doors. From that time forth they came no more, but as long as the shoemaker lived all went well with him, and all his undertakings prospered.

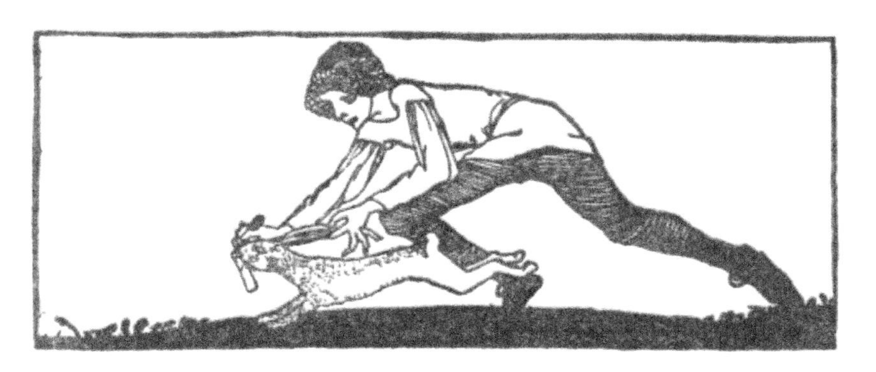

THE THREE BROTHERS

There was once a man who had three sons, and nothing else in the world but the house in which he lived. Now each of the sons wished to have the house after his father's death; but the father loved them all alike, and did not know what to do. He did not wish to sell the house, because it had belonged to his forefathers, else he might have divided the money amongst them.

At last a plan came into his head, and he said to his sons, "Go into the world, and try each of you to learn a trade. When you all come back, he who makes the best masterpiece shall have the house."

The sons were well content with this, and the eldest determined to be a blacksmith, the second a barber, and the third a fencing-master. They fixed a time when they should all come home again, and then each went his way.

It chanced that they all found skilful masters, who taught them their trades well. The blacksmith had to shoe the King's horses, and he thought to himself, "The house is mine, without doubt." The barber shaved only great people, and he too already looked upon the house as his own. The fencing-master got many a blow, but he only bit his lip, and let nothing vex him; "for," said he to himself, "if you are afraid of a blow, you'll never win the house."

When the appointed time had gone by, the three brothers came back home to their father. But they did not know how to find the best opportunity for showing their skill, so they sat down and consulted together.

As they were sitting thus, all at once a hare came running across the field. "Ah, ha, just in time!" said the barber. So he took his basin and soap, and lathered away until the hare came up. Then he soaped and shaved off the hare's whiskers whilst he was running at the top of his speed, and did not even cut his skin or injure a hair on his body.

"Well done!" said the old man, "your brothers will have to exert themselves wonderfully, or the house will be yours."

Soon after, up came a nobleman in his coach, dashing along at full speed. "Now you shall see what I can do, Father," said the blacksmith. So away he ran after the coach, took all four shoes off the feet of one of the horses whilst he was galloping, and put on four new shoes without stopping him.

"You are a fine fellow, and as clever as your brother," said his father. "I do not know to which I ought to give the house."

Then the third son said, "Father, let me have my turn, if you please." And, as it was beginning to rain, he drew his sword, and flourished it backward and forward above his head so fast that not a drop fell upon him. It rained still harder and harder, till at last it came down in torrents. But he only flourished his sword faster and faster, and remained as dry as if he were sitting in a house.

When his father saw this he was amazed, and said, "This is the masterpiece, the house is yours!"

His brothers were satisfied with this, as was agreed beforehand. And, as they loved one another very much, they all three stayed together in the house, followed their trades, and, as they had learnt them so well and were so clever, they earned a great deal of money.

Thus they lived together Happily, until they grew old. And at last, when one of them fell sick and died, the two others grieved so sorely about it that they also fell ill, and soon after died. And because they had been so clever, and had loved one another so much, they were all laid in the same grave.

LITTLE TABLE SET THYSELF, GOLD-ASS, AND CUDGEL OUT OF THE SACK

There was once upon a time, a tailor, who had three sons and only one goat. But as the goat supported the whole of them with her milk, she was obliged to have good food, and to be taken every day to pasture. The sons, therefore, did this, in turn.

Once, the eldest took her to the churchyard, where the finest herbs were to be found, and let her eat and run about there. At night, when it was time to go home, he asked, "Goat, have you had enough?"

The goat answered:

"I have eaten so much,
Not a leaf more I'll touch,
Ma! Ma!"

"Come home, then," said the youth, and took hold of the cord round her neck, led her into the stable and tied her up securely.

"Well," said the old tailor, "has the goat had as much food as she ought?"

"Oh," answered the son, "she has eaten so much, not a leaf more she'll touch."

But the father wished to satisfy himself, and went down to the stable, stroked the dear animal and asked, "Goat, are you satisfied?"

The goat answered:

"With what should I be satisfied?
Among the graves I leapt about,
And found no food, so went without,
Ma! Ma!"

"What do I hear?" cried the tailor, and ran up-stairs and said to the youth, "Hollo, you liar; you said the goat had had enough, and have let her go hungry!" and in his anger, he took the yard-measure from the wall, and drove him out with blows.

Next day, it was the turn of the second son, who looked out for a place in the fence of the garden, where nothing but good herbs grew. And the goat cleared them all off.

At night, when he wanted to go home, he asked, "Goat, are you satisfied?"

The goat answered:

"I have eaten so much,
Not a leaf more I'll touch,
Ma! Ma!"

"Come home, then," said the youth, and led her home and tied her up in the stable.

"Well," said the old tailor, "has the goat had as much food as she ought?"

"Oh," answered the son, "she has eaten so much, not a leaf more she'll touch."

The tailor would not rely on this, but went down to the stable and said, "Goat, have you had enough?"

The goat answered:

"*With what should I be satisfied?*
Among the graves I leapt about,
And found no food, so went without,
Ma! Ma!"

"The godless wretch!" cried the tailor, "to let such a good animal go hungry," and he ran up and drove the youth out of doors with the yard-measure.

Now came the turn of the third son, who wanted to do the thing well, and sought out some bushes with the finest leaves, and let the goat devour them.

In the evening when he wanted to go home, he asked, "Goat, have you had enough?"

The goat answered:

"*I have eaten so much,*
Not a leaf more I'll touch,
Ma! Ma!"

"Come home, then," said the youth, and led her into the stable, and tied her up.

"Well," said the old tailor, "has the goat had a proper amount of food?"

"She has eaten so much, not a leaf more she'll touch."

The tailor did not trust to that, but went down and asked, "Goat, have you had enough?"

The wicked beast answered:

"With what should I be satisfied?
Among the graves I leapt about,
And found no leaves, so went without,
Ma! Ma!"

"Oh, the brood of liars!" cried the tailor, "each as wicked and forgetful of his duty as the other! Ye shall no longer make a fool of me," and, quite beside himself with anger, he ran up-stairs and belabored the poor young fellow so vigorously with the yard-measure that he sprang out of the house.

The old tailor was now alone with his goat. Next morning he went down into the stable, caressed the goat and said, "Come, my dear little animal, I myself will take you to feed."

He took her by the rope and conducted her to green hedges, and amongst milfoil, and whatever else goats like to eat. "There you may for once eat to your heart's content," said he to her, and let her browse till evening.

Then he asked, "Goat, are you satisfied?" She replied:

"I have eaten so much,
Not a leaf more I'll touch,
Ma! Ma!"

"Come home, then," said the tailor, and led her into the stable, and tied her fast.

When he was going away, he turned round again and said, "Well, are you satisfied for once?"

But the goat did not behave better to him, and cried:

"With what should I be satisfied?
Among the graves I leapt about,
And found no leaves, so went without,

Ma! Ma!"

When the tailor heard that, he was shocked, and saw clearly that he had driven away his three sons without cause. "Wait, you ungrateful creature," cried he, "it is not enough to drive you forth, I will mark you so that you will no more dare to show yourself amongst honest tailors!"

In great haste, he ran up-stairs, fetched his razor, lathered the goat's head, and shaved her as clean as the palm of his hand. And as the yard-measure would have been too good for her, he brought the horsewhip, and gave her such cuts with it that she ran away with mighty leaps.

When the tailor was thus left quite alone in his house, he fell into great grief, and would gladly have had his sons back again. But no one knew whither they were gone.

The eldest had apprenticed himself to a joiner, and learnt industriously and unweariedly, and when the time came for him to go on his travels, his master presented him with a little table which had no unusual appearance, and was made of common wood. But it had one good property; if any one put it down, and said:

"*Little Table!*
Set thyself!"

the good Little Table was at once covered with a clean little cloth. And a plate was there, and a knife and fork beside it, and dishes with boiled meats and roasted meats, as many as there was room for, and a great glass of red wine shone so that it made the heart glad.

The young journeyman thought, "With this you have enough for your whole life!" and went joyously about the world, and never troubled himself whether an inn was good or bad, or if anything was to be found in it or not. When it suited him he did not enter an inn at all, but either in the plain, a wood, a meadow, or wherever he fancied, he took his Little Table off his back, set it down before him, and said:

"*Little Table!*
Set thyself!"

and then everything appeared that his heart desired.

At length, he took it into his head to go back to his father, whose anger would now be appeased, and who would now willingly receive him with his Wishing-Table. It came to pass that on his way home, he arrived, one evening, at an inn which was filled with guests. They bade him welcome, and invited him to sit and eat with them, for otherwise he would have difficulty in getting anything.

"No," answered the joiner, "I will not take the few bites out of your mouths. Rather than that, you shall be my guests."

They laughed, and thought he was joking. He, however, placed his wooden Little Table in the middle of the room, and said:

"*Little Table!*
Set thyself!"

Instantly it was covered with food, so good that the host could never have procured it, and the smell of it arose pleasantly to the noses of the guests.

"Fall to, dear Friends," said the joiner.

And the guests, when they saw that he meant it, did not need to be asked twice, but drew near, pulled out their knives and attacked it valiantly. And what surprised them most, was that when a dish became empty, a full one instantly took its place. The innkeeper stood in one corner and watched the doings. He did not know what to say, but thought, "I could easily find use for such a cook as that in my kitchen."

The joiner and his comrades made merry until late into the night. At length they lay down to sleep, and the young apprentice also went to bed, and set his Magic Table against the wall.

The host's thoughts, however, let him have no rest. It occurred to him that there was a little old table in his lumber-room, which looked just like the apprentice's. And he brought it out quite softly, and exchanged it for the Wishing-Table.

Next morning, the joiner paid for his bed, took up his table, never thinking that he had got a false one, and went his way.

At midday, he reached his father, who received him with great joy. "Well, my dear son, what have you learnt?" said he to him.

"Father, I have become a joiner."

"A good trade," replied the old man; "but what have you brought back with you from your apprenticeship?"

"Father, the best thing which I have brought back with me is this Little Table."

The tailor examined it on all sides and said, "You did not make a masterpiece, when you made that. It is a bad old table."

"But it is a table which furnishes itself," replied the son. "When I put it down, and tell it to set itself, the most beautiful dishes stand on it, and a wine also which gladdens the heart. Just invite all our relations and friends. They shall refresh and enjoy themselves for once, for the table will give them all they require."

When the company was assembled, he put his table in the middle of the room and said:

"Little Table!
Set thyself!"

but the little table did not bestir itself, and remained just as bare as any other table which did not understand language. Then the poor apprentice became aware that his table had been changed, and was ashamed at having to stand there like a liar.

The relations, however, mocked him, and were forced to go home without having eaten or drunk. The father brought out his patches, and began to tailor again, but the son went to a master in the craft.

The second son had gone to a miller and had apprenticed himself to him. When his years were over, the master said, "As you have conducted yourself so well, I give you an Ass of a peculiar kind, which neither draws a cart nor carries a sack."

"To what use is he put, then?" asked the young apprentice.

"He lets gold drop from his mouth," answered the miller. "If you set him on a cloth, and say:

"'*Bricklebrit!*'

the good animal will drop gold pieces for you."

"That is a fine thing," said the apprentice, and thanked the master, and went out into the world. When he had need of gold, he had only to say:

"*Bricklebrit!*"

to his Ass, and it rained gold pieces, and he had nothing to do but pick them off the ground. Wheresoever he went, the best of everything was good enough for him, and the dearer the better, for he had always a full purse.

When he had looked about the world for some time, he thought, "You must seek out your father; if you go to him with the Gold-Ass, he will forget his anger, and receive you well."

It came to pass, that he reached the same public-house in which his brother's table had been exchanged. He led his Ass by the bridle, and the host was about to take the animal from him to tie him up, but the young apprentice said, "Don't trouble yourself. I will take my gray horse into the stable, and tie him up myself, for I must know where he stands."

This struck the host as odd, and he thought that a man who was forced to look after his Ass himself, could not have much to spend. But when the stranger put his hand in his pocket and brought out two gold pieces, and said he was to provide something good for him, the host opened his eyes wide, and ran and sought out the best he could muster.

After dinner, the guest asked what he owed. The host did not see why he should not double the reckoning, and said the apprentice must give two more gold pieces.

He felt in his pocket, but his gold was just at an end. "Wait an instant, sir host," said he, "I will go and fetch some money;" but he took the tablecloth with him.

The host could not imagine what this could mean, and being curious, stole after him, and as the guest bolted the stable-door, he peeped through a hole left by a knot in the wood.

The stranger spread out the cloth under the animal and cried:

"*Bricklebrit!*"

and immediately the beast began to let gold pieces fall, so that it fairly rained down money on the ground.

"Eh, my word!" said the host, "ducats are quickly coined there! A purse like that is not amiss."

The guest paid his score, and went to bed, but in the night the host stole down into the stable, led away the master of the mint, and tied up another ass in his place. Early next morning, the apprentice went away with the ass, and thought that he had his Gold-Ass.

At midday he reached his father, who rejoiced to see him again, and gladly took him in. "What have you made of yourself, my Son?" asked the old man.

"A miller, dear Father," he answered.

"What have you brought back with you from your travels?"

"Nothing else but an ass."

"There are asses enough here," said the father. "I would rather have had a good goat."

"Yes," replied the son, "but it is no common ass, but a Gold-Ass. When I say:

"'*Bricklebrit!*'

the good beast opens its mouth and drops a whole sheetful of gold pieces. Just summon all our relations hither, and I will make them rich folk."

"That suits me well," said the tailor, "for then I shall have no need to torment myself any longer with the needle;" and he ran out and called the relations together.

As soon as they were assembled, the miller bade them make way, spread out his cloth, and brought the ass into the room. "Now watch," said he, and cried:

"*Bricklebrit!*"

but no gold pieces fell, and it was clear that the animal knew nothing of the art, for every ass does not attain such perfection.

Then the poor miller pulled a long face, saw that he was betrayed, and begged pardon of the relatives, who went home as poor as they came. There was no help for it, the old man had to betake him to his needle once more, and the youth hired himself to a miller.

The third brother had apprenticed himself to a turner, and as that is skilled labor, he was the longest in learning. His brothers, however, told him in a letter how badly things had gone with them, and how the innkeeper had cheated them of their beautiful wishing-gifts on the last evening before they reached home.

When the turner had served his time, and had to set out on his travels, as he had conducted himself so well, his master presented him with a sack, and said, "There is a Cudgel in it."

"I can put on the sack," said he, "and it may be of good service to me, but why should the Cudgel be in it? It only makes it heavy."

"I will tell you why," replied the master; "if any one has done anything to injure you, do but say:

"'*Cudgel!*
Out of the sack!'

and the Cudgel will leap forth among the people, and play such a dance on their backs, that they will not be able to stir or move for a week, and it will not leave off until you say:

"'*Cudgel!*
Into the sack!'"

The apprentice thanked him, put the sack on his back, and when any one came too near him, and wished to attack him, he said:

"*Cudgel!*
Out of the sack!"

and instantly the Cudgel sprang out, and dusted the coat or jacket of one after the other on their backs, and never stopped until it had stripped it off them. And it was done so quickly, that before any one was aware, it was already his own turn.

In the evening, the young turner reached the inn where his brothers had been cheated. He laid his sack on the table before him, and began to talk of all the wonderful things which he had seen in the world. "Yes," said he, "people may easily find a Little Table which will cover itself, a Gold-Ass, and things of that kind —extremely good things which I by no means despise—but these are nothing in comparison with the treasure which I have won for myself, and am carrying about with me in my sack there."

The innkeeper pricked up his ears. "What in the world can that be?" thought he. "The sack must be filled with nothing but jewels. I ought to get them cheap too, for all good things go in threes."

When it was time for sleep, the guest stretched himself on the bench, and laid his sack beneath him for a pillow. When the innkeeper thought his guest was lying in a sound sleep, he went to him and pushed and pulled quite gently and carefully at the sack to see if he could possibly draw it away and lay another in its place. The turner had, however, been waiting for this for a long time; and now, just as the innkeeper was about to give a hearty tug, he cried:

"Cudgel!
Out of the sack!"

Instantly the little Cudgel came forth, and fell on the innkeeper, and gave him a sound thrashing.

The host cried for mercy. But the louder he cried, so much the more heavily the Cudgel beat time on his back, until at length he fell to the ground exhausted.

Then the turner said, "If you do not give back the Little Table that sets itself, and the Gold-Ass, the dance shall begin afresh."

"Oh, no," cried the host, quite humbly, "I will gladly bring out everything, only make the accursed Kobold creep back into the sack!"

Then said the apprentice, "I will let mercy take the place of justice, but beware of getting into mischief again!" So he cried:

"Cudgel!
Into the sack!"

and let him have rest.

Next morning, the turner went home to his father with the Wishing-Table, and the Gold-Ass. The tailor rejoiced when he saw him once more, and asked him likewise what he had learned in foreign parts.

"Dear Father," said he, "I have become a turner."

"A skilled trade," said the father. "What have you brought back with you from your travels?"

"A precious thing, dear Father," replied the son, "a Cudgel in the sack."

"What!" cried the father, "a Cudgel! That's worth your trouble, indeed! From every tree you can cut one for yourself."

"But not one like this, dear Father. If I say:

"'*Cudgel!*
Out of the sack!'

the Cudgel springs out and leads any one, who means ill by me, a weary dance, and never stops until he lies on the ground and prays for fair weather. Look you, with this Cudgel have I got back the Wishing-Table and the Gold-Ass, which the thievish innkeeper took away from my brothers. Now let them both be sent for, and invite all our kinsmen. I will give them to eat and to drink, and will fill their pockets with gold into the bargain."

The old tailor would not quite believe, but nevertheless got the relatives together. Then the turner spread a cloth in the room, and led in the Gold-Ass, and said to his brother, "Now, dear Brother, speak to him."

The miller said:

"*Bricklebrit!*"

and instantly the gold pieces fell down on the cloth like a thunder-shower, and the Ass did not stop until every one of them had so much that he could carry no more. (I can see in your face that you also would have liked to be there!)

Then the turner brought the Little Table, and said, "Now, dear Brother, speak to it." And scarcely had the carpenter said:

"Little Table!
Set thyself!"

than it was spread, and covered with the most exquisite dishes. Then such a meal took place as the good tailor had never yet known in his house. The whole party of kinsmen stayed together till far in the night, and were all merry and glad. The tailor locked away needle and thread, yard-measure and goose, in a press, and lived with his three sons in joy and splendor.

What, however, has become of the goat, who was to blame for the tailor driving out his three sons? That I will tell you.

She was ashamed that she had a bald head, and ran to a fox's hole and crept into it. When the fox came home, he was met by two great eyes shining out of the darkness, and was terrified and ran away. A bear met him, and as the fox looked quite disturbed, he said, "What is the matter with you, brother Fox, why do you look like that?"

"Ah," answered Redskin, "a fierce beast is in my cave and stared at me with its fiery eyes."

"We will soon drive him out," said the bear, and went with him to the cave and looked in. But when he saw the fiery eyes, fear seized him likewise. He would have nothing to do with the furious beast, and took to his heels.

The bee met him, and as she saw that he was ill at ease, she said, "Bear, you are really pulling a very pitiful face. What has become of all your jollity?"

"It is all very well for you to talk," replied the bear, "a furious beast with staring eyes is in Redskin's house, and we can't drive him out."

The bee said, "Bear, I pity you! I am a poor weak creature, whom you would not turn aside to look at. Yet I believe I can help you." She flew into the fox's cave, lighted on the goat's clean, shaved head, and stung her so hard that she sprang up crying, "*Ma! ma!*" and ran forth into the world like mad; and to this hour no one knows where she has gone.

IRON JOHN

Once on a time there was a King who had a great forest near his palace, full of all kinds of wild animals. One day he sent out a huntsman to shoot him a roe, but he did not come back.

"Perhaps some accident has befallen him," said the King, and the next day he sent out two more huntsmen who were to search for him, but they too stayed away.

Then on the third day, he sent for all his huntsmen, and said, "Scour the whole forest through, and do not give up until ye have found all three." But of these also, none came home again, and of the pack of hounds which they had taken with them, none were seen more.

From that time forth, no one would any longer venture into the forest, and it lay in deep stillness and solitude. Nothing was seen but sometimes an eagle or a hawk flying over it. This lasted for many years, when a strange huntsman came to the King asking for work, and offered to go into the dangerous forest. The King, however, would not give his consent, and said, "It is not safe in there. I fear it would fare with you no better than with the others, and you would never come out again."

The huntsman replied, "Lord, I will venture it at my own risk; of fear I know nothing."

The huntsman therefore betook himself with his dog to the forest. It was not long before the dog fell in with some game, and wanted to pursue it. But hardly had the dog run two steps when he stood before a deep pool and could go no farther. Then a naked arm stretched itself out of the water, seized him, and drew him under.

When the huntsman saw that, he went back and fetched three men to come with buckets and bale out the water. When they could see the bottom, there lay a Wild Man whose body was brown like rusty iron, and whose hair hung over his face down to his knees. They bound him with cords, and led him away to the castle.

There was great astonishment over the Wild Man. The King had him put in an iron cage in his courtyard, and forbade the door to be opened on pain of death, and the Queen herself was to take the key into her keeping. And from this time forth, every one could once more go into the forest with safety.

The King had a son, eight years old, who one day was playing in the courtyard, and while he was playing, his golden ball fell into the cage. The boy ran thither and said, "Give me my ball."

"Not till you have opened the door for me," answered the man.

"No," said the boy, "I will not do that. The King has forbidden it," and ran away.

The next day he again went and asked for his ball. The Wild Man said, "Open my door," but the boy would not.

On the third day when the King had ridden out hunting, the boy went once more and said, "I cannot open the door even if I wished, for I have not the key."

Then the Wild Man said, "It lies under your mother's pillow. You can get it there."

The boy, who wanted to have his ball back, cast all thought to the winds, and brought the key. The door opened with difficulty, and the boy pinched his fingers. When it was open, the Wild Man stepped out, gave him the golden ball, and hurried away.

But the boy was afraid. He called and cried after him, "Oh, Wild Man, do not go away, or I shall be beaten!"

The Wild Man turned back, took him up, set him on his shoulder, and went with hasty steps into the forest.

When the King came home, he saw the empty cage, and asked the Queen how that had happened. She knew nothing about it, and sought the key, but it was gone. She called the boy, but no one answered. The King sent out people to seek for him in the fields, but they did not find him. Then he could easily guess what had happened, and much grief reigned in the Royal Court.

When the Wild Man had reached once more the dark forest, he took the boy down from his shoulder, and said to him, "You will never see your father and mother again, but I will keep you with me for you have set me free, and I pity you. If you do all I bid you, you shall fare well. Of treasure and gold have I enough, and more than any one in the world."

He made a bed of moss for the boy on which he slept. And the next morning, the man took him to a well, and said, "Behold, the gold well is as bright and clear as crystal; you shall sit beside it, and take care that nothing falls into it, or it will be polluted. I will come every evening to see if you have obeyed my order."

The boy placed himself by the margin of the well, and often saw a golden fish or a golden snake show itself therein, and he took care that nothing fell in. As he was sitting thus, his finger hurt him so violently that without thinking he put it in the water. He drew it quickly out again, but saw that it was quite gilded. And whatsoever pains he took to wash the gold off again, all was to no purpose.

In the evening, Iron John came back, looked at the boy, and said, "What has happened to the well?"

"Nothing, nothing," he answered, and held his finger behind his back, that the man might not see it.

But he said, "You have dipped your finger into the water. This time it may pass, but take care you do not again let anything get in."

At daybreak the boy was already sitting by the well and watching it. His finger hurt him again, and he passed it over his head, and then unhappily a hair fell down into the well. He took it quickly out, but it was quite gilded.

Iron John came, and already knew what had happened. "You have let a hair fall into the well," said he. "I will allow you to watch by it once more, but if this happens the third time, then the well will be polluted, and you can no longer remain with me."

On the third day, the boy sat by the well, and did not stir his finger, however much it hurt him. But the time was long to him, and he looked at the reflection of his face on the surface of the water. And as he still bent down more and more trying to look straight into the eyes, his long hair fell down from his shoulders into the water. He raised himself up quickly, but the whole of the hair of his head was golden, and shone like the sun.

You may imagine how terrified the poor boy was! He took his pocket-handkerchief and tied it round his head, in order that the man might not see it.

When he came, he already knew everything, and said, "Take off the handkerchief." Then the golden hair streamed forth, and let the boy excuse himself as he might, it was of no use. "You have not stood the trial, and can no longer stay here. Go forth into the world. There you will learn what poverty is. But as you have not a bad heart, and as I mean well by you, there is one thing I will grant you. If you fall into any difficulty, come to the forest and cry, 'Iron John,' and then I will come and help you. My power is great, greater than you think, and I have gold and silver in abundance."

Then the King's Son left the forest, and walked by beaten and unbeaten paths ever onward, until at length he reached a great city. There he looked for work, but could find none, and he had learnt nothing by which he could help himself.

At length, he went to the palace, and asked if they would take him in. The people about Court did not know what use to make of him, but they liked him, and told him to stay. At last, the cook took him into his service, and said he might carry wood and water, and rake the cinders together.

Once when it happened that no one else was at hand, the cook ordered him to carry the food to the royal table, but as he did not like to let his golden hair be seen, he kept his little hat on. Such a thing as that had never come under the King's notice, and he said, "When you serve at the royal table you must take off your hat."

He answered, "Ah, Lord, I cannot."

Then the King had the cook called before him. He scolded him, and asked how he could take such a boy as that into his service; and said that he was to turn him off at once. The cook, however, had pity on him, and exchanged him for the gardener's boy.

And now, the boy had to plant and water the garden, hoe and dig, and bear the wind and bad weather.

One day in summer when he was working alone in the garden, the day was so warm he took his little hat off that the air might cool him. As the sun shone on his hair it glittered and flashed so that the rays fell into the bedroom of the King's Daughter. Up she sprang to see what it could be. Then she saw the boy, and cried to him, "Boy, bring me a wreath of flowers."

He put his hat on with all haste, and gathered wild field-flowers and bound them together. When he was ascending the stairs with them, the gardener met him, and said, "How can you take the King's Daughter a garland of such common flowers?

Go quickly, and get another, and seek out the prettiest and rarest."

"Oh, no," replied the boy, "the wild ones have more scent, and will please her better."

When he went into the room, the King's Daughter said, "Take your cap off, it is not seemly to keep it on in my presence."

He again said, "I cannot."

She, however, caught at his hat and pulled it off, and then his golden hair rolled down on his shoulders. And it was splendid to behold.

THE KING'S DAUGHTER PULLED OFF HIS HAT

He wanted to run out, but she held him by the arm, and gave him a handful of ducats. With these he departed, but he cared nothing for the gold pieces. He took them to the gardener, and said, "I give them to your children, they may play with them."

The following day, the King's Daughter again called to him that he was to bring her a wreath of field-flowers. When he went in with it, she snatched at his hat, and wanted to take it away from him, but he held it fast with both hands. She again gave him a handful of ducats. But he would not keep them, and presented them to the gardener as playthings for his children.

On the third day, things went just the same. She could not get his hat away from him, and he would not have her money.

Not long afterward, the country was overrun by war. The King gathered together his people, and did not know whether or not he could overcome the enemy, who was superior in strength and had a mighty army.

Then said the gardener's boy, "I am grown up, and will go to the wars also, only give me a horse."

The others laughed, and said, "Seek one for yourself when we are gone. We will leave one behind us in the stable for you."

When they had gone forth, he went into the stable, and got the horse. It was lame of one foot, and limped *hobblety jig, hobblety jig*. Nevertheless he mounted it, and rode away to the dark forest. When he came to the outskirts, he called "Iron John" three times so loudly that it echoed through the trees.

Thereupon the Wild Man appeared immediately, and said, "What do you desire?"

"I want a strong steed, for I am going to the wars."

"That you shall have, and still more than you ask." Then the Wild Man went back into the forest, and it was not long before a stable-boy came out of it, who led a horse that snorted, and could hardly be restrained. Behind them followed a great troop of soldiers entirely equipped in iron, and their swords flashed in the sun. The youth made over his three-legged horse to the stable-boy, mounted the other, and rode at the head of the soldiers.

When he drew near the battle-field, a great part of the King's men had already fallen, and little was wanting to make the rest give way. Then the youth galloped thither with his iron soldiers, broke like a hurricane over the enemy, and beat down all who opposed him. They began to fly, but the youth pursued, and never stopped, until there was not a single man left.

Instead, however, of returning to the King, he conducted his troop by side-roads to the forest, and called Iron John.

"What do you desire?" asked the Wild Man.

"Take back your horse and troops, and give me my three-legged horse again." All that he asked was done, and soon he was riding on his three-legged horse.

When the King returned to his palace, his daughter went to meet him, and wished him joy of his victory. "I am not the one who carried away the victory," said he, "but a stranger Knight who came to my assistance with his soldiers." The daughter wanted to hear who the strange Knight was, but the King did not know, and said, "He followed the enemy, and I did not see him again."

She inquired of the gardener where his boy was, but he smiled, and said, "He has just come home on his three-legged horse, and the others have been mocking him, and crying, 'Here comes our hobblety jig back again!' They asked, too, 'Under what hedge have you been lying sleeping all the time?' He, however, answered, 'I did the best of all, and it would have gone badly without me.' And then he was ridiculed still more."

The King said to his daughter, "I will proclaim a great feast that shall last for three days, and you shall throw a Golden Apple. Perhaps the unknown will come to it."

When the feast was announced, the youth went out to the forest, and called Iron John.

"What do you desire?" asked he.

"That I may catch the King's Daughter's Golden Apple."

"It is as safe as if you had it already," said Iron John.

"You shall likewise have a suit of red armor for the occasion, and ride on a spirited chestnut horse."

When the day came, the youth galloped to the spot, took his place amongst the Knights, and was recognized by no one. The King's Daughter came forward, and threw a Golden Apple to the Knights. None of them caught it but he; only as soon as he had it, he galloped away.

On the second day, Iron John equipped him as a white Knight, and gave him a white horse. Again he was the only one who caught the apple, and he did not linger an instant, but galloped off with it.

The King grew angry, and said, "That is not allowed. He must appear before me and tell his name." He gave the order that if the Knight who caught the apple should go away again, they should pursue him, and, if he would not come back willingly, they should cut him down and stab him.

On the third day, he received from Iron John a suit of black armor and a black horse. Again he caught the apple. But when he was riding off with it, the King's attendants pursued him, and one of them got so near that he wounded the youth's leg with the point of his sword. The youth nevertheless escaped from them, but his horse leapt so violently that the helmet fell from his head, and they could see that he had golden hair. They rode back and announced this to the King.

The following day, the King's Daughter asked the gardener about his boy. "He is at work in the garden. The queer creature has been at the festival too, and only came home yesterday evening. He has likewise shown my children three Golden Apples which he has won."

The King had him summoned into his presence. He came and again had his hat on his head. But the King's Daughter went up to him and took it off. Then his golden hair fell down over his shoulders, and he was so handsome that all were amazed.

"Are you the Knight who came every day to the festival, always in different colors, and who caught the three Golden Apples?" asked the King.

"Yes," answered he, "and here are the apples," and he took them out of his pocket, and returned them to the King. "If you desire further proof, you may see the wound which your people gave me when they followed me. But I am likewise the Knight who helped you win your victory over your enemies."

"If you can perform such deeds as that, you are no gardener's boy. Tell me, who is your father?"

"My father is a mighty King, and gold have I in plenty as much as I require."

"I well see," said the King, "that I owe thanks to you. Can I do anything to please you?"

"Yes," answered he, "that indeed you can. Give me your daughter to wife."

The maiden laughed, and said, "He does not stand much on ceremony, but I have already seen by his golden hair that he is no gardener's boy," and then she went and kissed him.

His father and mother came to the wedding, and were in great delight, for they had given up all hope of ever seeing their dear son again. And as they were sitting at the marriage-feast, the music suddenly stopped, the doors opened, and a stately King came in with a great retinue.

He went up to the youth, embraced him and said, "I am Iron John, and was by enchantment a Wild Man, but you have set me free. All the treasures which I possess, shall be yours."

CLEVER ELSIE

There was once a man who had a daughter who was called Clever Elsie. And when she had grown up her father said, "We will get her married."

"Yes," said the mother, "if only any one would come who would have her."

At length a man came from a distance, and wooed her, who was called Hans. But he made one condition, that Clever Elsie should be really wise.

"Oh," said the father, "she's sharp enough."

And the mother said, "Oh, she can see the wind coming up the street, and hear the flies coughing."

"Well," said Hans, "if she is not really wise, I won't have her."

When they were sitting at dinner, and had eaten, the mother said, "Elsie, go into the cellar and fetch some beer."

Then Clever Elsie took the pitcher from the wall, went into the cellar, and tapped the lid briskly as she went that the time might not appear long. When she was below she fetched herself a chair, and set it before the barrel, so that she had no need to stoop, and did not hurt her back or do herself any unexpected injury.

Then she placed the can before her, and turned the tap, and while the beer was running, she would not let her eyes be idle, but looked up at the wall. And after much peering here and there, saw a pickaxe exactly above her, which the masons had left there by mistake.

Then Clever Elsie began to weep and said, "If I get Hans, and we have a child, and he grows big, and we send him into the cellar here to draw beer, then the pickaxe will fall on his head and kill him." Then she sat and wept and screamed with all the strength of her body, over the misfortune which lay before her.

Those upstairs waited for the drink, but Clever Elsie still did not come. Then the woman said to the servant, "Just go down into the cellar and see where Elsie is."

The maid went and found her sitting in front of the barrel, screaming loudly.

"Elsie, why do you weep?" asked the maid.

"Ah," she answered, "have I not reason to weep? If I get Hans, and we have a child, and he grows big, and has to draw beer here, the pickaxe may fall on his head, and kill him."

Then said the maid, "What a clever Elsie we have!" and sat down beside her and began loudly to weep over the misfortune.

After a while, as the maid did not come back, and those upstairs were thirsty for the beer, the man said to the boy, "Just go down into the cellar and see where Elsie and the girl are."

The boy went down, and there sat Clever Elsie and the girl both weeping together. Then he asked, "Why are you weeping?"

"Ah," said Elsie, "have I not reason to weep? If I get Hans, and we have a child, and he grows big, and has to draw beer here, the pickaxe will fall on his head and kill him."

Then said the boy, "What a clever Elsie we have!" and sat down by her, and likewise began to howl loudly.

Upstairs they waited for the boy, but as he did not return, the man said to the woman, "Just go down into the cellar and see where Elsie is!"

The woman went down, and found all three in the midst of their lamentations, and inquired what was the cause. Then Elsie told her also, that her future child was to be killed by the pickaxe, when it grew big and had to draw beer, and the pickaxe fell down.

Then said the mother likewise, "What a clever Elsie we have!" and sat down and wept with them.

The man upstairs waited a short time, but as his wife did not come back and his thirst grew ever greater, he said, "I must go into the cellar myself and see where Elsie is."

But when he got into the cellar, and they were all sitting together crying, and he heard the reason, and that Elsie's child was the cause, and that Elsie might perhaps bring one into the world some day, and that it might be killed by the pickaxe, if it should happen to be sitting beneath it, drawing beer just at the very time when it fell, he cried, "Oh, what a clever Elsie!" and sat down, and likewise wept with them.

The Bridegroom stayed up-stairs alone for a long time; then as no one came back he thought, "They must be waiting for me below. I, too, must go there and see what they are about."

When he got down, all five of them were sitting screaming and lamenting quite piteously, each outdoing the other.

"What misfortune has happened then?" asked he.

"Ah, dear Hans," said Elsie, "if we marry each other and have a child, and he is big, and we perhaps send him here to draw something to drink, then the pickaxe which has been left up there might dash his brains out, if it were to fall down, so have we not reason to weep?"

"Come," said Hans, "more understanding than that is not needed for my household, as you are such a clever Elsie, I will have you," and he seized her hand, took her upstairs with him, and married her.

After Hans had had her some time, he said, "Wife, I am going out to work and earn money for us. Go into the field and cut the corn, that we may have some bread."

"Yes, dear Hans, I will do that."

After Hans had gone away, she cooked herself some good broth, and took it into the field with her. When she came to the field she said to herself, "What shall I do? Shall I shear first, or shall I eat first? Oh, I will eat first."

Then she emptied her basin of broth, and when she was fully satisfied, she once more said, "What shall I do? Shall I shear first, or shall I sleep first? I will sleep first." Then she lay down among the corn and fell asleep.

Hans had been at home for a long time, but Elsie did not come. Then said he, "What a clever Elsie I have. She is so industrious, that she does not even come home to eat."

As, however, she still stayed away, and it was evening, Hans went out to see what she had cut. But nothing was cut, and she was lying among the corn, asleep. Then Hans hastened home and brought a fowler's net with little bells and hung it round about her, and she still went on sleeping. Then he ran home, shut the house-door, and sat down in his chair and worked.

At length, when it was quite dark, Clever Elsie awoke and when she got up there was a jingling all round about her, and the bells rang at each step which she took. Then she was frightened, and became uncertain whether she really was Clever Elsie or not, and said, "Is it I, or is it not I?"

But she knew not what answer to make to this, and stood for a time in doubt. At length she thought, "I will go home and ask if it be I, or if it be not I. They will be sure to know."

She ran to the door of her own house, but it was shut. Then she knocked at the window and cried, "Hans, is Elsie within?"

"Yes," answered Hans, "she is within."

Hereupon she was terrified, and said, "Ah, heavens! Then it is not I," and went to another door.

But when the people heard the jingling of the bells, they would not open it, and she could get in nowhere. Then she ran out of the village, and no one has seen her since.

THE BREMEN TOWN-MUSICIANS

A certain man had a Donkey, which had carried the corn-sacks to the mill faithfully for many a long year; but his strength was going, and he was growing more and more unfit for work.

Then his master began to consider how he might best save his keep; but the Donkey, seeing that no good wind was blowing, ran away and set out on the road to Bremen.

"There," he thought, "I can surely be town-musician."

When he had walked some distance, he found a Hound lying on the road, gasping like one who had run till he was tired.

"What are you gasping so for, you big fellow?" asked the Donkey.

"Ah," replied the Hound, "as I am old, and daily grow weaker and no longer can hunt, my master wants to kill me. So I have taken to flight. But now how am I to earn my bread?"

"I tell you what," said the Donkey, "I am going to Bremen, and shall be town-musician there. Come with me and engage yourself also as a musician. I will play the lute, and you shall beat the kettledrum."

The Hound agreed, and on they went.

Before long, they came to a Cat, sitting on the path, with a face like three rainy days!

"Now then, old shaver, what has gone askew with you?" asked the Donkey.

"Who can be merry when his neck is in danger?" answered the Cat. "Because I am now getting old, and my teeth are worn to stumps, and I prefer to sit by the fire and spin, rather than hunt about after mice, my mistress wants to drown me, so I have run away. But now good advice is scarce. Where am I to go?"

"Come with us to Bremen. You understand night-music, so you can be a town-musician."

The Cat thought well of it, and went with them.

After this the three fugitives came to a farmyard, where the Cock was sitting upon the gate, crowing with all his might.

"Your crow goes through and through one," said the Donkey. "What is the matter?"

"I have been foretelling fine weather, because it is the day on which Our Lady washes the Christ-child's little shirts, and wants to dry them," said the Cock. "But guests are coming for Sunday, so the housewife has no pity, and has told the cook that she intends to eat me in the soup to-morrow. This evening I am to have my head cut off. Now I am crowing at full pitch while I can."

"Ah, but Red-Comb," said the Donkey, "you had better come away with us. We are going to Bremen. You can find something better than death everywhere. You have a good voice, and if we make music together, it must have some quality!"

The Cock agreed to this plan, and all four went on together.

They could not, however, reach the city of Bremen in one day, and in the evening they came to a forest where they meant to pass the night. The Donkey and the Hound laid themselves down under a large tree. The Cat and the Cock settled themselves in the branches; but the Cock flew right to the top, where he was most safe.

Before he went to sleep, he looked round on all the four sides, and thought he saw in the distance a little spark burning. So he called out to his companions that there must be a house not far off, for he saw a light.

The Donkey said, "If so, we had better get up and go on, for the shelter here is bad."

The Hound thought that a few bones with some meat would do him good too!

They made their way to the place where the light was, and soon saw it shine brighter and grow larger, until they came to a well-lighted robber's house. The Donkey, as the biggest, went to the window and looked in.

"What do you see, my Grey-Horse?" asked the Cock.

"What do I see?" answered the Donkey; "a table covered with good things to eat and drink, and robbers sitting at it enjoying themselves."

"That would be the sort of thing for us," said the Cock.

"Yes, yes! ah, how I wish we were there!" said the Donkey.

Then the animals took counsel together as to how they could drive away the robbers, and at last they thought of a plan. The Donkey was to place himself with his forefeet upon the window-ledge, the Hound was to jump on the Donkey's back, the Cat was to climb upon the Hound, and lastly the Cock was to fly up and perch upon the head of the Cat.

When this was done, at a given signal, they began to perform their music together. The Donkey brayed, the Hound barked, the Cat mewed, and the Cock crowed. Then they burst through the window into the room, so that the glass clattered!

At this horrible din, the robbers sprang up, thinking no otherwise than that a ghost had come in, and fled in a great fright out into the forest.

The four companions now sat down at the table, well content with what was left, and ate as if they were going to fast for a month.

As soon as the four minstrels had done, they put out the light, and each sought for himself a sleeping-place according to his nature and to what suited him. The Donkey laid himself down upon some straw in the yard, the Hound behind the door, the Cat upon the hearth near the warm ashes, and the Cock perched himself upon a beam of the roof. Being tired with their long walk, they soon went to sleep.

When it was past midnight, the robbers saw from afar that the light was no longer burning in their house, and all appeared quiet.

The captain said, "We ought not to have let ourselves be frightened out of our wits;" and ordered one of them to go and examine the house.

The messenger finding all still, went into the kitchen to light a candle, and, taking the glistening fiery eyes of the Cat for live coals, he held a lucifer-match to them to light it. But the Cat did not understand the joke, and flew in his face, spitting and scratching.

He was dreadfully frightened, and ran to the back door, but the Dog, who lay there, sprang up and bit his leg.

Then, as he ran across the yard by the straw-heap, the Donkey gave him a smart kick with his hind foot. The Cock, too, who had been awakened by the noise, and had become lively, cried down from the beam:

"*Kicker-ee-ricker-ee-ree!*"

Then the robber ran back as fast as he could to his captain, and said, "Ah, there is a horrible Witch sitting in the house, who spat on me and scratched my face with her long claws. By the door stands a man with a knife, who stabbed me in the leg. In the yard there lies a black monster, who beat me with a wooden club. And above, upon the roof, sits the judge, who called out:

"'*Bring the rogue here to me!*'

so I got away as well as I could."

After this the robbers did not trust themselves in the house again. But it suited the four musicians of Bremen so well that they did not care to leave it any more.

And the mouth of him who last told this story, is still warm.

THE SIX SWANS

Once upon a time, a certain King was hunting in a great forest, and he chased a wild beast so eagerly that none of his attendants could follow him. When evening drew near, he stopped and looked around him, and saw that he had lost his way. He sought a way out, but could find none. Then he perceived an Old Woman with a head which nodded all the time, who came toward him, but she was a Witch.

"Good woman," said he to her, "can you not show me the way through the forest?"

"Oh, yes, Lord King," she answered, "that I certainly can, but on one condition, and if you do not fulfill that, you will never get out of the forest, and will die of hunger in it."

"What kind of a condition is it?" asked the King.

"I have a daughter," said the old woman, "who is as beautiful as any one in the world, and well deserves to be your wife. If you will make her your Queen, I will show you the way out of the forest."

In the anguish of his heart the King consented, and the old woman led him to her little hut, where her daughter was sitting by the fire. She received the King as if she had been expecting him. He saw that she was very beautiful, but still she did not please him, and he could not look at her without secret horror.

After he had taken the maiden up on his horse, the old woman showed him the way, and the King reached his royal palace again, where the wedding was celebrated.

The King had already been married once, and had by his first wife, seven children, six boys and a girl, whom he loved better than anything else in the world. As he now feared that the new Queen might not treat them well, and even do them some injury, he took them to a lonely castle which stood in the midst of a forest. It lay concealed, and the way was so difficult to find, that he himself would not have found it at all, if a Wise Woman had not given him a ball of yarn with wonderful properties. When he threw it down before him, it unrolled itself and showed him his path.

The King, however, went so frequently to visit his dear children, that the Queen noticed his absence. She was curious and wanted to know what he did when he was alone in the forest. She gave a great deal of money to his servants, and they betrayed the secret to her, and told her likewise of the ball which alone could point out the way.

And now she knew no rest until she had learnt where the King kept the ball of yarn. Then she made little shirts of white silk, and as she had learnt the art of witchcraft from her mother, she sewed a charm inside them. And one day, when the King had ridden forth to hunt, she took the little shirts and went into the forest, and the ball showed her the way.

The children, who saw from a distance that some one was approaching, thought that their dear father was coming to them, and full of joy, ran to meet him. Then she threw one of the little shirts over each of them. And no sooner had the shirts touched their bodies than they were changed into Swans, and flew away over the forest.

The Queen went home quite delighted, and thought she had got rid of all the children, but the girl had not run out with her brothers, and the Queen knew nothing about her.

Next day, the King went to visit his children, but found no one but the little girl.

"Where are your brothers?" asked the King.

"Alas, dear Father," she answered, "they have gone away and left me alone!" and she told him that she had seen from her little window, how her brothers had flown away over the forest in the shape of Swans. And she showed him the feathers, which they had let fall in the courtyard, and which she had picked up.

The King mourned, but he did not think that the Queen had done this wicked deed. And as he feared that the girl also would be stolen from him, he wanted to take her away. But she was afraid of the Queen, and entreated the King to let her stay just one night more in the forest-castle.

The poor girl thought, "I can no longer remain here. I will go and seek my brothers." And when night came, she ran away, and went straight into the forest.

She walked the whole night long, and next day also without stopping, until she could go no farther for weariness. Then she saw a forest-hut, and went into it, and found a room with six little beds. She did not venture to get into any of them, but crept under one, and lay down on the hard ground, to pass the night there. Just before sunset she heard a rustling, and saw six Swans come flying in at the window. They alighted on the ground and blew at each other, and blew all the feathers off, and their swan's skins stripped off like a shirt.

Then the maiden looked at them and recognized her brothers. She rejoiced and crept forth from beneath the bed. The brothers were not less delighted to see their little sister, but their joy was short.

"Here can you not abide," they said to her. "This is a shelter for robbers. If they come home and find you, they will kill you."

"But can you not protect me?" asked the little sister.

"No," they replied, "only for one quarter of an hour each evening, can we lay aside our swan's skins and have our human form. After that, we are once more turned into Swans."

The little sister wept, and said, "Can you not be set free?"

"Alas, no," they answered, "the conditions are too hard! For six years you may neither speak nor laugh, and in that time you must sew together six little shirts of Star-Flowers for us. And if one single word falls from your lips, all your work will be lost."

And when the brothers had said this, the quarter of an hour was over, and they flew out of the window again as Swans.

THE PRINCESS WENT OUT AND GATHERED STAR-FLOWERS

The maiden, however, resolved to deliver her brothers, even if it should cost her her life. She left the hut, went into the midst of the forest, seated herself on a tree, and there passed the night. Next morning, she went out and gathered Star-Flowers and began to sew. She could not speak to any one, and she had no wish to laugh. She sat there and looked at nothing but her work.

When she had spent a long time there, it came to pass that the King of the country was hunting in the forest, and his huntsmen came to the tree on which the maiden was sitting.

They called to her, and said, "Who are you?" But she made no answer. "Come down to us," said they. "We will not do you any harm."

She only shook her head. As they pressed her further with questions, she threw her golden necklace down to them, and thought to content them with that. They, however, did not cease, and then she threw her girdle down to them, and as this also was to no use, her garters, and little by little everything which she had on that she could do without, until she had nothing left but her shift. The huntsmen, however, did not let themselves be turned aside by that, but climbed the tree and fetched the maiden down and led her before the King.

The King asked, "Who are you? What are you doing on the tree?"

But she did not answer. He put the question in every language that he knew, but she remained as mute as a fish. As she was so beautiful, the King's heart was touched, and he was smitten with a great love for her. He put his mantle on her, took her before him on his horse, and carried her to his castle.

Then he caused her to be dressed in rich garments, and she shone in her beauty like bright daylight, but no word could be drawn from her. He placed her by his side at table, and her modest bearing and courtesy pleased him so much, that he said,

"She is the one whom I wish to marry, and no other woman in the world." And a few days after, he united himself to her.

The King, however, had a wicked mother, who was dissatisfied with his marriage and spoke ill of the young Queen.

"Who knows," said she, "from whence comes the creature, who can't speak? She is not worthy of a King!"

After a year had passed, when the Queen brought her first child into the world, the old woman took it away from her and smeared her mouth with blood as she slept. Then she went to the King and accused the Queen of being a man-eater. The King would not believe it, and would not suffer any one to do her injury. She, however, sat continually sewing at the shirts, and cared for nothing else.

The next time, when she again bore a beautiful boy, the false old woman used the same treachery, but the King could not bring himself to believe her words. He said, "She is too pious and good to do anything of that kind. If she were not dumb, and could defend herself, her innocence would come to light."

But when the old woman stole away the newly-born child for the third time, and accused the Queen, who did not utter one word of defense, the King could do no otherwise than deliver her over to justice; and she was sentenced to be burned.

When the day came for the sentence to be executed, it was the last day of the six years during which she was not to speak or laugh, and she had delivered her dear brothers from the power of the enchantment. The six shirts were ready, only the left sleeve of the sixth was wanting.

When, therefore, she was led to the stake, she laid the shirts on her arm. And when she stood on high and the fire was just going to be lighted, she looked around and six Swans came flying through the air toward her. Then she saw that her deliverance was near, and her heart leapt with joy.

The Swans swept toward her and sank down so that she could throw the shirts over them. And as they were touched by them, their swan's skins fell off, and her brothers stood in their own form before her, vigorous and handsome. The youngest lacked only his left arm, and had in its place a swan's wing on his shoulder.

They embraced and kissed each other, and the Queen went to the King, who was greatly moved, and she began to speak, and said, "Dearest Husband, now I may speak and declare to you that I am innocent, and falsely accused." And she told him of the treachery of the old woman who had taken away her three children, and hidden them.

To the great joy of the King, they were brought back. And as a punishment, the wicked woman was bound to the stake and burned to ashes.

But the King and the Queen, with their six brothers, lived many years in happiness and peace.

THE POOR MILLER'S BOY AND THE CAT

In a certain mill, lived an old miller who had neither wife nor child. Three apprentices served under him.

As they had been with him several years, he one day said to them, "I am old, and want to sit in the chimney-corner. Go out, and whichsoever of you brings me the best horse, to him will I give the mill. And in return for it, he shall take care of me till my death."

The third of the boys was, however, the drudge, who was looked on as foolish by the others. They begrudged the mill to him, and afterward he would not have it.

Then all three went out together, and when they came to the village, the two said to stupid Hans, "You may just as well stay here; as long as you live you will never get a horse."

Hans, however, went with them, and when it was night they came to a cave in which they lay down to sleep. The two sharp ones waited until Hans had fallen asleep, then they got up, and went away leaving him where he was. They thought they had done a very clever thing, but it was certain to turn out ill for them.

When the sun arose, and Hans woke up, he was lying in a deep cavern. He looked around on every side and exclaimed, "Oh, alas! where am I?"

Then he got up and clambered out of the cave, into the forest, thinking:

"Here I am quite alone and deserted, how shall I obtain a horse now?"

Whilst he was thus walking full of thought, he met a small Tabby-Cat which said quite kindly, "Hans, where are you going?"

"Alas, you cannot help me."

"I well know your desire," said the Cat. "You wish to have a beautiful horse. Come with me, and be my faithful servant for seven years, and then I will give you a horse more beautiful than any you have ever seen in your whole life."

"Well, this is a wonderful Cat!" thought Hans, "but I am determined to see if she is telling the truth."

So she took him with her into her enchanted castle, where there were nothing but cats who were her servants. They leapt nimbly upstairs and downstairs, and were merry and happy.

In the evening when they sat down to dinner, three of them had to make music. One played the bassoon, the other the fiddle, and the third put the trumpet to his lips, and blew out his cheeks as much as he possibly could.

When they had dined, the table was carried away, and the Cat said, "Now, Hans, come and dance with me."

"No," said he, "I won't dance with a pussy cat. I have never done that yet."

"Then take him to bed," said she to the cats.

So one of them lighted him to his bedroom, one pulled his shoes off, one his stockings, and at last one of them blew out the candle.

Next morning they returned and helped him out of bed, one put his stockings on for him, one tied his garters, one brought his shoes, one washed him, and one dried his face with her tail.

"That feels very soft!" said Hans.

He, however, had to serve the Cat, and chop some wood every day. And to do that, he had an axe of silver, while the wedge and saw were of silver and the mallet of copper. So he chopped the wood small.

He stayed there in the house and had good meat and drink, but never saw any one but the Tabby-Cat and her servants.

Once she said to him, "Go and mow my meadow, and dry the grass," and gave him a scythe of silver, and a whetstone of gold, but bade him deliver them up again carefully.

So Hans went thither, and did what he was bidden, and when he had finished the work, he carried the scythe, whetstone, and hay to the house, and asked if it was not yet time for her to give him his reward.

"No," said the Cat, "you must first do something more for me of the same kind. There is timber of silver, carpenter's axe, square, and everything that is needful, all of silver, with these build me a small house."

Then Hans built the small house, and said that he had now done everything, and still he had no horse.

Nevertheless, the seven years had gone by with him as if they were six months. The Cat asked him if he would like to see her horses?

"Yes," said Hans.

Then she opened the door of the small house. And when she had opened it, there stood twelve horses,—such horses, so bright and shining, that his heart rejoiced at the sight of them.

And now she gave him to eat and to drink, and said, "Go home. I will not give you your horse to take away with you. But in three days' time, I will follow you and bring it."

So Hans set out, and she showed him the way to the mill. She had, however, never once given him a new coat, and he had been obliged to keep on his dirty old smock-frock, which he had brought with him, and which during the seven years had everywhere become too small for him.

When he reached home, the two other apprentices were there again, and each of them certainly had brought a horse with him.

But one of them was blind and the other lame. They asked Hans where his horse was.

"It will follow me in three days' time."

Then they laughed and said, "Indeed, stupid Hans! where will you get a horse? It will be a fine one!"

Hans went into the parlor, but the miller said he should not sit down to table for he was so ragged and torn, that they would all be ashamed of him if any one came in. So they gave him a mouthful of food outside.

At night, when they went to rest, the two others would not let him have a bed, and at last he was forced to creep into the goose-house, and lie down on a little hard straw.

In the morning, when he awoke, the three days had passed, and a coach came with six horses and they shone so bright that it was delightful to see them!—and a servant brought a seventh as well, which was for the poor miller's boy.

And a magnificent Princess alighted from the coach, and went into the mill. And this Princess was the little Tabby-Cat whom poor Hans had served for seven years.

She asked the miller where the miller's boy and drudge was.

Then the miller said, "We will not have him here in the mill, he is so ragged. He is lying in the goose-house."

Then the King's Daughter said that they were to fetch him immediately.

So they brought him; and he had to hold his little smock together to cover himself.

Her servants unpacked splendid garments, and washed him and dressed him. And when it was done, no King could have looked more handsome.

Then the Princess desired to see the horses, which the other apprentices had brought home with them. One of them was blind and the other lame. So she ordered her servants to bring the seventh horse.

When the miller saw it, he said such a horse as that had never before entered his yard.

"And that is for the third miller's boy," said she.

"Then he must have the mill," said the miller.

But the Princess said that the horse was for himself, and that he was to keep his mill as well. Then she took her faithful Hans, set him in the coach, and drove away with him.

They first drove to the little house, which he had built with the silver tools. Behold! it was a great castle! Everything inside it was of silver and gold!

Then she married him; and he was rich, so rich that he had enough for all the rest of his life.

After this, let no one say that any one who is silly can never become a person of importance.

LITTLE RED-CAP

Once upon a time, there was a sweet little girl, who was loved by every one who looked at her, and most of all by her Grandmother. There was nothing that she would not have given the child!

Once she gave her a little cap of red velvet, which suited her so well that she would not wear anything else. So she was always called Little Red-Cap.

One day, her Mother said to her, "Come, Little Red-Cap, here is a piece of cake and a bottle of wine. Take them to your Grandmother. She is ill and weak, and they will do her good. Set out before it gets hot. Walk nicely and quietly. Do not run off the path, or you may fall and break the bottle; then your Grandmother will get nothing! When you go into her room, don't forget to say 'Good morning,' and don't stop to peep into every corner, before you do it."

"I'll take great care," said Little Red-Cap to her Mother, and gave her hand on it.

The Grandmother lived in the wood, half an hour's distance from the village, and just as Little Red-Cap entered the wood, a Wolf met her. Red-Cap did not know what a wicked creature he was, and was not at all afraid of him.

"Good-day, Little Red-Cap," said he.

"Thank you kindly, Wolf."

"Whither away so early, Little Red-Cap?"

"To my Grandmother's."

"What have you got in your apron?"

"Cake and wine. Yesterday was baking-day, so poor sick Grandmother is to have something good, to make her stronger."

"Where does your Grandmother live, Little Red-Cap?"

"A good quarter of an hour farther on in the wood. Her house stands under the three large oak-trees; the nut-trees are just below. You surely must know it," replied Little Red-Cap.

The Wolf thought to himself, "What a tender young creature! what a nice plump mouthful—she will be better to eat than the old woman. I must act craftily, so as to catch both."

He walked for a short time by the side of Little Red-Cap, and then he said, "See, Little Red-Cap, how pretty the flowers are about here—why do you not look round? I believe, too, that you do not hear how sweetly the little birds are singing. You walk gravely along as if you were going to school, while everything else in the wood is merry."

Little Red-Cap raised her eyes, and when she saw the sunbeams dancing here and there through the trees, and pretty flowers growing everywhere, she thought, "Suppose I take Grandmother a fresh nosegay. That would please her too. It is so early in the day that I shall still get there in good time."

And so she ran from the path into the wood to look for flowers. And whenever she had picked one, she fancied that she saw a still prettier one farther on, and ran after it, and thus got deeper and deeper into the wood.

Meanwhile, the Wolf ran straight to the Grandmother's house and knocked at the door.

"Who is there?"

"Little Red-Cap," replied the Wolf. "She is bringing cake and wine. Open the door."

"Lift the latch," called out the Grandmother, "I am too weak, and cannot get up."

The Wolf lifted the latch, the door flew open, and without saying a word he went straight to the Grandmother's bed, and devoured her. Then he put on her clothes, dressed himself in her cap, laid himself in bed, and drew the curtains.

Little Red-Cap, however, had been running about picking flowers. When she had gathered so many that she could carry no more, she remembered her Grandmother, and set out on the way to her.

She was surprised to find the cottage-door standing open. And when she went into the room, she had such a strange feeling, that she said to herself, "Oh dear! how uneasy I feel to-day, and at other times I like being with Grandmother so much."

She called out, "Good morning," but received no answer. So she went to the bed and drew back the curtains. There lay her Grandmother with her cap pulled far over her face, and looking very strange.

"Oh! Grandmother," she said, "what big ears you have!"

"The better to hear you with, my Child," was the reply.

"But, Grandmother, what big eyes you have!" she said.

"The better to see you with, my dear."

"But, Grandmother, what large hands you have!"

"The better to hug you with."

"Oh! but Grandmother, what a terrible big mouth you have!"

"The better to eat you with!" And scarcely had the Wolf said this, than with one bound he was out of bed and swallowed up Red-Cap.

When the Wolf had satisfied his appetite, he lay down again in the bed, fell asleep and began to snore very loud. The huntsman was just passing the house, and thought to himself, "How the old woman is snoring! I must just see if she wants anything."

So he went into the room, and when he came to the bed, he saw the Wolf lying in it. "Do I find thee here, thou old sinner!" said he. "I have long sought thee!"

Then just as he was going to fire at him, it occurred to him that the Wolf might have devoured the grandmother, and that she might still be saved. So he did not fire, but took a pair of scissors, and began to cut open the stomach of the sleeping Wolf.

When he had made two snips, he saw the little Red-Cap shining, and then he made two snips more, and the little girl sprang out, crying, "Ah, how frightened I have been! How dark it was inside the Wolf!"

And after that the aged grandmother came out alive also, but scarcely able to breathe.

Red-Cap then quickly fetched great stones with which they filled the Wolf's body. And when he awoke, he wanted to run away, but the stones were so heavy that he tumbled down at once, and fell dead.

Then all three were delighted. The huntsman drew off the Wolf's skin and went home with it. The grandmother ate the cake and drank the wine which Red-Cap had brought, and grew strong again.

But Red-Cap thought to herself, "As long as I live, I will never leave the path to run into the wood, when my mother has forbidden me to do so."

KING THRUSHBEARD

A King had a daughter who was beautiful beyond all measure, but so proud and haughty withal that no suitor was good enough for her. She sent away one after the other, and made fun of them as well.

Once the King gave a great feast and invited thereto, from far and near, all the young men likely to marry. They were marshalled in a row according to their rank and standing. First came the Kings, then the Grand-dukes, then the Princes, the Earls, the Barons, and the gentry.

Then the King's Daughter was led through the ranks, but to every one she had some objection to make. One was too fat, "The wine-cask," she said. Another was too tall, "Long and thin has little in." The third was too short, "Short and thick is never quick." The fourth was too pale, "As pale as death." The fifth too red, "A fighting-cock." The sixth was not straight enough, "A green log dried behind the stove."

So she had something to say against every one. But she made herself especially merry over a good King, who stood quite high up in the row, and whose chin had grown a little crooked. "Well," she cried and laughed, "he has a chin like a thrush's beak!" and from that time he got the name of King Thrushbeard.

But the old King, when he saw that his daughter did nothing but mock people, and despised all the suitors who were gathered there, was very angry, and swore that she should have for her husband the very first beggar that came to his doors.

A few days afterward, a fiddler came and sang beneath the windows, trying to earn a small alms. When the King heard him, he said, "Let him come up."

So the fiddler came up, in his dirty, ragged clothes, and sang before the King and his daughter. When he had ended he asked for a trifling gift.

The King said, "Your song has pleased me so well that I will give you my daughter there, to wife."

The King's Daughter shuddered, but the King said, "I have taken an oath to give you to the very first beggar man, and I will keep it."

All she could say was in vain; the priest was brought, and she had to let herself be wedded to the fiddler on the spot.

When that was done the King said, "Now it is not proper for you, a beggar woman, to stay any longer in my palace, you may go away with your husband."

The beggar man led her out by the hand, and she was obliged to go away on foot with him. When they came to a large forest she asked, "To whom does that beautiful forest belong?"

"It belongs to King Thrushbeard. If you had taken him, it would have been yours." "Ah, unhappy girl that I am! If I had but taken King Thrushbeard!"

Afterward, they came to a meadow, and she asked again, "To whom does this beautiful green meadow belong?"

"It belongs to King Thrushbeard. If you had taken him, it would have been yours."

"Ah, unhappy girl that I am! If I had but taken King Thrushbeard!"

Then they came to a large town, and she asked again, "To whom does this fine large town belong?"

"It belongs to King Thrushbeard. If you had taken him, it would have been yours."

"Ah, unhappy girl that I am! If I had but taken King Thrushbeard!"

"It does not please me," said the fiddler, "to hear you always wishing for another husband. Am I not good enough for you?"

"WELL," SHE LAUGHED, "HE HAS A CHIN LIKE A THRUSH'S BEAK"

At last they came to a very little hut, and she said, "Oh, goodness! what a small house! To whom does this miserable, mean hovel belong?"

The fiddler answered, "That is my house and yours, where we shall live together."

She had to stoop in order to go in at the low door. "Where are the servants?" said the King's Daughter.

"What servants?" answered the beggar man. "You must do what you wish to have done. Just make a fire at once, and set on water to cook my supper. I am quite tired."

But the King's Daughter knew nothing about lighting fires or cooking, and the beggar man had to lend a hand himself to get anything fairly done. When they had finished their scanty meal they went to bed; but he forced her to get up quite early in the morning in order to look after the house.

For a few days, they lived in this way as well as might be, and ate up all the food in the house.

Then the man said, "Wife, we cannot go on any longer eating and drinking here and earning nothing. You must weave baskets."

He went out, cut some willows, and brought them home. Then she began to weave, but the tough willows wounded her delicate hands.

"I see that this will not do," said the man; "you had better spin; perhaps you can do that."

She sat down and tried to spin, but the hard thread soon cut her soft fingers so that the blood ran down.

"See," said the man, "you are fit for no sort of work. I have made a bad bargain with you. Now, I will try to earn a living by selling pots and earthenware. You must sit in the market-place and sell the ware."

"Alas," thought she, "if any of the people from my father's kingdom come to the market and see me sitting there, selling, how they will mock me!" But it was of no use, she had to yield unless she chose to die of hunger.

For the first time, she succeeded well, for the people were glad to buy the woman's wares because she was good-looking, and they paid her what she asked. Many even gave her the money and left the pots with her as well. So they lived on what she had earned as long as it lasted.

Then the husband bought a lot of new crockery. With this she sat down at the corner of the market-place, and set it around her ready for sale. But suddenly there came a drunken soldier galloping along, and he rode right amongst the pots, so that they were all broken into a thousand bits.

She began to weep, and did not know what to do for fear. "Alas! what will happen to me?" cried she; "what will my husband say to this?" She ran home and told him of the misfortune.

"Who would seat herself at a corner of the market-place with crockery?" said the man. "Leave off crying. I see very well that you cannot do ordinary work, so I have been to our King's palace and have asked whether they cannot find a place for a kitchen-maid. They have promised me to take you. In that way, you will get your food for nothing."

The King's Daughter was now a kitchen-maid, and had to be at the cook's beck and call, and do the dirtiest work. In each of her pockets she fastened a little jar, in which she took home her share of the leavings, and upon this they lived.

It happened that the wedding of the King's eldest son was to be celebrated. So the poor woman went up and placed herself by the door of the hall to look on. When all the candles were lit, and people, each more beautiful than the other, entered, and all was full of pomp and splendor, she thought of her lot with a sad heart, and cursed the pride and haughtiness which had humbled her, and brought her to so great poverty.

The smell of the delicious dishes which were being taken in and out reached her, and now and then the servants threw her a few morsels. These she put in her jars to take home.

All at once, the King's Son entered, clothed in velvet and silk, with gold chains about his neck. And when he saw the beautiful woman standing by the door he seized her by the hand, and would have danced with her. But she refused and shrank back with fear, for she saw that it was King Thrushbeard, her suitor whom she had driven away with scorn.

Her struggles were of no use; he drew her into the hall. But the string by which her pockets were fastened, broke, the pots fell down, the soup ran out, and the scraps were scattered all around. And when the people saw it, there arose laughter and derision, and she was so ashamed that she would rather have been a thousand fathoms below ground.

She sprang to the door and would have run away, but on the stairs a man caught her and brought her back. And when she looked at him it was King Thrushbeard!

He said to her kindly, "Do not be afraid, I and the fiddler who has been living with you in that wretched hovel are one. For love of you I disguised myself so. And I, also, was the soldier who rode through your crockery. This was all done to humble your proud spirit, and to punish you for the insolence with which you mocked me."

Then she wept bitterly and said, "I have done great wrong, and am not worthy to be your wife."

But he said, "Be comforted. The evil days are past. Now we will celebrate our wedding."

Then the maids-in-waiting came, and put the most splendid clothing on her. Her father and his whole Court arrived, and wished her happiness in her marriage to King Thrushbeard. And the joy now began in earnest. I wish you and I had been there too!

THE GOLD-CHILDREN

There was once a poor man and a poor woman who had nothing but a little cottage. They earned their bread by fishing, and always lived from hand to mouth.

But it came to pass one day, when the man was sitting by the waterside and casting his net, that he drew out a fish entirely of gold.

As he was looking at the fish, full of astonishment, it began to speak and said, "Hark you, Fisherman, if you will throw me back again into the water, I will change your little hut into a splendid castle."

Then the fisherman answered, "Of what use is a castle to me, if I have nothing to eat?"

The Gold Fish continued, "That shall be taken care of. There will be a cupboard in the castle in which, when you open it, shall be dishes of the most delicate meats, and as many of them as you may desire."

"If that be true," said the man, "then I can well do you a favor."

"Yes," said the Fish, "there is, however, the condition that you shall tell no one in the world, whosoever he may be, whence your good luck has come. If you speak but one single word, all will be over."

Then the man threw the wonderful Fish back again into the water, and went home.

Where his hovel had formerly stood, now stood a great castle. He opened wide his eyes, entered, and saw his wife dressed in beautiful clothes, sitting in a splendid room.

She was quite delighted, and said, "Husband, how has all this come to pass? It suits me very well."

"Yes," said the man, "it suits me too. But I am frightfully hungry, just give me something to eat."

Said the wife, "But I have got nothing and don't know where to find anything in this new house."

"There is no need of your knowing," said the man, "for I see yonder a great cupboard, just unlock it."

When she opened it, lo! there stood cakes, meat, fruit, wine.

Then the woman cried joyfully, "What more can you want, my dear?" and they sat down, and ate and drank together.

When they had had enough, the woman said, "But, Husband, whence come all these riches?"

"Alas," answered he, "do not question me about it, for I dare not tell you anything. If I disclose it to any one, then all our good fortune will fly."

"Very good," said she, "if I am not to know anything, then I do not want to know anything."

However, she was not in earnest. She never rested day or night, and she goaded her husband until in his impatience he revealed that all was owing to a wonderful Gold Fish which he had caught, and to which in return he had given its liberty.

And as soon as the secret was out, the splendid castle with the cupboard immediately disappeared. They were once more in the old fisherman's hut, and the man was obliged to follow his former trade and fish.

But fortune would so have it, that he once more drew out the Gold Fish. "Listen," said the Fish, "if you will throw me back into the water again, I will once more give you the castle with the cupboard full of roast and boiled meats. Only be firm; for your life's sake don't reveal from whom you have it, or you will lose it all again!"

"I will take good care," answered the fisherman, and threw the fish back into the water.

Now at home, everything was once more in its former magnificence. The wife was overjoyed at their good fortune. But curiosity left her no peace, so that after a couple of days she began to ask again how it had come to pass, and how he had managed to secure it.

The man kept silence for a short time, but at last she made him so angry that he broke out and betrayed the secret. In an instant the castle disappeared, and they were back again in their old hut.

"Now you have got what you want," said he; "and we can gnaw at a bare bone again."

"Ah," said the woman, "I had rather have no riches; if I am not to know from whom they come, then I have no peace."

The man went back to fish, and after a while he chanced to draw out the Gold Fish for a third time.

"Listen," said the Fish, "I see very well that I am fated to fall into your hands. Take me home and cut me into six pieces. Give your wife two of them to eat, two to your horse, and bury two of them in the ground. Then they will bring you a blessing."

The fisherman took the Fish home with him, and did as it had bidden him.

It came to pass that from the two pieces that were buried in the ground, two Golden Lilies sprang up; that the horse had two Golden Foals; and the fisherman's wife bore two children who were made entirely of gold.

The children grew up, became tall and handsome, and the lilies and horses grew likewise.

Then the lads said, "Father, we want to mount our Golden Steeds and travel out in the world."

But he answered sorrowfully, "How shall I bear it, if you go away and I know not how it fares with you?"

Then they said, "The two Golden Lilies remain here. By them you may see how it is with us. If they are fresh, then we are in health. If they are withered, we are ill. If they perish, then we are dead."

So they rode forth and came to an inn, in which were many people. They perceived the Gold-Children and began to laugh, and jeer.

When one of them heard the mocking he felt ashamed and would not go out into the world, but turned back and went home again to his father. But the other rode forward and reached a great forest.

As he was about to enter it, the people said, "It is not safe for you to ride through; the wood is full of robbers, who would treat you badly. You will fare ill. When they see that you are all of gold and your horse likewise, they will assuredly kill you."

But he would not allow himself to be frightened, and said, "I must and will ride through it."

Then he took bear-skins and covered himself and his horse with them, so that the gold was not seen, and rode fearlessly into the forest. When he had ridden onward a little, he heard a rustling in the bushes, and heard voices speaking together.

From one side came cries of, "There is one!" but from the other, "Let him go! 'tis an idle fellow, as poor and bare as a church-mouse. What should we gain from him?"

So the Gold-Child rode joyfully through the forest, and no evil befell him.

One day he entered a village wherein he saw a maiden, who was so beautiful that he did not believe that any more beautiful than she existed in the world.

And as such a mighty love took possession of him, he went up to her and said, "I love you with my whole heart. Will you be my wife?"

THE MAIDEN SAID, "I WILL BE TRUE TO YOU, YOUR LIFE LONG"

He, too, pleased the maiden so much that she agreed and said, "Yes, I will be your wife, and be true to you your whole life long."

They were married. Then just as they were in the greatest happiness, home came the father of the Bride. When he saw that his daughter's wedding was being celebrated, he was astonished, and said, "Where is the Bridegroom?"

They showed him the Gold-Child, who, however, still wore his bear-skins.

Then the father said wrathfully, "A vagabond shall never have my daughter!" and was about to kill him.

Then the Bride begged as hard as she could, and said, "He is my husband, and I love him with all my heart!" until at last he allowed himself to be appeased.

Nevertheless the idea never left his thoughts, so that next morning he rose early, wishing to see whether his daughter's husband was a common ragged beggar. But when he peeped in, he saw a magnificent golden man in the bed, and the cast-off bear-skins lying on the ground.

Then he went back, and thought, "What a good thing it was that I restrained my anger! I should have committed a great crime."

But the Gold-Child dreamed that he rode out to the chase of a splendid stag, and when he awoke in the morning, he said to his wife, "I must go out hunting."

She was uneasy, and begged him to stay there, and said, "You might easily meet with a great misfortune."

But he answered, "I must and will go."

Thereupon he got up, and rode forth into the forest. It was not long before a fine stag crossed his path exactly according to his dream. He aimed and was about to shoot it, when the stag ran away. He gave chase over hedges and ditches for the whole day without feeling tired. In the evening the stag vanished from his sight, and when the Gold-Child looked round him, he was standing before a little house, wherein was a Witch.

He knocked, and a little old woman came out and asked, "What are you doing so late in the midst of the great forest?"

"Have you not seen a stag?"

"Yes," answered she, "I know the stag well," and thereupon a little dog which had come out of the house with her, barked at the man violently.

"Will you be silent, you odious toad," said he, "or I will shoot you dead."

Then the Witch cried out in a passion, "What! will you slay my little dog?" and immediately she transformed him, so that he lay like a stone.

Meanwhile his Bride awaited him in vain, and thought, "That which I so greatly dreaded, which lay so heavily on my heart, has come upon him!"

But at home, the other brother was standing by the Gold-Lilies, when one of them suddenly drooped. "Alas!" said he, "my brother has met with some great misfortune! I must away to see if I can possibly rescue him."

Then he mounted his Golden Horse, and rode forth and entered the great forest, where his brother lay turned to stone. The old Witch came out of her house and called him, wishing to entrap him also.

He did not go near her, but said, "I will shoot you, if you do not bring my brother to life again."

She touched the stone, though very unwillingly, with her forefinger. Then he was immediately restored to his human shape.

The two Gold-Children rejoiced, when they saw each other again. They kissed and caressed each other, and rode away together out of the forest, the one home to his Bride, the other to his father.

The father then said, "I knew well that you had rescued your brother, for the Golden Lily suddenly rose up and blossomed out again."

Then they lived happily, and all prospered with them until their death.

LITTLE SNOW-WHITE

Once upon a time, in the middle of winter, when the flakes of snow were falling like feathers from the sky, a Queen sat at a window sewing, and the frame of the window was made of black ebony.

And whilst she was sewing and looking out of the window at the snow, she pricked her finger with the needle, and three drops of blood fell upon the snow. And the red looked pretty upon the white snow, and she thought to herself, "Would that I had a child as white as snow, as red as blood, and as black as the wood of the window-frame."

Soon after that she had a little daughter, who was as white as snow, and as red as blood, and her hair was as black as ebony. She was therefore called little Snow-White. And when the child was born, the Queen died.

After a year had passed the King took to himself another wife. She was a beautiful woman, but proud and haughty, and she could not bear that any one else should surpass her in beauty. She had a wonderful looking-glass, and when she stood in front of it and looked at herself in it, and said:

"Looking-Glass, Looking-Glass, on the wall,
Who in this land is the fairest of all?"

the Looking-Glass answered:

"Thou, O Queen, art the fairest of all!"

Then she was satisfied, for she knew that the Looking-Glass spoke the truth.

But little Snow-White was growing up, and grew more and more beautiful. When she was seven years old she was as beautiful as the day, and more beautiful than the Queen herself. And once when the Queen asked her Looking-Glass:

"Looking-Glass, Looking-Glass, on the wall,
Who in this land is the fairest of all?"

it answered:

"Thou art fairer than all who are here, Lady Queen.
But more beautiful still is Snow-White, I ween."

Then the Queen was shocked, and turned yellow and green with envy. From that hour, whenever she looked at little Snow-White, her heart heaved in her breast, she hated the maiden so much.

And envy and pride grew higher and higher in her heart like a weed, so that she had no peace day or night. She called a huntsman, and said, "Take the child away into the forest. I will no longer have her in my sight. Kill her."

The huntsman obeyed, and took her away. But when he had drawn his knife, and was about to pierce little Snow-White's innocent heart, she began to weep, and said, "Ah, dear Huntsman, leave me my life! I will run away into the wild forest, and never come home again."

And as she was so beautiful, the huntsman had pity on her and said, "Run away, then, you poor child." "The wild beasts will soon have devoured you," thought he, and yet it seemed as if a stone had been rolled from his heart since it was no longer needful for him to kill her.

But now, the poor child was all alone in the great forest, and so terrified that she looked at every leaf of every tree, and did not know what to do. Then she began to run, and ran over sharp stones and through thorns, and the wild beasts ran past her, but did her no harm.

She ran as long as her feet would go, until it was almost evening. Then she saw a little cottage and went into it to rest herself. Everything in the cottage was small, but neater and cleaner than can be told. There was a table on which was a white cover, and seven little plates, and on each plate a little spoon. Moreover, there were seven little knives and forks, and seven little mugs. Against the wall stood seven little beds side by side, and covered with snow-white counterpanes.

Little Snow-White was so hungry and thirsty, that she ate some vegetables and bread from each plate and drank a drop of wine out of each mug, for she did not wish to take all from one only. Then, as she was so tired, she laid herself down on one of the little beds, but none of them suited her. One was too long, another too short, but at last she found that the seventh one was right, so she remained in it, said a prayer and went to sleep.

When it was quite dark the owners of the cottage came back. They were seven Dwarfs who dug and delved in the mountains for ore. They lit their seven candles, and, as it was now light within the cottage, they saw that some one had been there, for everything was not in the same order in which they had left it.

The first said, "Who has been sitting on my chair?"

The second, "Who has been eating off my plate?"

The third, "Who has been taking some of my bread?"

The fourth, "Who has been eating my vegetables?"

The fifth, "Who has been using my fork?"

The sixth, "Who has been cutting with my knife?"

The seventh, "Who has been drinking out of my mug?"

Then the first looked round and saw that there was a little hole on his bed, and he said, "Who has been getting into my bed?"

The others came up and each called out, "Somebody has been lying in my bed too."

But the seventh when he looked at his bed saw little Snow-White, who was lying fast asleep therein. And he called the others, who came running up, and they cried out with astonishment, and brought their seven little candles and let the light fall on little Snow-White.

"Oh, oh!" cried they, "what a lovely child!" and they were so glad that they did not wake her up, but let her sleep on in the bed. And the seventh Dwarf slept with his companions, one hour with each, and so got through the night.

The next morning, little Snow-White awoke, and was frightened when she saw the seven Dwarfs. But they were friendly and asked her what her name was.

"My name is little Snow-White," she answered.

"How have you come to our house?" said the Dwarfs.

Then she told them that the wicked Queen had wished to have her killed, but that the huntsman had spared her life, and that she had run for the whole day, until at last she had found their dwelling.

The Dwarfs said, "If you will take care of our house, cook, make the beds, wash, sew, and knit, and if you will keep everything neat and clean, you may stay with us and you shall want for nothing."

"Yes," said little Snow-White, "with all my heart," and she stayed with them.

She kept the house in order for them. In the mornings they went to the mountains and looked for copper and gold, in the evenings they came back, and then their supper had to be ready.

The maiden was alone the whole day, so the good Dwarfs warned her and said, "Beware of the Queen, she will soon know that you are here. Be sure to let no one come in."

But the Queen, believing that little Snow-White was dead, could not but think that she herself was again the first and most beautiful of all. She went to her Looking-Glass, and said:

"*Looking-Glass, Looking-Glass, on the wall,*
Who in this land is the fairest of all?"

and the Glass answered:

"*Oh, Queen, thou art fairest of all I see,*
But over the hills, where the Seven Dwarfs dwell,
Little Snow-White is alive and well,
And none is so fair as she."

Then she was astounded, for she knew that the Looking-Glass never spoke falsely, and she knew that the huntsman had betrayed her, for that little Snow-White was still alive.

And so she thought and thought again how she might kill her, for so long as she herself was not the fairest in the whole land, envy let her have no rest. And when she had at last thought of something to do, she painted her face, and dressed herself like an old pedler-woman, and no one could have known her.

In this disguise she went over the Seven Mountains to the Seven Dwarfs, and knocked at the door and cried, "Pretty things to sell, very cheap, very cheap!"

Little Snow-White looked out at the window, and called, "Good-day, my dear woman, what have you to sell?"

"Good things, pretty things," she answered; "stay-laces of all colors," and she pulled out one which was woven of bright-colored silk.

"I may let the worthy old woman in," thought little Snow-White, and she unbolted the door and bought the pretty laces.

"Child," said the old woman, "what a fright you look. Come, I will lace you properly for once."

Little Snow-White had no suspicion, but stood before her, and let herself be laced with the new laces. But the old woman laced so quickly and laced so tightly that little Snow-White lost her breath and fell down as if dead.

"Now I am the most beautiful," said the Queen to herself, and ran away.

Not long afterward, in the evening, the Seven Dwarfs came home. But how shocked they were when they saw their dear little Snow-White lying on the ground, and that she neither stirred nor moved, and seemed to be dead. They lifted her up, and, as they saw that she was laced too tightly, they cut the laces. Than she began to breathe a little, and after a while came to life again.

When the Dwarfs heard what had happened, they said, "The old pedler-woman was no one else than the wicked Queen. Take care and let no one come in when we are not with you."

But the wicked woman, when she had reached home, went in front of the Glass and asked:

"Looking-Glass, Looking-Glass, on the wall,
Who in this land is the fairest of all?"

and it answered as before:

"Oh, Queen, thou art fairest of all I see,
But over the hills, where the Seven Dwarfs dwell,
Little Snow-White is alive and well,
And none is so fair as she."

When she heard that, all her blood rushed to her heart with fear, for she saw plainly that little Snow-White was again alive. "But now," she said, "I will think of something that shall put an end to you," and by the help of witchcraft, which she understood, she made a poisonous comb.

Then she disguised herself, and took the shape of another old woman. So she went over the Seven Mountains to the Seven Dwarfs, knocked at the door, and cried, "Good things to sell, cheap, cheap!"

Little Snow-White looked out, and said, "Go away. I cannot let any one come in."

"I suppose you may look," said the old woman, and pulled the poisonous comb out and held it up.

It pleased the maiden so well that she let herself be beguiled, and opened the door. When they had made a bargain, the old woman said, "Now I will comb you properly for once."

Poor little Snow-White had no suspicion, and let the Old Woman do as she pleased. But hardly had she put the comb in her hair, then the poison in it took effect, and the maiden fell down senseless.

"You paragon of beauty," said the wicked woman, "you are done for now!" and she went away.

But fortunately it was almost evening, and the Seven Dwarfs came home. When they saw little Snow-White lying as if dead upon the ground, they at once suspected the Queen. They looked and found the poisoned comb. Scarcely had they taken it out, when little Snow-White came to herself, and told them what had happened. Then they warned her once more to be upon her guard, and to open the door to no one.

The Queen, at home, went in front of the Glass and said:

"Looking-Glass, Looking-Glass, on the wall,
Who in this land is the fairest of all?"

then it answered as before:

"Oh, Queen, thou art fairest of all I see,
But over the hills, where the Seven Dwarfs dwell,
Little Snow-White is alive and well,
And none is so fair as she."

When she heard the Glass speak thus, she trembled and shook with rage. "Little Snow-White shall die," she cried, "even if it costs me my life!"

Thereupon she went into a secret, lonely room, where no one ever came, and there she made a very poisonous apple. Outside it looked pretty, white with a red cheek, so that every one who saw it longed for it. But whoever ate a piece of it must surely die.

When the apple was ready, she painted her face, and dressed herself as a countrywoman, and so she went over the Seven Mountains to the Seven Dwarfs. She knocked at the door. Little Snow-White put her head out of the window and said, "I cannot let any one in. The Seven Dwarfs have forbidden me."

"It is all the same to me," answered the woman, "I shall soon get rid of my apples. There, I will give you one."

"No," said little Snow-White, "I dare not take anything."

"Are you afraid of poison?" said the old woman. "Look, I will cut the apple in two pieces. You eat the red cheek, and I will eat the white."

The apple was so cunningly made that only the red cheek was poisoned. Little Snow-White longed for the fine apple, and when she saw that the woman ate part of it, she could resist no longer, and stretched out her hand and took the poisonous half. But hardly had she a bit of it in her mouth, than she fell down dead.

Then the Queen looked at her with a dreadful look, and laughed aloud, and said, "White as snow, red as blood, black as ebony-wood! This time the Dwarfs cannot wake you up again!"

And when she asked of the Looking-Glass at home:

"Looking-Glass, Looking-Glass, on the wall,

Who in this land is the fairest of all?"
it answered at last:
"Oh, Queen, in this land thou art fairest of all."

Then her envious heart had rest, so far as an envious heart can have rest.

The Dwarfs, when they came home in the evening, found little Snow-White lying upon the ground. She breathed no longer and was dead. They lifted her up, looked to see whether they could find anything poisonous, unlaced her, combed her hair, washed her with water and wine, but it was all of no use. The poor child was dead, and remained dead. They laid her upon a bier, and all seven of them sat round it and wept for her, and wept three days long.

Then they were going to bury her, but she still looked as if she was living, and still had her pretty red cheeks. They said, "We could not bury her in the dark ground," and they had a transparent coffin of glass made, so that she might be seen from all sides. They laid her in it, and wrote her name upon it in golden letters, and that she was a King's Daughter.

Then they put the coffin out upon the mountain, and one of them always stayed by it to watch it. And birds came too, and wept for little Snow-White; first an owl, then a raven, and last a dove.

And now little Snow-White lay a long, long time in the coffin. She did not change, but looked as if she were asleep; for she was as white as snow, as red as blood, and her hair was as black as ebony.

It happened, however, that a King's Son came into the forest, and went to the Dwarfs' house to spend the night. He saw the coffin on the mountain, and the beautiful little Snow-White within it, and read what was written upon it in golden letters.

Then he said to the Dwarfs, "Let me have the coffin. I will give you whatever you want for it."

But the Dwarfs answered, "We will not part with it for all the gold in the world."

Then he said, "Let me have it as a gift, for I cannot live without seeing little Snow-White. I will honor and prize her as my dearest possession," As he spoke in this way the good Dwarfs took pity upon him, and gave him the coffin.

And now the King's Son had it carried away by his servants on their shoulders. And it happened, that they stumbled over a tree-stump, and with the shock the poisonous piece of apple, which little Snow-White had bitten off, came out of her throat. And before long she opened her eyes, lifted up the lid of the coffin, sat up, and was once more alive.

"Oh, where am I?" she cried.

The King's Son, full of joy, said, "You are with me," and told her what had happened, and said, "I love you more than everything in the world. Come with me to my father's palace, you shall be my wife."

And little Snow-White was willing, and went with him, and their wedding was held with great show and splendor. But the wicked Queen was also bidden to the feast. When she had arrayed herself in beautiful clothes, she went before the Looking-Glass, and said:

"Looking-Glass, Looking-Glass, on the wall,
Who in this land is the fairest of all?"

the Glass answered:

"Oh, Queen, of all here the fairest art thou,
But the young Queen is fairer by far, I trow!"

Then the wicked woman uttered a curse, and was so wretched, so utterly wretched, that she knew not what to do. At first she would not go to the wedding at all, but she had no peace, and must go to see the young Queen.

And when she went in she knew little Snow-White. And she stood still with rage and fear, and could not stir. But iron slippers had already been put upon the fire, and they were brought in with tongs, and set before her. Then she was forced to put on the red-hot shoes, and dance until she dropped down dead.

RUMPELSTILTSKIN

Once there was a miller who was poor, but who had a beautiful daughter. Now it happened that he had to speak to the King, and in order to make himself appear important he said to him, "I have a daughter who can spin straw into gold."

The King said to the miller, "That is an art which pleases me well. If your daughter is as clever as you say, bring her to-morrow to my palace, and I will try what she can do."

And when the girl was brought to him, he took her into a room which was quite full of straw, gave her a spinning-wheel and a reel, and said, "Now set to work. If by to-morrow morning early, you have not spun this straw into gold, you must die."

There upon he himself locked up the room, and left her in it alone. So there sat the poor miller's daughter, and for her life could not tell what to do. She had no idea how straw could be spun into gold; and she grew more and more miserable, until at last she began to weep.

But all at once the door opened, and in came a Little Man, and said, "Good evening, Mistress Miller. Why are you crying so?"

"Alas!" answered the girl, "I have to spin straw into gold, and I do not know how to do it."

"What will you give me," said the Little Man, "if I do it for you?"

"My necklace," said the girl.

The Little Man took the necklace, seated himself in front of the wheel, and *whirr, whirr, whirr,* three turns, and the reel was full. Then he put another on, and *whirr, whirr, whirr,* three times round, and the second was full too. And so it went on till the morning, when all the straw was spun, and all the reels were full of gold.

By daybreak, the King was there, and when he saw the gold, he was astonished and delighted, but his heart became only more greedy. He had the miller's daughter taken into another room full of straw, which was much larger, and commanded her to spin that also in one night if she valued her life.

The girl knew not how to help herself, and was crying, when the door again opened, and the Little Man appeared, and said, "What will you give me if I spin the straw into gold for you?"

"The ring on my finger," answered the girl.

The Little Man took the ring, again began to turn the wheel, and, by morning, had spun all the straw into glittering gold.

The King rejoiced beyond measure at the sight, but still he had not gold enough. He had the miller's daughter taken into a still larger room full of straw, and said, "You must spin this, too, in the course of this night. But if you succeed, you shall be my wife." "Even if she be a miller's daughter," thought he, "I could not find a richer wife in the whole world."

When the girl was alone the Little Man came again for the third time, and said, "What will you give me if I spin the straw for you this time also?"

"I have nothing left that I could give," answered the girl.

"Then promise me, if you should become Queen, your first child."

"Who knows whether that will ever happen?" thought the miller's daughter. And, not knowing how else to help herself in this difficulty, she promised the Little Man what he wanted. And for that he once more span the straw into gold.

And when the King came in the morning, and found all as he had wished, he took her in marriage. And the pretty miller's daughter became a Queen.

A year after, she had a beautiful child, and she never gave a thought to the Little Man. But suddenly he came into her room, and said, "Now give me what you promised."

The Queen was horror-struck, and offered the Little Man all the riches of the kingdom if he would leave her the child.

But the Little Man said, "No, something that is alive, is dearer to me than all the treasures in the world."

Then the Queen began to weep and cry, so that the Little Man pitied her. "I will give you three days' time," said he; "if by that time you find out my name, then you shall keep your child."

So the Queen thought the whole night of all the names that she had ever heard, and she sent a messenger over the country to inquire, far and wide, for any other names there might be.

When the Little Man came the next day, she began with *Caspar, Melchior, Balthazar,* and said all the names she knew, one after another. But to every one the Little Man said, "That is not my name."

On the second day, she had inquiries made in the neighborhood as to the names of the people there. And she repeated to the Little Man the most uncommon and curious, "Perhaps your name is *Shortribs*, or *Sheepshanks*, or *Laceleg*?" but he always answered, "That is not my name."

On the third day, the messenger came back again, and said, "I have not been able to find a single new name. But as I came to a high mountain at the end of the forest, where the fox and the hare bid each other good night, there I saw a little house. Before the house a fire was burning, and round about the fire a funny Little Man was jumping. He hopped upon one leg, and shouted:

"To-day I brew, to-morrow I bake,
And next, I shall the Queen's child take!
Ah! well it is, none knows the same—

That Rumpelstiltskin is my name!"

You may think how glad the Queen was when she heard the name! And when soon afterward the Little Man came in, and asked, "Now, Mistress Queen, what is my name?" she said:

"Is your name *Conrad*?"

"No."

"Is your name *Harry*?"

"No."

"Perhaps your name is *Rumpelstiltskin*?"

"The devil has told you that! the devil has told you that!" cried the Little Man, and in his anger he stamped his right foot so deep into the earth that his whole leg went in. And then in rage, he pulled at his left leg so hard with both hands, that he tore himself in two.

"PERHAPS," SAID SHE, "YOUR NAME IS RUMPELSTILTSKIN?"

LITTLE BRIAR-ROSE

Along time ago, there were a King and Queen who said every day, "Ah, if only we had a child!" but they never had one.

But it happened that once when the Queen was bathing, a Frog crept out of the water on to the land, and said to her, "Your wish shall be fulfilled. Before a year has gone by, you shall have a daughter."

What the Frog had said came true, and the Queen had a little girl, who was so pretty that the King could not contain himself for joy, and ordered a great feast. He invited not only his kindred, friends and acquaintance, but also the Wise Women, in order that they might be kind and well-disposed toward the child. There were thirteen of them in his kingdom. But, as he had only twelve golden plates for them to eat out of, one of them had to be left at home.

The feast was held with all manner of splendor. When it came to an end the Wise Women bestowed their magic gifts upon the baby. One gave Virtue, another Beauty, a third Riches, and so on with everything in the world that one can wish for.

When eleven of them had made their promises, suddenly the thirteenth came in. She wished to avenge herself for not having been invited, and without greeting, or even looking at any one, she cried with a loud voice, "The King's Daughter, in her fifteenth year, shall prick herself with a spindle, and fall down dead." And, without saying a word more, she turned round and left the room.

They were all shocked. But the twelfth, whose good wish still remained unspoken, came forward, and as she could not undo the evil sentence, but only soften it, she said, "It shall not be death, but a deep sleep of a hundred years, into which the Princess shall fall."

The King, who wished to keep his dear child from the misfortune, gave orders that every spindle in the whole kingdom should be burnt. Meanwhile, the gifts of the Wise Women were fulfilled on the young girl, for she was so beautiful, modest, sweet tempered, and wise, that every one who saw her, was bound to love her.

It happened that on the very day, when she was fifteen years old, the King and Queen were not at home, and the maiden was left in the palace quite alone. So she went round into all sorts of places, looked into rooms and bedchambers just as she liked, and at last came to an old tower. She climbed up the narrow winding-staircase, and reached a little door. A rusty key was in the lock, and when she turned it the door sprang open. There in a little room sat an Old Woman with a spindle, busily spinning flax.

"Good day, old Dame," said the King's Daughter; "what are you doing there?"

"I am spinning," said the Old Woman, and nodded her head.

"What sort of thing is that, which rattles round so merrily?" said the maiden, and she took the spindle and wanted to spin too. But scarcely had she touched the spindle when the magic decree was fulfilled, and she pricked her finger with it.

And, in the very moment when she felt the prick, she fell down upon the bed that stood there, and lay in a deep sleep. And this sleep extended over the whole palace.

The King and Queen, who had just come home, and had entered the great hall, began to go to sleep, and the whole of the Court with them. The horses, too, went to sleep in the stable, the dogs in the yard, the pigeons upon the roof, the flies on the wall. Even the fire, that was flaming on the hearth, became quiet and slept. The roast meat left off frizzling, and the cook, who was just going to pull the hair of the scullery boy, because he had forgotten something, let him go, and went to sleep. And the wind fell; and on the trees before the castle not a leaf moved again.

But round about the castle, there began to grow a hedge of thorns. Every year it became higher, and at last grew close up round the castle and all over it, so that there was nothing of it to be seen, not even the flag upon the roof.

But the story of the beautiful sleeping "Briar-Rose," for so the Princess was named, went about the country, so that from time to time Kings' Sons came and tried to get through the thorny hedge into the castle. But they found it impossible, for the thorns held fast together, as if they had hands, and the youths were caught in them, could not get loose again, and died a miserable death.

After long, long years, again a King's Son came to that country. He heard an old man talking about the thorn-hedge, and that a castle was said to stand behind it in which a wonderfully beautiful Princess, named Briar-Rose, had been asleep for a hundred years; and that the King and Queen and the whole Court were asleep likewise. He had heard, too, from his grandfather, that many Kings' Sons had come, and had tried to get through the thorny hedge, but they had remained sticking fast in it, so had died a pitiful death.

Then the youth said, "I am not afraid. I will go and see the beautiful Briar-Rose." The good old man might dissuade him as he would, he did not listen to his words.

But by this time the hundred years had just passed. The day was come when Briar-Rose was to awake again. When the King's Son came near to the thorn-hedge, it was nothing but large and beautiful flowers, which parted from each other of their own accord, and let him pass unhurt. Then they closed again behind him like a hedge.

In the castle-yard he saw the horses and the spotted hounds lying asleep. On the roof, sat the pigeons with their heads under their wings. And when he entered the house, the flies were asleep upon the wall, the cook in the kitchen was still holding out his hand to seize the boy, and the maid was sitting by the black hen which she was going to pluck.

He went on farther, and in the great hall he saw the whole of the Court lying asleep, and by the throne lay the King and Queen.

Then he went on still farther, and all was so quiet that a breath could be heard. At last he came to the tower, and opened the door into the little room where Briar-Rose was sleeping. There she lay, so beautiful that he could not turn his eyes away. He stooped down and gave her a kiss. But as soon as he kissed her, Briar-Rose opened her eyes and awoke, and looked at him quite sweetly.

Then they went down together, and the King awoke, and the Queen, and the whole Court, and gazed at each other in great astonishment. And the horses in the courtyard stood up and shook themselves. The hounds jumped up and wagged their tails. The pigeons upon the roof pulled out their heads from under their wings, looked round, and flew into the open country. The flies on the wall crept again. The fire in the kitchen burned up and flickered and cooked the meat. The joint began to turn and frizzle, and the cook gave the boy such a box on the ear that he screamed, and the maid plucked the fowl ready for the spit.

And then the marriage of the King's Son and Briar-Rose was celebrated with all splendor, and they lived contented to the end of their days.

THE THREE LITTLE MEN IN THE WOOD

There was once a man whose wife died, and a woman whose husband died; and the man had a daughter, and the woman also had a daughter.

The girls were acquainted with each other. They went walking together, and came to the woman's house. Then she said to the man's daughter:

"Listen! Tell your father that I would like to marry him. Then you shall wash yourself in milk every morning and drink wine; but my own daughter shall wash herself in water and drink water."

The girl went home, and told her father what the woman had said. The man said, "What shall I do? Marriage is a joy, also a torment!"

At last, as he could not decide, he pulled off his boot, and said, "Take this boot. It has a hole in the sole of it. Go with it upstairs to the loft. Hang it on the big nail. Then pour water into it. If it holds the water, then I will again take a wife. But if it runs through, I will not!"

The girl did as she was ordered, but the water drew the hole together, and the boot became full to the top. She informed her father how it had turned out.

Then he himself went up, and when he saw that she was right, he went to the widow and wooed her, and the wedding was celebrated.

The next morning, when the two girls got up, there stood before the man's daughter, milk for her to wash in and wine for her to drink. But before the woman's daughter, stood water to wash herself with and water for drinking.

On the second morning, stood water for washing and water for drinking before the man's daughter as well as before the woman's daughter.

And on the third morning, stood water for washing and water for drinking before the man's daughter, and milk for washing and wine for drinking, before the woman's daughter, and so it continued.

The woman became bitterly unkind to the man's daughter, and day by day did her best to treat her still worse. She was envious too because the man's daughter was beautiful and lovable, and her own daughter ugly and repulsive.

One day, in winter, when everything was frozen as hard as a stone, and hill and vale lay covered with snow, the woman made a frock of paper, called the man's daughter and said, "Here, put on this dress and go out into the wood, and fetch me a little basketful of strawberries,—I have a fancy for some."

"Alas!" said the girl, "no strawberries grow in winter! The ground is frozen, and besides the snow has covered everything. And why am I to go in this paper frock? It is so cold outside that one's very breath freezes! The wind will blow through the frock, and the thorns will tear it off my body."

"Will you contradict me again?" said the woman. "See that you go, and do not show your face again until you have the basketful of strawberries!"

Then she gave her a little piece of hard bread, and said, "This will last you the day," and thought, "You will die of cold and hunger outside, and will never be seen again by me."

Then the girl obeyed, and put on the paper frock, and went out with the basket. Far and wide there was nothing but snow, and not a green blade to be seen.

When she got into the wood she saw a small house out of which peeped three little Dwarfs. She wished them good day, and knocked modestly at the door. They cried, "Come in," and she entered the room and seated herself on the bench by the stove, where she began to warm herself and eat her breakfast.

The Dwarfs said, "Give us some of it."

"Willingly," said she, and divided her bit of bread in two, and gave them the half.

They asked, "What do you here in the forest in the winter time, in your thin dress?"

"Ah," she answered, "I am to look for a basketful of strawberries, and am not to go home until I can take them with me."

When she had eaten her bread, they gave her a broom and said, "Sweep away the snow at the back door with it."

But when she was outside, the three Little Men said to one another, "What shall we give her as she is so good, and has shared her bread with us?"

Then said the first, "My gift is, that every day she shall grow more beautiful."

The second said, "My gift is, that gold pieces shall fall out of her mouth every time she speaks."

The third said, "My gift is, that a King shall come and take her to wife."

The girl, however, did as the Little Men had bidden her, swept away the snow behind the little house with the broom. And what did she find but real ripe strawberries, which came up quite dark-red out of the snow! In her joy she hastily gathered her basket full, thanked the Little Men, shook hands with each of them, and ran home to take the woman what she had longed for so much.

When she went in and said good-evening, a piece of gold at once fell out of her mouth. Thereupon she related what had happened to her in the wood. But with every word she spoke, gold pieces fell from her mouth, until very soon the whole room was covered with them.

"Now look at her pride," cried the woman's daughter, "to throw about gold in that way!" but she was secretly envious of it, and wanted to go into the forest to seek strawberries.

Her mother said, "No, my dear little Daughter, it is too cold, you might die of cold."

However, as her daughter let her have no peace, the mother at last yielded, made her a magnificent dress of fur, which she was obliged to put on, and gave her bread-and-butter and cake to take with her.

The girl went into the forest and straight up to the little house. The three Little Men peeped out again, but she did not greet them. Without looking round at them and without speaking to them, she went awkwardly into the room, seated herself by the stove, and began to eat her bread-and-butter and cake.

"Give us some of it," cried the Little Men.

But she replied, "There is not enough for myself, so how can I give it away to other people?"

When she had done eating, they said, "There is a broom for you, sweep all clean for us outside by the back-door."

"Humph! Sweep for yourselves," she answered, "I am not your servant."

When she saw that they were not going to give her anything, she went out the door. Then the Little Men said to each other, "What shall we give her as she is so naughty, and has a wicked envious heart, that will never let her do a good turn to any one?"

The first said, "I grant that she may grow uglier every day."

The second said, "I grant that at every word she says, a toad shall spring out of her mouth."

The third said, "I grant that she may die a miserable death."

The maiden looked for strawberries outside, but as she found none, she went angrily home. And when she opened her mouth, and was about to tell her mother what had happened to her in the wood, with each word she said, a toad sprang out of her mouth, so that everybody was seized with horror of her.

Then her mother was still more enraged, and thought of nothing but how to do every possible injury to the man's daughter, whose beauty, however, grew daily greater. At length she took a cauldron, set it on the fire, and boiled yarn in it. When it was boiled, she flung it on the poor girl's shoulder, and gave her an axe in order that she might go on the frozen river, cut a hole in the ice, and rinse the yarn.

She was obedient, went thither and cut a hole in the ice. And while she was in the midst of her cutting, a splendid carriage came driving up, in which sat the King. The carriage stopped, and the King asked, "My Child, who are you, and what are you doing here?"

"I am a poor girl, and I am rinsing yarn."

Then the King felt compassion, and when he saw that she was so very beautiful, he said to her, "Will you go away with me?"

"Ah, yes, with all my heart," she answered, for she was glad to get away from the mother and sister.

So she got into the carriage and drove away with the King, and when they arrived at his palace, the wedding was celebrated with great pomp, as the Little Men had granted to the maiden.

THE GOLDEN BIRD

In the olden time, there was a King, who had behind his palace a beautiful pleasure-garden, in which there was a tree that bore Golden Apples. When the apples were getting ripe they were counted, but on the very next morning one was missing. This was told to the King, and he ordered that a watch should be kept every night beneath the tree.

The King had three sons, the eldest of whom he sent, as soon as night came, into the garden. But when it was midnight, he could not keep himself from sleeping, and next morning again an apple was gone.

The following night, the second son had to keep watch, it fared no better with him. As soon as twelve o'clock had struck he fell asleep, and in the morning an apple was gone.

Now, it came to the turn of the third son to watch. He was quite ready, but the King had not much trust in him, and thought that he would be of less use than his brothers. But at last he let him go.

The youth lay down beneath the tree, but kept awake, and did not let sleep master him. When it struck twelve, something rustled through the air, and in the moonlight he saw a bird coming whose feathers were shining with gold. The bird alighted on the tree, and had just plucked off an apple, when the youth shot an arrow at him. The bird flew off, but the arrow had struck his plumage, and one of his golden feathers fell down.

The youth picked it up, and the next morning took it to the King and told him what he had seen in the night. The King called his council together, and every one declared that a feather like this was worth more than the whole kingdom.

"If the feather is so precious," declared the King, "one alone will not do for me. I must and will have the whole bird!"

The eldest son set out. He trusted to his cleverness, and thought that he would easily find the Golden Bird. When he had gone some distance he saw a Fox sitting at the edge of a wood, so he cocked his gun and took aim at him.

The Fox cried, "Do not shoot me! And in return I will give you some good counsel. You are on the way to the Golden Bird. This evening you will come to a village in which stand two inns opposite to one another. One of them is lighted up brightly, and all goes on merrily within, but do not enter it. Go rather into the other, even though it seems a bad one."

"How can such a silly beast give wise advice?" thought the King's Son, and he pulled the trigger. But he missed the Fox, who stretched out his tail and ran quickly into the wood.

So he pursued his way, and by evening came to the village where the two inns were. In one they were singing and dancing. The other had a poor, miserable look.

"I should be a fool, indeed," he thought, "if I were to go into the shabby tavern, and pass by the good one." So he went into the cheerful one, lived there in riot and revel, and forgot the bird and his father, and all good counsels.

Some time had passed, and when the eldest son, month after month, did not come home, the second set out, wishing to find the Golden Bird. The Fox met him as he had met the eldest, and gave him the good advice, of which he took no heed. He came to the two inns. His brother was standing at the window of the one from which came the music, and called to him. He could not resist, but went inside, and lived only for pleasure.

IN THE MOONLIGHT HE SAW A BIRD

Again some time passed, and then the youngest King's Son wanted to set off and try his luck. But his father would not allow it. "It is of no use," said he, "he will be less likely to find the Golden Bird than his brothers. And if a mishap were to befall him, he knows not how to help himself. He is a little wanting at the best." But at last, as he had no peace, he let him go.

Again the Fox was sitting outside the wood, and begged for his life, and offered his good advice. The youth was good-natured, and said, "Be easy, little Fox, I will do you no harm."

"You shall not repent it," answered the Fox; "and that you may proceed more quickly, get up behind on my tail."

And scarcely had he seated himself, when the Fox began to run, and away he went over stock and stone till his hair whistled in the wind. When they came to the village, the youth got off. He followed the good advice, and without looking round turned into the little inn, where he spent the night quietly.

The next morning, as soon as he got into the open country, there sat the Fox already, and said, "I will tell you further what you have to do. Go straight forward. At last you will come to a castle, in front of which a whole regiment of soldiers is lying, but do not trouble yourself about them, for they will all be asleep and snoring.

"Go through the midst of them straight into the castle. Go through all the rooms, till at last you will come to a chamber where a Golden Bird is hanging in a wooden cage. Close by, there stands an empty gold cage for show. Beware of taking the bird out of the common cage and putting it into the fine one, or it may go badly with you."

With these words the Fox again stretched out his tail, and the King's Son seated himself upon it. Away he went over stock and stone, till his hair whistled in the wind.

When he came to the castle he found everything as the Fox had said. The King's Son went into the chamber where the Golden Bird was shut up in a wooden cage, whilst a golden one stood hard by; and the three Golden Apples lay about the room.

"But," thought he, "it would be absurd if I were to leave the beautiful bird in the common and ugly cage," so he opened the door, laid hold of it, and put it into the golden cage. But at the same moment the bird uttered a shrill cry.

The soldiers awoke, rushed in, and took him off to prison. The next morning he was taken before a court of justice, and as he confessed everything, was sentenced to death.

The King, however, said that he would grant him his life on one condition—namely, if he brought him the Golden Horse which ran faster than the wind. And in that case he should receive, over and above, as a reward, the Golden Bird.

The King's Son set off, but he sighed and was sorrowful, for how was he to find the Golden Horse? But all at once he saw his old friend the Fox sitting on the road.

"Look you," said the Fox, "this has happened because you did not give heed to me. However, be of good courage. I will help you, and tell you how to get to the Golden Horse. You must go straight on, and you will come to a castle, where in the stable stands the horse. The grooms will be lying in front of the stable.

"They will be asleep and snoring, and you can quietly lead out the Golden Horse. But of one thing you must take heed. Put on him the common saddle of wood and leather, and not the golden one, which hangs close by, else it will go ill with you."

Then the Fox stretched out his tail, the King's Son seated himself upon it. Away he went over stock and stone, until his hair whistled in the wind.

Everything happened just as the Fox had said. The King's Son came to the stable in which the Golden Horse was standing, but just as he was going to put the common saddle upon him, he thought, "It will be a shame to such a beautiful beast, if I do not give him the good saddle which belongs to him by right."

But scarcely had the golden saddle touched the horse than he began to neigh loudly. The grooms awoke, seized the youth, and threw him into prison. The next morning he was sentenced by the court to death; but the King promised to grant him his life, and the

Golden Horse as well, if he would rescue the beautiful Princess from the Golden Castle.

With a heavy heart the youth set out. Yet luckily for him he soon found the trusty Fox.

"I ought to leave you to your ill-luck," said the Fox, "but I pity you, and will help you once more out of your trouble. This road takes you straight to the Golden Castle. You will reach it by eventide. And at night, when everything is quiet, the beautiful Princess goes to the bathing-house to bathe. When she enters it, run up to her and give her a kiss. Then she will follow you, and you can take her away with you. Only do not allow her to say farewell to her parents first, or it will go ill with you."

Then the Fox stretched out his tail, the King's Son seated himself upon it. Away the Fox went, over stock and stone, till his hair whistled in the wind.

When he reached the Golden Castle it was just as the Fox had said. He waited until midnight, when everything lay in deep sleep, and the beautiful Princess was going to the bathing-house. Then he sprang out and gave her a kiss. She said that she would like to go with him, but she asked him pitifully, and with tears, to be allowed to take leave of her parents.

At first he withstood her prayer, but when she wept more and more, and fell at his feet, he at last gave in. But no sooner had the maiden reached the bedside of her father, than he and all the rest in the castle awoke, and the youth was laid hold of and put into prison.

The next morning, the King said to him, "Your life is forfeited, and you can only find mercy if you take away the hill which stands in front of my windows, and prevents my seeing beyond it. And you must finish it all within eight days. If you do that you shall have my daughter as your reward."

The King's Son began, and dug and shovelled without leaving off. But after seven days when he saw how little he had done, and how all his work was as good as nothing, he fell into great sorrow and gave up all hope.

On the evening of the seventh day the Fox appeared and said, "You do not deserve that I should take any trouble about you. Nevertheless, go away and lie down to sleep. I will do the work for you."

The next morning, when he awoke and looked out of the window, the hill had gone. Full of joy, the youth ran to the King, and told him that the task was fulfilled. And whether he liked it or not, the King had to hold to his word and give him his daughter.

So the two set forth together, and it was not long before the trusty Fox came up with them. "You have certainly got what is best," said he, "but the Golden Horse also belongs to the maiden of the Golden Castle."

"How shall I get it?" asked the youth.

"That I will tell you," answered the Fox; "first take the beautiful maiden to the King who sent you to the Golden Castle. There will be unheard-of rejoicing. They will gladly give you the Golden Horse, and will bring it out to you."

All was brought to pass successfully, and the King's Son carried off the beautiful Princess on the Golden Horse.

The Fox did not remain behind, and he said to the youth, "Now I will help you to get the Golden Bird. When you come near to the castle where the Golden Bird is to be found, let the maiden get down, and I will take her into my care. Then ride with the Golden Horse into the castle-yard. There will be great rejoicing at the sight, and they will bring out the Golden Bird for you."

When all was accomplished and the King's Son was about to ride home with his treasures, the Fox said, "Now you shall reward me for my help."

"What do you require for it?" asked the youth.

"When you get into the wood yonder, shoot me dead, and chop off my head and feet."

"That would be fine gratitude," said the King's Son, "I cannot possibly do that for you."

The Fox said, "If you will not do it I must leave you. But before I go away I will give you a piece of good advice. Be careful about two things. Buy no gallows'-flesh, and do not sit at the edge of any well." And then he ran into the wood.

The youth thought, "That is a wonderful beast, he has strange whims. Who is going to buy gallows'-flesh? and the desire to sit at the edge of a well has never yet seized me."

He rode on with the beautiful maiden, and his road took him again through the village in which his two brothers had remained. There was a great stir and noise, and, when he asked what was going on, he was told that two men were going to be hanged. As he came nearer to the place he saw that they were his brothers, who had been playing all kinds of wicked pranks, and had squandered their entire wealth. He inquired whether they could not be set free.

"If you will pay for them," answered the people; "but why should you waste your money on wicked men, and buy them free?"

He did not think twice about it, but paid for them. And when they were set free they all went on their way together.

They came to the wood where the Fox had first met them, and, as it was cool and pleasant within it, whilst the sun shone hotly, the two brothers said, "Let us rest a little by the well, and eat and drink."

He agreed, and whilst they were talking he forgot himself, and sat down upon the edge of the well without foreboding any evil. But the two brothers threw him backwards into the well, took the maiden, the Horse, and the Bird, and went home to their father. "Here we bring you not only the Golden Bird," said they; "we have won the Golden Horse also, and the maiden from the Golden Castle."

Then was there great joy. But the Horse would not eat, the Bird would not sing, and the maiden sat and wept.

But the youngest brother was not dead. By good fortune the well was dry, and he fell upon soft moss without being hurt. But he could not get out again. Even in this strait, the faithful Fox did not leave him. He came and leapt down to him, and upbraided him for having forgotten his advice. "But yet I cannot give it up so," he said; "I will help you up again into daylight." He bade him grasp his tail and keep tight hold of it; and then he pulled him up.

"You are not out of all danger yet," said the Fox. "Your brothers were not sure of your death, and have surrounded the wood with watchers, who are to kill you if you let yourself be seen."

But a poor man was sitting upon the road, with whom the youth changed clothes, and in this way he got to the King's palace.

No one knew him, but the Bird began to sing, the Horse began to eat, and the beautiful maiden left off weeping. The King, astonished, asked, "What does this mean?"

Then the maiden said, "I do not know, but I have been so sorrowful and now I am so happy! I feel as if my true Bridegroom had come." She told him all that had happened, although the other brothers had threatened her with death if she were to betray anything.

The King commanded that all people, who were in his castle, should be brought before him; and amongst them came the youth in his ragged clothes. But the maiden knew him at once and fell upon his neck. The wicked brothers were seized and put to death, but he was married to the beautiful maiden and declared heir to the King.

But how did it fare with the poor Fox? Long afterward, the King's Son was once again walking in the wood, when the Fox met him and said, "You have everything now that you can wish for. But there is never an end to my misery, and yet it is in your power to free me," and again he asked him with tears to shoot him dead and to chop off his head and feet.

So he did it, and scarcely was it done when the Fox was changed into a man, and was no other than the brother of the beautiful Princess, who at last was freed from the magic charm which had been laid upon him.

And now nothing more was wanting to their happiness as long as they lived.

THE QUEEN BEE

Two King's Sons once went out in search of adventures, and fell into a wild, disorderly way of living, so that they never came home again. The youngest, who was called Simpleton, set out to seek his brothers. When at length he found them, they mocked him for thinking that he with his simplicity could get through the world, when they two could not make their way, and yet were so much cleverer.

They all three traveled away together, and came to an ant-hill. The two elder wanted to destroy it, to see the little ants creeping about in their terror, carrying their eggs away, but Simpleton said, "Leave the creatures in peace. I will not allow you to disturb them."

Then they went farther, and came to a lake, on which a great number of ducks were swimming. The two brothers wanted to catch a couple and roast them, but Simpleton would not permit it, and said, "Leave the creatures in peace. I will not suffer you to kill them."

At length they came to a bee's nest, in which there was so much honey, that it ran out of the trunk of the tree where it was.

The two wanted to make a fire under the tree, and suffocate the bees in order to take away the honey, but Simpleton again stopped them and said, "Leave the creatures in peace. I will not allow you to burn them."

At last the two brothers arrived at a castle where stone horses were standing in the stables, and no human being was to be seen. They went through all the halls until they came to a door in which were three locks. In the middle of the door there was a little pane, through which they could see into the room.

There they saw a little Gray Man sitting at a table. They called him, once, twice, but he did not hear. Then they called him for the third time, when he got up, opened the locks, and came out. He said nothing but led them to a handsomely-spread table; and when they had eaten and drunk, he took each of them to a bedroom.

Next morning, the little Gray Man came to the eldest, beckoned to him, and conducted him to a stone table, on which were inscribed three tasks, by the doing of which the castle could be delivered. The first was that in the forest, beneath the moss, lay the Princess's pearls, a thousand in number, which must be picked up. And if by sunset, one single pearl was wanting, he who had looked for them would be turned to stone.

The eldest went thither, and sought the whole day, but when it came to an end, he had found only one hundred, and what was written on the table came to pass, he was changed into stone.

Next day, the second brother undertook the adventure. It did not, however, fare much better with him than with the eldest. He did not find more than two hundred pearls, and was changed to stone.

At last, the turn came to Simpleton, who sought in the moss. But it was so hard to find the pearls, and he got on so slowly, that he seated himself on a stone, and wept. And while he was thus sitting, the King of the Ants, whose life he had once saved, came with five thousand ants, and before long the little creatures had got all the pearls together, and laid them in a heap.

The second task was to fetch out of the lake the key of the King's Daughter's bedchamber. When Simpleton came to the lake, the ducks which he had saved, swam up to him, dived down, and brought the key out of the water.

But the third task was the most difficult. From amongst the three sleeping daughters of the King, the youngest and dearest was to be sought out. They resembled each other exactly, and were only to be distinguished by their having eaten different sweetmeats before they fell asleep: the eldest a bit of sugar; the second a little syrup; and the youngest a spoonful of honey.

Then the Queen of the Bees, which Simpleton had protected from the fire, came and tasted the lips of all three. At last she remained sitting on the mouth which had eaten honey; and thus the King's Son recognized the right Princess.

Then the enchantment was at an end. Everything was released from sleep, and those who had been turned to stone received once more their natural forms. Simpleton married the youngest and sweetest Princess, and after her father's death became King, while his two brothers received the two other sisters.

BIRD-FOUND

There was once a forester, who went into the forest to hunt. When he entered it, he heard a screaming as if a little child was there.

He followed the sound, and at last came to a high tree. In the top of it a little child was sitting. His mother had fallen asleep under the tree with the child, and a bird of prey had seen him in her arms, flown down, and snatched him away, and set him on the high tree.

The forester climbed the tree, and brought the child down. And he thought to himself, "I will take him home, and bring him up with my Lina."

He took him home, and the two children grew up together. The one he had found in a tree, he called Bird-Found, because a bird had carried it away.

Bird-Found and Lina loved each other so dearly, that when they did not see each other they were sad.

The forester, however, had an old cook, who one evening took two pails and began to fetch water, and did not go once only, but many times, out to the spring.

Lina saw this and said, "Hark you, old Sanna, why are you fetching so much water?"

Then the cook said, "Early to-morrow morning, when the forester is out hunting, I will heat the water. When it is boiling in the kettle, I will throw in Bird-Found, and will boil him in it."

Betimes next morning, the forester got up and went out hunting, and when he was gone the children were still in bed. Then Lina said to Bird-Found, "If you will never leave me, I will never leave you."

Bird-Found said, "Neither now, nor ever, will I leave you."

Then said Lina, "I will tell you. Last night, old Sanna carried so many buckets of water into the house that I asked her why she was doing so. She said that early to-morrow morning, when Father was out hunting, she would set on the kettle full of water, throw you into it and boil you. But we will get up quickly, dress ourselves, and go away together."

The two children, therefore, got up, dressed themselves quickly, and went away. When the water in the kettle was boiling, the cook came into the bedroom to fetch Bird-Found and throw him into it. But when she came in, and went to the beds, both the children were gone.

Then she was terribly frightened, and she said to herself, "What shall I say now when the forester comes home and sees that the children are gone? They must be followed instantly and brought back."

Then the cook sent three servants after them, who were to run and overtake the children.

The children, however, were sitting outside the forest, and when they saw from afar the three servants running, Lina said to Bird-Found, "Never leave me, and I will never leave you."

Bird-Found said, "Neither now, nor ever."

Then said Lina, "Do you become a rose-tree, and I the rose upon it."

When the three servants came to the forest, nothing was there but a rose-tree and one rose on it; the children were nowhere. Said they, "There is nothing to be done here," and they went home and told the cook that they had seen nothing in the forest but a little rose-bush with one rose on it.

Then the old cook scolded and said, "You simpletons, you should have cut the rose-bush in two, and have broken off the rose and brought it home with you. Go, and do it at once."

They had therefore to go out and look for the second time. The children, however, saw them coming from a distance.

Then Lina said, "Bird-Found, never leave me, and I will never leave you."

Bird-Found said, "Neither now, nor ever."

Said Lina, "Then do you become a church, and I'll be the chandelier in it."

So when the three servants came, nothing was there but a church, with a chandelier in it. They said therefore to each other, "What can we do here? Let us go home." When they got home, the cook asked if they had not found them. They said no, they had found nothing but a church, and that there was a chandelier in it.

The cook scolded them and said, "You fools! Why did you not pull the church to pieces, and bring the chandelier home with you?"

And now the old cook herself got on her legs, and went, with the three servants, in pursuit of the children. The children saw from afar that the three servants were coming, and the cook waddling after them.

Then said Lina, "Bird-Found, never leave me, and I will never leave you."

Then said Bird-Found, "Neither now, nor ever."

Said Lina, "Be a fishpond, and I will be the duck upon it."

The cook, however, came up to them, and when she saw the pond she lay down by it, and was about to drink it up, when she fell into the water, and there the old Witch had to drown.

Then the children went home together, and were heartily delighted, and if they are not dead, they are living still.

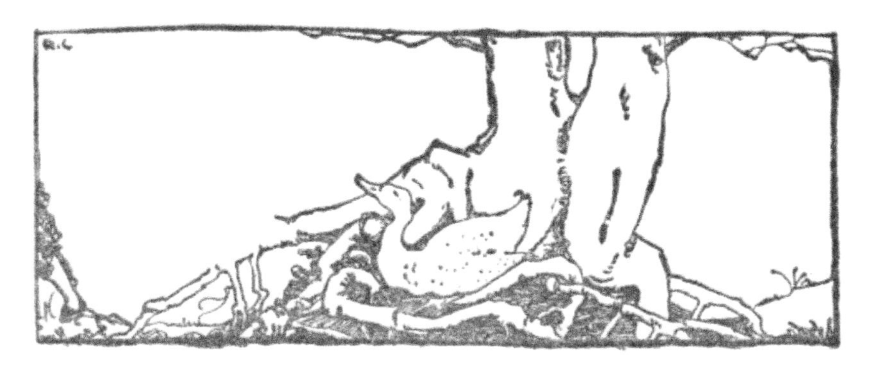

THE GOLDEN GOOSE

There was a man who had three sons, the youngest of whom was called Dunderhead, and was despised, mocked, and put down on every occasion.

It happened, that the eldest wanted to go into the forest to hew wood. Before he went his mother gave him a beautiful sweet cake and a bottle of wine, that he might not suffer from hunger or thirst.

When he entered the forest, there met him a little old Gray Man who bade him good-day, and said, "Do give me a piece of cake out of your pocket, and let me have a draught of your wine. I am so hungry and thirsty."

But the prudent youth answered, "If I give you my cake and wine, I shall have none for myself. Be off with you," and he left the Little Man standing and went on.

But when he began to hew down a tree, it was not long before he made a false stroke, and the axe cut him in the arm. So he had to go home and have it bound up. And this was the little Gray Man's doing.

After this, the second son went into the forest, and his mother gave him, like the eldest, a cake and a bottle of wine. The little old Gray Man met him likewise, and asked him for a piece of cake and a drink of wine. But the second son, too, said with much reason, "What I give you will be taken away from myself. Be off!" and he left the Little Man standing and went on.

His punishment, however, was not delayed. When he had made a few strokes at the tree, he struck himself in the leg. So he had to be carried home.

Then Dunderhead said, "Father, do let me go and cut wood."

The father answered, "Your brothers have hurt themselves doing so. Leave it alone. You do not understand anything about it."

But Dunderhead begged so long that at last he said, "Go then. You will get wiser by hurting yourself."

His mother gave him a cake made with water and baked in the cinders, and with it a bottle of sour beer.

When he came to the forest the little old Gray Man met him likewise, and greeting him said, "Give me a piece of your cake and a drink out of your bottle. I am so hungry and thirsty."

Dunderhead answered, "I have only cinder-cake and sour beer. If that pleases you, we will sit down and eat."

So they sat down, and when Dunderhead pulled out his cinder-cake, it was a fine sweet cake, and the sour beer had become good wine.

So they ate and drank, and after that the Little Man said, "Since you have a good heart, and are willing to divide what you have, I will give you good luck. There stands an old tree. Cut it down, and you will find something at the roots."

Then the old man took leave of him.

Dunderhead went and cut down the tree; and when it fell there was a Goose sitting in the roots, with feathers of pure gold. He lifted her up, and taking her with him, went to an inn, where he thought he would stay the night. Now the host had three daughters, who saw the Goose and were curious to know what such a wonderful bird might be. And each wanted one of its feathers.

The eldest thought, "I shall soon find an opportunity of pulling out a feather," and when Dunderhead was gone out, she seized the Goose by the wing. But her finger and hand remained sticking fast to it.

The second came in soon afterward, thinking only of how she might get a feather for herself, but she had scarcely touched her sister than she was held fast.

At last, the third came with the like intent, and the others screamed out, "Keep away! For goodness' sake keep away!"

But she did not understand why she was to keep away. "The others are there," she thought, "I may as well be there too," and ran to them. But as soon as she had touched her sister, she remained sticking fast to her. So they had to spend the night with the Goose.

The next morning, Dunderhead took the Goose under his arm and set out, without troubling himself about the three girls who were hanging on to it. They were obliged to run after him, now left, now right, just as he was inclined to go.

In the middle of the fields, the parson met them, and when he saw the procession he said, "For shame, you good-for-nothing girls! Why are you running across the fields after this young man? Is that seemly?" At the same time he seized the youngest by the hand in order to pull her away. But as soon as he touched her, he likewise stuck fast, and was obliged to run behind. Before long, the sexton came by and saw his master, the parson, running on foot behind three girls. He was astonished at this, and called out, "Hi! your Reverence! Whither away so quickly? Do not forget that we have a christening to-day!" and running after him he took him by the sleeve, but was also held fast.

While the five were trotting thus one behind the other, two laborers came with their hoes from the fields. The parson called out to them and begged that they would set him and the sexton free. But they had scarcely touched the sexton, when they were held fast. And now there were seven of them running behind Dunderhead and the Goose.

Soon afterward, he came to a city, where a King ruled who had a daughter who was so serious that no one could make her laugh. So he had put forth a decree that whosoever should make her laugh should marry her. When Dunderhead heard this, he went with his Goose and all her train before the King's Daughter.

As soon as she saw the seven people running on and on, one behind the other, she began to laugh very loudly as if she would never leave off. Thereupon Dunderhead asked to have her for his wife, and the wedding was celebrated.

After the King's death, Dunderhead inherited the Kingdom, and lived a long time contentedly with his wife.

MOTHER HOLLE

There was once a widow who had two daughters, one of whom was beautiful and industrious, whilst the other was ugly and lazy. But she was much fonder of the ugly and lazy one. Every day, the other, poor girl, had to sit by a well in the highway, and *spin, spin* till her fingers bled.

Now it happened, one day, that the shuttle was stained with her blood. She dipped it in the well to wash the stains off, and it dropped out of her hand and fell to the bottom. She began to weep, and ran to the woman, and told her of the mishap.

She scolded her hard, and was so cruel as to say, "Since you have let the shuttle fall in, you must fetch it out again."

So the girl went back to the well, and did not know what to do. Then in the anguish of her heart, she jumped into the well to get the shuttle. She lost her senses. But when she awoke and came to herself, she was in a lovely meadow, where the sun was shining and thousands of flowers were growing.

Along this meadow she went, and at length came to a baker's oven full of bread. And the bread cried:

"*Oh, take me out! Take me out!*
Or I shall burn. I am well baked!"

So she went up to it, and, with the bread shovel, took out all the loaves one after the other.

After that, she went on till she came to a tree covered with apples, and it called to her:

"Oh, shake me! Shake me!
We apples are all ripe!"

So she shook the tree till the apples fell like rain, and went on shaking till they were all down. And when she had gathered them into a heap, she went on her way.

At last, she came to a little house out of which an Old Woman was peeping. She had such large teeth that the girl was frightened, and was about to run away.

But the Old Woman called out to her, "What are you afraid of, my Child? Stay with me. If you will do the work in my house carefully, you shall be the better for it! Only you must take care to make my bed well, and to shake it thoroughly till the feathers fly —for then it snows on earth. I am Mother Holle."

As the Old Woman spoke so kindly to her, the girl took heart, and willingly entered her service. She did everything to the Old Woman's satisfaction, and always shook her bed so hard that the feathers flew about like snowflakes. So she lived happily with her, never an angry word, and boiled or roasted meat every day.

She stayed some time with Mother Holle, then she grew sad. At first she did not know what was the matter with her, but, by and by, she found that it was homesickness. Although she was many thousand times better off here than at home, still she had a longing to be there.

At last, she said to the Old Woman, "I am longing for home. However well off I am down here, I cannot stay any longer. I must go up again to my own people."

Mother Holle said, "I am pleased that you long for your home again. You have served me so faithfully, that I myself will take you up again."

Thereupon she took her by the hand, and led her to a large door. The door was opened, and just as the girl was standing beneath the doorway, a heavy shower of Gold-Rain fell, and all the gold stuck to her so that she was covered with it.

"You shall have that because you are so industrious," said Mother Holle. And at the same time, she gave her back the shuttle which she had let fall into the well.

Thereupon the door closed, and the girl found herself again upon the earth, not far from her mother's house.

As she went into the yard, the cock was standing by the well, and cried:

"*Cock-a-doodle-doo!*
Your Golden Girl's came back to you!"

So she went into her mother. And as she was thus covered with gold, she was welcomed by both her and the sister.

The girl told all that had happened to her. As soon as the mother heard how she had come by such great riches, she was anxious for the same good fortune to befall her ugly and lazy daughter. She had to seat herself by the well and spin. And in order that her shuttle might be stained with blood, she stuck her hand into a thorn-bush, and pricked her finger. Then she threw her shuttle into the well, and jumped in after it.

She came like the other to the beautiful meadow, and walked along the very same path. When she got to the oven, the bread cried again:

"*Oh, take me out! Take me out!*
Or I shall burn. I am well baked!"

A HEAVY SHOWER OF GOLD-RAIN FELL

But the lazy thing answered, "As if I wanted to soil myself!" and on she went.

Soon she came to the apple-tree, which cried:

"Oh, shake me! Shake me!
We apples are all ripe!"

But she answered, "I like that! One of you might fall on my head!" and on she went.

When she came to Mother Holle's house, she was not afraid, for she had already heard about her big teeth. She hired herself out immediately.

The first day, she made herself work diligently, and obeyed Mother Holle, when she told her to do anything, for she was thinking of all the gold that she would give her.

But on the second day, she began to be lazy, and on the third day stall more so, for then she would not get up in the morning. Neither did she make Mother Holle's bed carefully, nor shake it so as to make the feathers fly up.

Mother Holle was soon tired of this, and gave her notice to leave. The lazy girl was willing to go, and thought that now the Gold-Rain would come. Mother Holle led her to the great doorway. But while she was standing under it, instead of gold, a big kettleful of pitch was emptied over her.

"That is the reward of your service," said Mother Holle, and shut the door.

So the lazy girl went home. She was covered with pitch, and the cock by the well, as soon as he saw her, cried out:

"Cock-a-doodle-doo!
Your Pitchy Girl's come back to you!"

But the pitch stuck fast to her, and could not be got off so long as she lived.

THE TWO TRAVELERS

Hill and vale do not come together, but the children of men do, good and bad. In this way a shoemaker and a tailor once met with each other in their travels.

The tailor was a handsome little fellow who was always merry and full of enjoyment. He saw the shoemaker coming toward him from the other side, and as he observed by his bag what kind of a trade he plied, he sang a little mocking song to him:

Sew me the seam,
Draw me the thread,
Spread it with pitch,
Knock the nail on the head.

The shoemaker, however, could not endure a joke. He pulled a face as if he had drunk vinegar, and made a gesture as if he were about to seize the tailor by the throat.

But the little fellow began to laugh, reached him his bottle, and said, "No harm was meant, take a drink, and swallow your anger down."

The shoemaker took a very hearty drink, and the storm on his face began to clear away.

He gave the bottle back to the tailor, and said, "I spoke civilly to you. One speaks well after much drinking, but not after much thirst. Shall we travel together?"

"All right," answered the tailor, "if only it suits you to go into a big town where there is no lack of work."

"That is just where I want to go," answered the shoemaker. "In a small nest there is nothing to earn; and in the country, people like to go barefoot."

They traveled therefore onward together, and always set one foot before the other like a weazel in the snow.

Both of them had time enough, but little to bite and to break. When they reached a town, they went about and paid their respects to the tradesmen.

Because the tailor looked so lively and merry, and had such pretty red cheeks, every one gave him work willingly. And when luck was good, the master's daughters gave him a kiss beneath the porch, as well. When he again fell in with the shoemaker, the tailor had always the most in his bundle.

The ill-tempered shoemaker made a wry face, and thought, "The greater the rascal the more the luck."

But the tailor began to laugh and to sing, and shared all he got with his comrade. If a couple of pence jingled in his pockets, he ordered good cheer, and thumped the table in his joy till the glasses danced, and it was lightly come, lightly go, with him.

When they had traveled for some time, they came to a great forest through which passed the road to the capital. Two foot-paths, however, led through it, one of them a seven days' journey, and the other only two. But neither of the travelers knew which way was the short one.

They seated themselves beneath an oak-tree, and took counsel together as to what they should do and for how many days they should provide themselves with bread.

The shoemaker said, "One must look before one leaps. I will take with me bread for a week."

"What!" said the tailor, "drag bread for seven days on one's back like a beast of burden, and not be able to look about. I shall trust in God, and not trouble myself about anything! The money I have in my pocket is as good in summer as in winter; but in hot weather bread gets dry and mouldy into the bargain. Even my coat does not go as far as it might. Besides, why should we not find the right way? Bread for two days, and that's enough."

Each, therefore, bought his own bread. And then they tried their luck in the forest.

It was as quiet there as in a church. No wind stirred, no brook murmured, no bird sang, and through the thickly-leaved branches, no sunbeam forced its way.

The shoemaker spoke never a word, the heavy bread weighed down his back until the perspiration streamed down his cross and gloomy face.

The tailor, however, was quite merry; he jumped about, whistled on a leaf, or sang a song, and thought to himself, "God in Heaven must be pleased to see me so happy."

This lasted two days, but on the third the forest would not come to an end, and the tailor had eaten up all his bread, so after all his heart sank down a yard deeper. In the meantime, he did not lose courage, but relied on God and on his luck.

On the third day, he lay down in the evening hungry under a tree, and rose again next morning hungry still.

So also passed the fourth day, and when the shoemaker seated himself on a fallen tree and devoured his dinner, the tailor was only a looker-on.

If he begged for a little piece of bread the other laughed mockingly, and said, "You have always been so merry, now you can try for once what it is to be sad. The birds which sing too early in the morning, are struck by the hawk in the evening," in short he was pitiless.

But on the fifth morning, the poor tailor could no longer stand up, and was hardly able to utter one word for weakness. His cheeks were white, and his eyes red.

Then the shoemaker said to him, "I will give you a bit of bread to-day, but in return for it, I will put out your right eye."

The unhappy tailor, who still wished to save his life, could not do it in any other way. He wept once more with both eyes, and then held them out. The shoemaker, who had a heart of stone, put out his right eye with a sharp knife.

The tailor called to remembrance what his mother had formerly said to him when he had been eating secretly in the pantry, "Eat what one can, and suffer what one must."

When he had consumed his dearly-bought bread, he got on his legs again, forgot his misery and comforted himself with the thought that he could always see enough with one eye.

But on the sixth day, hunger made itself felt again, and gnawed him almost to the heart. In the evening he fell down by a tree, and on the seventh morning he could not raise himself up for faintness, and death was close at hand.

Then said the shoemaker, "I will show mercy and give you bread once more, but you shall not have it for nothing. I shall put out your other eye for it."

And now the tailor felt how thoughtless his life had been, prayed to God for forgiveness, and said, "Do what you will, I will bear what I must, but remember that our Lord God does not always look on passively, and that an hour will come when the evil deed, which you have done to me and which I have not deserved of you, will be requited. When times were good with me, I shared what I had with you. My trade is of that kind that each stitch must always be exactly like the other. If I no longer have my eyes and can sew no more, I must go a-begging. At any rate, do not leave me here alone when I am blind, or I shall die of hunger."

The shoemaker, however, who had driven God out of his heart, took the knife and put out his left eye. Then he gave him a bit of bread to eat, held out a stick to him, and drew him on behind him.

When the sun went down, they got out of the forest, and before them in the open country stood the gallows. Thither the shoemaker guided the blind tailor, and then left him alone and went his way.

Weariness, pain, and hunger made the wretched man fall asleep, and he slept the whole night. When day dawned he awoke, but knew not where he lay.

Two poor sinners were hanging on the gallows, and a crow sat on the head of each of them. Then one of the men who had been hanged began to speak, and said, "Brother, are you awake?"

"Yes, I am awake," answered the second.

"Then I will tell you something," said the first; "the dew which this night has fallen down over us from the gallows, gives every one who washes himself with it, his eyes again. If blind people did but know this, how many would regain their sight who do not believe that to be possible!"

When the tailor heard that, he took his pocket-handkerchief, pressed it on the grass, and when it was moist with dew, washed the sockets of his eyes with it. Immediately was fulfilled what the man on the gallows had said, and a couple of healthy new eyes filled the sockets.

It was not long before the tailor saw the sun rise behind the mountains. In the plain before him, lay the great royal city with its magnificent gates and hundred towers. The golden balls and crosses which were on the spires began to shine. He could distinguish every leaf on the trees, saw the birds which flew past, and the midges which danced in the air. He took a needle out of his pocket, and as he could thread it as well as ever he had done, his heart danced with delight.

He threw himself on his knees, thanked God for the mercy he had shown him, and said his morning prayer.

Then he took his bundle on his back, and soon forgot the pain of heart he had endured, and went on his way singing and whistling.

The first thing he met was a brown foal running about the fields at large. He caught it by the mane, and wanted to spring on it and ride into the town.

The foal, however, begged to be set free. "I am still too young," it said, "even a light tailor such as you are would break my back in two—let me go till I have grown strong. A time may come when I can reward you for it."

"Run off," said the tailor, "I see you are still a giddy thing."

He gave it a touch with a switch over its back, whereupon it kicked up its hind legs for joy, leapt over hedges and ditches, and galloped away into the open country.

But the little tailor had eaten nothing since the day before. "The sun to be sure fills my eyes," said he, "but the bread does not fill my mouth. The first thing that comes across me and is even half eatable, will have to suffer for it."

In the meantime a stork stepped solemnly over the meadow toward him.

"Halt, halt!" cried the tailor, and seized him by the leg. "I don't know if you are good to eat or not, but my hunger leaves me no great choice. I must cut your head off, and roast you."

"Don't do that," replied the stork; "I am a sacred bird which brings mankind great profit, and no one ever does me an injury. Leave me my life, and I may do you good in some other way."

"Well, be off, Cousin Longlegs," said the tailor.

The stork rose up, let its long legs hang down, and flew gently away.

"What's to be the end of this?" said the tailor to himself at last; "my hunger grows greater and greater, and my stomach more and more empty. Whatsoever comes in my way now is lost."

At this moment, he saw a couple of young ducks which were on a pond, come swimming toward him.

"You come just at the right moment," said he, and laid hold of one of them and was about to wring its neck.

On this an old duck, which was hidden among the reeds, began to scream loudly and swam to him with open beak, and begged him urgently to spare her dear children.

"Can you not imagine," said she, "how your mother would mourn if any one wanted to carry you off, and give you your death blow?"

"Only be quiet," said the good-tempered tailor; "you shall keep your children," and he put the prisoner back into the water.

When he turned round, he was standing in front of an old tree which was partly hollow, and saw some wild bees flying in and out of it.

"There I shall at once find the reward of my good deed," said the tailor; "the honey will refresh me."

But the Queen-Bee came out, threatened him and said, "If you touch my people, and destroy my nest, our stings shall pierce your skin like ten thousand red-hot needles. But if you will leave us in peace and go your way, we will do you a service for it another time."

The little tailor saw that here also nothing was to be done. "Three dishes empty and nothing on the fourth is a bad dinner!" He dragged himself therefore with his starved-out stomach into the town. It was just striking twelve, all was ready-cooked for him in the inn, and he was able to sit down at once to dinner.

When he was satisfied, he said, "Now I will get to work."

He went round the town, sought a master, and soon found a good situation. As he had thoroughly learned his trade, it was not long before he became famous, and every one wanted to have a new coat made by the little tailor, whose importance increased daily.

"I can go no further in skill," said he, "and yet things improve every day."

At last the King appointed him court-tailor.

But how things do happen in the world! On the very same day his former comrade, the shoemaker, also became court-shoemaker. When the latter caught sight of the tailor, and saw that he had once more two healthy eyes, his conscience troubled him.

"Before he takes revenge on me," thought he to himself, "I must dig a pit for him."

He, however, who digs a pit for another, falls into it himself.

In the evening when work was over and it had grown dusk, he stole to the King and said, "Lord King, the tailor is an arrogant fellow and has boasted that he will get the gold crown back again, which was lost in ancient times."

"That would please me very much," said the King.

He caused the tailor to be brought before him next morning, and ordered him to get the crown back again, or to leave the town for ever.

"Oho!" thought the tailor, "a rogue gives more than he has got. If the surly King wants me to do what can be done by no one, I will not wait till morning, but will go out of the town at once, to-day."

He packed up his bundle, but when he was without the gate, he could not help being sorry to give up his good fortune and turn his back on the town in which all had gone so well with him. He came to the pond where he had made the acquaintance of the ducks.

At that very moment the old one whose young ones he had spared was sitting there by the shore, pluming herself with her beak. She knew him again and asked why he was hanging his head.

"You will not be surprised when you hear what has befallen me," replied the tailor, and told her his fate.

"If that be all," said the duck, "we can help you. The crown fell into the water, and lies at the bottom. We will soon bring it up again for you. In the meantime just spread out your handkerchief on the bank."

She dived down with her twelve young ones. And in five minutes she was up again with the crown resting on her wings. The twelve young ones were swimming round about and had put their beaks under it, and were helping to carry it. They all swam to the shore and put the crown on the handkerchief.

No one can imagine how magnificent the crown was. When the sun shone on it, it gleamed like a hundred thousand carbuncles. The tailor tied his handkerchief together by the four corners, and carried it to the King, who was full of joy, and put a gold chain round the tailor's neck.

When the shoemaker saw that one stroke had failed, he contrived a second, and went to the King and said, "Lord King, the tailor has become insolent again. He boasts that he will copy in wax the whole of the royal palace, with everything that pertains to it, loose or fast, inside and out."

The King sent for the tailor and ordered him to copy in wax the whole of the royal palace, with everything that pertained to it, movable or immovable, within and without. And if he did not succeed in doing this, or if so much as one nail on the wall were wanting, he should be imprisoned for his whole life underground.

The tailor thought, "It gets worse and worse! No one can endure that!" and threw his bundle on his back, and went forth.

When he came to the hollow tree, he sat down and hung his head. The bees came flying out, and the Queen-Bee asked him if he had a stiff neck, since he held his head so awry.

"Alas, no," answered the tailor, "something quite different weighs me down," and he told her what the King had demanded of him.

The bees began to buzz and hum amongst themselves, and the Queen-Bee said, "Just go home again. But come back to-morrow at this time, and bring a large sheet with you, and then all will be well."

So he turned back again, but the bees flew to the royal palace and straight into it through the open windows, crept round about into every corner, and inspected everything most carefully.

Then they hurried back and modeled the palace in wax with such rapidity that any one looking on would have thought it was growing before his eyes. By the evening all was ready.

And when the tailor came next morning, the whole of the splendid building was there, and not one nail in the wall or tile of the roof was wanting, and it was delicate withal and white as snow, and smelt sweet as honey.

The tailor wrapped it carefully in his cloth and took it to the King, who could not admire it enough, placed it in his largest hall, and in return for it presented the tailor with a large stone house.

The shoemaker, however, did not give up, but went for the third time to the King and said, "Lord King, it has come to the tailor's ears that no water will spring up in the courtyard of the castle. He has boasted that it shall rise up in the midst of the courtyard to a man's height and be clear as crystal."

Then the King ordered the tailor to be brought before him and said, "If a stream of water does not rise in my courtyard by to-morrow as you have promised, the executioner shall in that very place make you shorter by the head."

The poor tailor did not take long to think about it, but hurried out to the gate, and because this time it was a matter of life and death to him, tears rolled down his face.

Whilst he was thus going forth full of sorrow, the foal to which he had formerly given its liberty, and which had now become a beautiful chestnut horse, came leaping toward him.

"The time has come," it said to the tailor, "when I can repay you for your good deed. I know already what is needful to you, but you shall soon have help. Get on me, my back can carry two such as you."

The tailor's courage came back to him. He jumped up in one bound; and the horse went full speed into the town, and right up to the courtyard of the castle. It galloped as quick as lightning thrice round it, and at the third time it fell violently down. At the same instant there was a terrific clap of thunder, a fragment of earth in the middle of the courtyard sprang like a cannon ball into the air, and over the castle. Directly after it, a jet of water rose as high as a man on horseback, and the water was as pure as crystal, and the sunbeams began to dance on it.

When the King saw that he arose in amazement, and went and embraced the tailor in the sight of all men.

But good fortune did not last long. The King had daughters in plenty, each one prettier than the other, but he had no son.

So the malicious shoemaker betook himself for the fourth time to the King, and said, "Lord King, the tailor has not given up his arrogance. He has now boasted that if he liked, he could cause a son to be brought to the Lord King through the air."

The King commanded the tailor to be summoned, and said, "If you cause a son to be brought to me within nine days, you shall have my eldest daughter to wife."

"The reward is indeed great," thought the little tailor. "One would willingly do something for it, but the cherries grow too high for me. If I climb for them, the bough will break beneath me, and I shall fall."

He went home, seated himself cross-legged on his work-table, and thought over what was to be done.

"It can't be managed," cried he at last. "I will go away. After all I can't live in peace here."

He tied up his bundle and hurried away to the gate. When he got to the meadow, he perceived his old friend the stork, who was walking backward and forward like a philosopher. Sometimes he stood still, took a frog into close consideration, and at length swallowed it down.

The stork came to him and greeted him. "I see," he began, "that you have your pack on your back. Why are you leaving the town?"

The tailor told him what the King had required of him, and how he could not perform it, and lamented his misfortune.

"Don't let your hair grow gray about that," said the stork. "I will help you out of your difficulty. For a long time past, I have carried the children in swaddling-clothes into the town. So for once, I can fetch a little Prince out of the well. Go home and be easy. In nine days from this time repair to the royal palace, and there will I come."

The little tailor went home, and at the appointed time was at the castle. It was not long before the stork came flying thither and tapped at the window. The tailor opened it, and Cousin Longlegs came carefully in, and walked with solemn steps over the smooth marble pavement.

He had a baby in his beak that was as lovely as an angel, and stretched out its little hands to the Queen. The stork laid it in her lap, and she caressed it and kissed it, and was beside herself with delight.

Before the stork flew away he took his traveling bag off his back and handed it over to the Queen. In it there were little paper parcels full of colored sweetmeats, and they were divided amongst the little Princesses.

The eldest, however, had none of them, but got the merry tailor for a husband.

"It seems to me," said he, "just as if I had won the highest prize. My mother was right after all; she always said that whoever trusts in God and his own fortune can never fail."

The shoemaker had to make the shoes in which the little tailor danced at the wedding festival. After which he was commanded to quit the town for ever.

The road to the forest led him to the gallows. Worn out with anger, rage, and the heat of the day, he threw himself down. When he had closed his eyes and was about to sleep, the two crows flew down from the heads of the men who were hanging there, and pecked his eyes out.

In his madness he ran into the forest and must have died there of hunger, for no one has ever either seen him again or heard of him.

THE ELDEST GOT THE MERRY TAILOR FOR A HUSBAND

JORINDA AND JORINGEL

There was once an old castle in the midst of a large and thick forest, and in it an old woman, who was a Witch, dwelt all alone.

In the daytime, she changed herself into a cat or a screech-owl, but in the evening she took her proper shape again as a human being. She could lure wild beasts and birds to her, then she killed and boiled and roasted them.

If any one came within one hundred paces of the castle he was obliged to stand still, and could not stir from the place until she bade him be free. But whenever an innocent maiden came within this circle, she changed her into a bird, shut her up in a wicker-work cage, and carried the cage into a room in the castle. She had about seven thousand cages of rare birds in the castle.

Now, there was once a maiden who was called Jorinda, who was fairer than all other girls. She and a handsome youth named Joringel had promised to marry each other, and their greatest happiness was being together.

One day, in order that they might be able to talk together in quiet, they went for a walk in the forest.

"Take care," said Joringel, "that you do not go too near the castle."

It was a beautiful evening. The sun shone brightly between the trunks of the trees into the dark green of the forest, and the turtledoves sang mournfully upon the young boughs of the birch-trees.

Jorinda wept now and then. She sat down in the sunshine and was sorrowful. Joringel was sorrowful too. They were as sad as if they were about to die. Then they looked around them, and were quite at a loss, for they did not know by which way to go home. The sun was half above the mountain and half set.

Joringel looked through the bushes, and saw the old walls of the castle close at hand. He was horror-stricken and filled with deadly fear.

Jorinda was singing:

"*My little Bird, with the necklace red,*
Sings sorrow, sorrow, sorrow,
He sings that the Dove must soon be dead,
Sings sorrow, sor— —jug, jug, jug!"

Joringel looked for Jorinda. She was changed into a Nightingale, and sang "*jug, jug, jug!*"

A screech-owl with glowing eyes flew three times round about her, and three times cried, "*to-whoo, to-whoo, to-whoo!*"

Joringel could not move. He stood there like a stone, and could neither weep nor speak, nor move hand or foot.

The sun had now set. The owl flew into the thicket. Directly afterward there came out of it a crooked Old Woman, yellow and lean, with large red eyes and a hooked nose, the point of which reached to her chin. She muttered to herself, caught the Nightingale, and took it away in her hand.

Joringel could neither speak nor move from the spot. The Nightingale was gone.

At last the woman came back, and said in a hollow voice, "Greet thee, Zachiel. If the moon shines on the cage, Zachiel, let him loose at once."

Then Joringel was freed. He fell on his knees before the woman and begged that she would give him back his Jorinda. But she said that he should never have her again, and went away. He called, he wept. He lamented, but all in vain, "Ah, what is to become of me?"

Joringel went away, and at last came to a strange village. There he kept sheep for a long time. He often walked round and round the castle, but not too near to it. One night he dreamt that he found a Blood-Red Flower, in the middle of which was a beautiful large pearl; that he picked the flower and went with it to the castle, and that everything he touched with the flower was freed from enchantment. He also dreamt that by means of it, he recovered his Jorinda.

In the morning, when he awoke, he began to seek over hill and dale to find such a flower. He sought until the ninth day, and then, early in the morning, he found the Blood-Red Flower. In the middle of it, there was a large dew-drop, as big as the finest pearl.

Day and night, he journeyed with this flower to the castle.

When he was within a hundred paces of it he was not held fast, but walked on to the door.

Joringel was full of joy. He touched the door with the flower, and it sprang open. He walked in through the courtyard, and listened for the sound of the birds. At last he heard it. He went on, and found the room from whence it came. There the Witch was feeding the birds in the seven thousand cages.

When she saw Joringel, she was angry, very angry, and scolded and spat poison and gall, but she could not come within two paces of him. He did not take any notice of her, but went and looked at the cages with the birds. But there were many hundred Nightingales, how was he to find his Jorinda again?

Just then he saw the Old Woman quietly take away a cage with a bird in it, and go toward the door.

Swiftly he sprang toward her, touched the cage with the flower, and also the Old Woman.

She could now no longer bewitch any one. And Jorinda was standing there, clasping him round the neck, and she was as beautiful as ever!

HOW SIX MEN GOT ON IN THE WORLD

There was once a man who understood all kinds of arts. He served in war, and behaved well and bravely, but when the war was over he received his dismissal, and three farthings for his expenses on the way. "Stop," said he, "I shall not be content with this. If I can but meet with the right people, the King will have to give me all the treasure of the country."

Then full of anger he went into the forest, and saw a man standing therein who had plucked up six trees as if they were blades of corn. He said to him, "Will you be my servant and go with me?"

"Yes," he answered, "but, first, I will take this little bundle of sticks home to my mother," and he took one of the trees, and wrapped it round the five others, lifted the bundle on his back and carried it away.

Then he returned and went with his master, who said, "We two ought to be able to get through the world very well."

When they had walked on for a short while they found a huntsman who was kneeling, had shouldered his gun, and was about to fire. The master said to him, "Huntsman, what are you going to shoot?"

He answered, "Two miles from here a fly is sitting on the branch of an oak-tree, and I want to shoot its left eye out."

"Oh, come with me," said the man, "if we three are together, we certainly ought to be able to get on in the world!"

The huntsman was ready, and went with him.

They came to seven windmills whose sails were turning round with great speed, and yet no wind was blowing either on the right or the left, and no leaf was stirring. Then said the man, "I know not what is driving the windmills, not a breath of air is stirring," and he went onward with his servants, and when they had walked two miles they saw a man sitting on a tree, who was shutting one nostril, and blowing out of the other. "Good gracious! what are you doing up there?"

He answered, "Two miles from here are seven windmills. Look, I am blowing them till they turn round."

"Oh, come with me," said the man. "If we four are together, we shall carry the whole world before us!"

Then the blower came down and went with him.

After a while they saw a man who was standing on one leg and had taken off the other, and laid it beside him. Then the master said, "You have arranged things very comfortably to have a rest."

"I am a runner," he replied, "and to stop myself running far too fast, I have taken off one of my legs, for if I run with both, I go quicker than any bird can fly."

"Oh, come with me. If we five are together, we shall carry the whole world before us."

So he went with them.

It was not long before they met a man who wore a cap, but had put it quite on one ear. Then the master said to him, "Gracefully! gracefully! don't stick your cap on one ear, you look just like a tom-fool!"

"I must not wear it otherwise," said he, "for if I set my hat straight, a terrible frost comes on, and all the birds in the air are frozen, and drop dead on the ground."

“Oh, come with me,” said the master. “If we six are together, we can carry the whole world before us.”

Now the six came to a town where the King had proclaimed that whosoever ran a race with his daughter and won the victory, should be her husband, but whosoever lost it, must lose his head.

Then the man presented himself and said, “I will, however, let my servant run for me.”

The King replied, “Then his life also must be staked, so that his head and thine are both set on the victory.”

When that was settled and made secure, the man buckled the other leg on the runner, and said to him, “Now be nimble, and help us to win.”

It was fixed that the one who was the first to bring some water from a far distant well, was to be the victor. The runner received a pitcher, and the King’s Daughter one too, and they began to run at the same time. But in an instant, when the King’s Daughter had got a very little way, the people who were looking on could see no more of the runner, it was just as if the wind had whistled by.

In a short time he reached the well, filled his pitcher with water, and turned back. Half-way home, however, he was overcome with fatigue, and set his pitcher down, lay down himself, and fell asleep. He had, however, made a pillow of a horse’s skull which was lying on the ground, in order that he might lie uncomfortably, and soon wake up again.

In the meantime, the King’s Daughter, who could also run very well—quite as well as any ordinary mortal can—had reached the well, and was hurrying back with her pitcher full of water, and when she saw the runner lying there asleep, she was glad and said, “My enemy is delivered over into my hands,” emptied his pitcher, and ran on.

And now all would have been lost if by good luck the huntsman had not been standing at the top of the castle, and had not seen everything with his sharp eyes. Then said he, “The King’s Daughter shall still not prevail against us.”

He loaded his gun, and shot so cleverly, that he shot the horse's skull away from under the runner's head without hurting him. Then the runner awoke, leapt up, and saw that his pitcher was empty, and that the King's Daughter was already far in advance. He did not lose heart, however, but ran back to the well with his pitcher, again drew some water, and was still at home again, ten minutes before the King's Daughter. "Behold!" said he, "I have not bestirred myself till now. It did not deserve to be called running before."

But it pained the King, and still more his daughter, that she should be carried off by a common disbanded soldier like that. So they took counsel with each other how to get rid of him and his companions.

Then said the King to her, "I have thought of a way. Don't be afraid, they shall not come back again." And he said to them, "You shall now make merry together, and eat and drink."

He conducted them to a room which had a floor of iron, and the doors also were of iron, and the windows were guarded with iron bars. There was a table in the room covered with delicious food, and the King said to them, "Go in, and enjoy yourselves."

And when they were inside, he ordered the doors to be shut and bolted. Then he sent for the cook, and commanded him to make a fire under the room until the iron became red-hot. This the cook did, and the six who were sitting at table began to feel quite warm, and they thought the heat was caused by the food. But as it became still greater, and they wanted to get out, and found that the doors and windows were bolted, they became aware that the King had an evil intention, and wanted to suffocate them.

"He shall not succeed, however," said the one with the cap. "I will cause a frost to come, before which the fire shall be ashamed, and creep away."

Then he put his cap on straight, and immediately there came such a frost that all heat disappeared, and the food on the dishes began to freeze.

When an hour or two had passed by, and the King believed that they had perished in the heat, he had the doors opened to behold them himself. But when the doors were opened, all six were standing there, alive and well, and said that they should very much like to get out to warm themselves, for the very food was fast frozen to the dishes with the cold.

Then, full of anger, the King went down to the cook, scolded him and asked why he had not done what he had been ordered to do. But the cook replied, "There is heat enough there, just look yourself." Then the King saw that a fierce fire was burning under the iron room, and perceived that there was no getting the better of the six in this way.

Again the King considered how to get rid of his unpleasant guests, and caused their chief to be brought and said, "If you will take gold and renounce my daughter, you shall have as much as you wish."

"Oh, yes, Lord King," he answered, "give me as much as my servant can carry, and I will not ask for your daughter."

On this the King was satisfied, and the other continued, "In fourteen days, I will come and fetch it."

Thereupon he summoned together all the tailors in the whole kingdom, and they were to sit for fourteen days and sew a sack. And when it was ready, the strong one who could tear up trees had to take it on his back, and go with it to the King.

Then said the King, "Who can that strong fellow be who is carrying a bundle of linen on his back that is as big as a house?" and he was alarmed and said, "What a lot of gold he can carry away!"

Then he commanded a ton of gold to be brought. It took sixteen of his strongest men to carry it, but the strong one snatched it up in one hand, put it in his sack, and said, "Why don't you bring more at the same time?—that hardly covers the bottom!"

Then, little by little, the King caused all his treasure to be brought thither, and the strong one pushed it into the sack, and still the sack was not half full with it. "Bring more," cried he, "these few crumbs don't fill it."

Then seven thousand carts with gold had to be gathered together in the whole kingdom, and the strong one thrust them and the oxen harnessed to them into his sack. "I will examine it no longer," said he, "but will just take what comes, so long as the sack is but full."

When all that was inside, there was still room for a great deal more. Then he said, "I will just make an end of the thing. People do sometimes tie up a sack even when it is not full." So he took it on his back, and went away with his comrades.

When the King now saw how one single man was carrying away the entire wealth of the country, he became enraged, and bade his horsemen mount and pursue the six, and ordered them to take the sack away from the strong one. Two regiments speedily overtook the six, and called out, "You are prisoners. Put down the sack with the gold, or you will all be cut to pieces!"

"What say you?" cried the blower, "that we are prisoners! Rather than that should happen, all of you shall dance about in the air." And he closed one nostril, and with the other blew on the two regiments. Then they were driven away from each other, and carried into the blue sky over all the mountains—one here, the other there.

One sergeant cried for mercy. He had nine wounds, and was a brave fellow who did not deserve ill-treatment. The blower stopped a little so that he came down without injury, and then the blower said to him, "Now go home to your King, and tell him he had better send some more horsemen, and I will blow them all into the air."

When the King was informed of this he said, "Let the rascals go. They have the best of it."

Then the six conveyed the riches home, divided it amongst them, and lived in content until their death.

THE GOOSE-GIRL

There was once upon a time, an old Queen, whose husband had been dead for many years, and she had a beautiful daughter.

When the Princess grew up, she was betrothed to a Prince who lived very far away. When the time came for her to be married, and she had to journey forth into the distant kingdom, the aged Queen packed up for her many costly vessels of silver and gold, and trinkets, also of gold and silver, and cups and jewels, in short, everything which appertained to a royal dowry, for she loved her child with all her heart.

She likewise sent her maid-in-waiting, who was to ride with her, and hand her over to the Bridegroom. Each had a horse for the journey, but the horse of the King's Daughter was called Falada, and could speak.

So when the hour of parting had come, the aged mother went into her bedroom, took a small knife and cut her finger with it until it bled. Then she held a white handkerchief to it, into which she let three drops of blood fall.

She gave the handkerchief to her daughter and said, "Dear Child, preserve this carefully. It will be of service to you on your way."

So they took a sorrowful leave of each other. The Princess put the piece of cloth in her bosom, mounted her horse, and then went away to her Bridegroom.

After she had ridden for a while she felt a burning thirst, and said to her waiting-maid, "Dismount, and take my cup which you have brought with you, and get me some water from the stream, for I should like to drink."

"If you are thirsty," said the waiting-maid, "get off your horse yourself, and lie down and drink out of the water. I don't choose to be your servant."

So in her great thirst the Princess alighted, bent down over the water in the stream and drank, and was not allowed to drink out of the golden cup. Then she said, "Ah, Heaven!" and the three drops of blood answered:

"If thy Mother only knew,
'Twould surely break her heart in two!"

But the King's Daughter was humble, said nothing, and mounted her horse again.

She rode some miles further, but the day was warm, the sun scorched her, and she was thirsty once more. When they came to a stream of water, she again cried to her waiting-maid, "Dismount, and give me some water in my golden cup," for she had long ago forgotten the girl's ill words.

But the waiting-maid said still more haughtily, "If you wish to drink, drink as you can, I don't choose to be your maid."

Then in her great thirst the King's Daughter alighted, bent over the flowing stream, wept and said, "Ah, Heaven!" and the drops of blood again replied:

"If thy Mother only knew,
'Twould surely break her heart in two!"

And as she was thus drinking and leaning right over the stream, the handkerchief with the three drops of blood fell out of her bosom, and floated away with the water without her observing it, so great was her trouble. The waiting-maid, however, had seen it, and she rejoiced to think that she had now power over the Bride, for since the Princess had lost the drops of blood, she had become weak and powerless.

So now, when she wanted to mount her horse again, the one that was called Falada, the waiting-maid said, "Falada is more suitable for me, and my nag will do for you," and the Princess had to be content with that.

Then the waiting-maid, with many hard words, bade the Princess exchange her royal apparel for her own shabby clothes; and at length she was compelled to swear by the clear sky above her, that she would not say one word of this to any one at the Royal Court. And if she had not taken this oath she would have been killed on the spot. But Falada saw all this, and observed it well.

The waiting-maid now mounted Falada, and the true Bride the bad horse, and thus they traveled onward, until they entered the royal palace. There were great rejoicings over her arrival, and the Prince sprang forward to meet her, lifted the waiting-maid from her horse, and thought she was his Bride. She was conducted up-stairs, but the real Princess was left standing below.

Then the old King looked out of the window and saw her standing in the courtyard, and how dainty and delicate and beautiful she was. He instantly went to the royal apartment, and asked the Bride about the girl she had with her, who was standing down below in the courtyard, and who she was.

"I picked her up on my way for a companion. Give the girl something to work at, that she may not stand idle."

But the old King had no work for her, and knew of none, so he said, "I have a little boy who tends the geese, she may help him."

The boy was called Conrad, and the true Bride had to help him to tend the geese.

Soon afterward the false Bride said to the young King, "Dearest Husband, I beg you to do me a favor."

He answered, "I will do so most willingly."

"Then send for the butcher, and have the head of the horse on which I rode here, cut off, for it vexed me on the way." In reality, she was afraid that the horse might tell how she had behaved to the King's Daughter.

Then she succeeded in making the King promise that it should be done, and the faithful Falada was to die. This came to the ears of the real Princess, and she secretly promised the butcher a piece of gold if he would perform a small service for her. There was a great dark-looking gateway in the town, through which, morning and evening, she had to pass with the geese: would he be so good as to nail up Falada's head on it, so that she might see him again? The butcher promised to do that, and cut off the head, and nailed it fast beneath the dark gateway.

Early in the morning, when she and Conrad drove out their flock beneath this gateway, she said in passing:

"*Alas, Falada, hanging there!*"

Then the head answered:

"*Alas! young Queen, how ill you fare!*
If this your tender Mother knew,
Her heart would surely break in two!"

Then they went still farther out of the town, and drove their geese into the country. And when they had come to the meadow, she sat down and unbound her hair which was like pure gold. Conrad saw it and delighted in its brightness, and wanted to pluck out a few hairs. Then she said:

"*Blow, blow, thou gentle Wind, I say,*
Blow Conrad's little hat away,
And make him chase it here and there,
Until I've braided all my hair,
And bound it up again."

And there came such a violent wind that it blew Conrad's hat far away across county, and he was forced to run after it.

When he came back she had finished combing her hair and was putting it up again and he could not get any of it. Then Conrad was angry, and would not speak to her. And thus they watched the geese until the evening, and then they went home.

THE HEAD ANSWERED, "ALAS! YOUNG QUEEN HOW ILL YOU FARE"

Next day when they were driving the geese out through the dark gateway, the maiden said:

"Alas, Falada, hanging there!"
Falada answered:

"Alas! young Queen, how ill you fare!
If this your tender Mother knew,
Her heart would surely break in two!"

And she sat down again in the field and began to comb out her hair. Conrad ran and tried to clutch it, so she said in haste:

"Blow, blow, thou gentle Wind, I say,
Blow Conrad's little hat away,
And make him chase it here and there,
Until I've braided all my hair,
And bound it up again."

Then the wind blew, and blew his little hat off his head and far away, and Conrad was forced to run after it. When he came back, her hair had been put up a long time, and he could get none of it. So they looked after their geese till evening came.

But in the evening, after they had got home, Conrad went to the old King, and said, "I won't tend the geese with that girl any longer!"

"Why not?" inquired the old King.

"Oh, because she vexes me the whole day long."

Then the old King commanded him to relate what it was that she did to him.

And Conrad said, "In the morning, when we pass beneath the dark gateway with the flock, there is a sorry horse's head on the wall, and she says to it:

"'*Alas, Falada, hanging there!*'
And the head replies:

"'*Alas! young Queen, how ill you fare!*
If this your tender Mother knew,
Her heart would surely break in two!'"

And Conrad went on to relate what happened on the goose-pasture, and how when there he had to chase his hat.

The old King commanded him to drive his flock out again next day, and as soon as morning came, he placed himself behind the dark gateway, and heard how the maiden spoke to the head of Falada. Then he went into the country, and hid himself in the thicket in the meadow. There he soon saw with his own eyes, the goose-girl and the goose-boy bringing their flock, and how after a while she sat down and unplaited her hair, which shone with radiance. And soon she said:

"*Blow, blow, thou gentle Wind, I say,*
Blow Conrad's little hat away,
And make him chase it here and there,
Until I've braided all my hair,
And bound it up again."

Then came a blast of wind and carried off Conrad's hat, so that he had to run far away, while the maiden quietly went on combing and plaiting her hair. All of which the King observed.

Then, quite unseen, he went away, and when the goose-girl came home in the evening, he called her aside, and asked why she did all these things.

"I may not tell you that, and I dare not lament my sorrows to any human being, for I have sworn not to do so by the heaven which is above me. If I had not done that, I should have lost my life."

He urged her and left her no peace, but he could draw nothing from her. Then said he, "If you will not tell me anything, tell your sorrows to the iron stove there," and he went away.

Then she crept into the iron stove, and began to weep and lament, and emptied her whole heart, and said, "Here am I deserted by the whole world, and yet I am a King's Daughter, and a false waiting-maid has by force brought me to such a pass, that I have been compelled to put off my royal apparel. She has taken my place with my Bridegroom, and I have to do the mean work of a goose-girl.

"If my Mother only knew,
'Twould surely break her heart in two!"

The old King was standing outside by the pipe of the stove, and was listening to what she said, and heard it. Then he came back again, and bade her come out of the stove. And royal garments were placed on her, and it was marvelous how beautiful she was! The old King called his son, and revealed to him, that he had got the false Bride who was only a waiting-maid, but that the true one was standing there, as the goose-girl.

The young King rejoiced with all his heart when he saw her beauty and youth, and a great feast was made ready to which all the people and all good friends were invited. At the head of the table sat the Bridegroom with the King's Daughter at one side of him, and the waiting-maid on the other, but the waiting-maid was blinded, and did not recognize the Princess in her dazzling array.

When they had eaten and drunk, and were merry, the old King asked the waiting-maid as a riddle, what a person deserved who had behaved in such and such a way to her master, and at the same time related the whole story, and asked what sentence such a one merited?

Then the false Bride said, "She deserves no better fate than to be put in a barrel which is studded inside with pointed nails, and two white horses should be harnessed to it, to drag her along through one street after another, till she is dead."

"It is you," said the old King, "and you have pronounced your own sentence. Thus shall it be done unto you."

And when the sentence had been carried out, the young King married his true Bride, and both of them reigned over their kingdom in peace and happiness.

THE SINGING, SOARING LARK

There was once on a time, a man who was about to set out on a long journey. At parting he asked his three daughters what he should bring back for them.

Whereupon the eldest wished for pearls, the second wished for diamonds, but the third said, "Dear Father, I should like a Singing, Soaring Lark."

The father said, "Yes, if I can get it, you shall have it," kissed all three, and set out.

Now, when the time had come for him to return home, he had brought pearls and diamonds for the two eldest. But he had sought everywhere in vain for a Singing, Soaring Lark for the youngest, and he was very unhappy about it, for she was his favorite child.

Then his road lay through a forest, and in the midst of it was a splendid castle. Near the castle stood a tree, and quite on the top of the tree, he saw a Singing, Soaring Lark.

"Aha, you come just at the right moment!" he said, quite delighted, and called to his servant to climb up and catch the little creature.

But as he approached the tree, a Lion leapt from beneath it, shook himself, and roared till the leaves on the tree trembled. "He who tries to steal my Singing, Soaring Lark," he cried, "will I devour."

Then the man said, "I did not know that the bird belonged to you. I will make amends for the wrong I have done, and ransom myself with a large sum of money, only spare my life."

The Lion said, "Nothing can save you, unless you will promise to give me for mine own what first meets you on your return home. But if you will do that, I will grant you your life, and you shall have the bird for your daughter, into the bargain."

The man hesitated and said, "That might be my youngest daughter, she loves me best, and always runs to meet me on my return home."

The servant, however, was terrified and said, "Why should your daughter be the very one to meet you, it might as easily be a cat, or dog?"

Then the man allowed himself to be persuaded, took the Singing, Soaring Lark, and promised to give the Lion whatsoever should first meet him on his return home.

When he reached home and entered his house, the first who met him was no other than his youngest and dearest daughter, who came running up, kissed and embraced him. When she saw that he had brought with him a Singing, Soaring Lark, she was beside herself with joy.

The father, however, could not rejoice, but began to weep, and said, "My dearest Child, I have bought the little bird at a great cost! In return for it, I have been obliged to promise you to a savage Lion. When he has you he will tear you in pieces and devour you," and he told her all, just as it had happened, and begged her not to go thither, come what might.

But she consoled him and said, "Dearest Father, indeed your promise must be fulfilled. I will go thither and soften the Lion, so that I may return to you safely."

Next morning, she had the road pointed out to her, took leave, and went fearlessly out into the forest. The Lion, however, was an enchanted Prince and was by day a Lion, and all his people were Lions with him. But in the night, they resumed their natural human shapes.

On her arrival, she was kindly received and led into the castle. When night came, the Lion turned into a handsome man, and their wedding was celebrated with great magnificence. They lived happily together, remained awake at night, and slept in the daytime.

One day, he came and said, "To-morrow there is a feast in your father's house, because your eldest sister is to be married, and if you are inclined to go there, my Lions shall conduct you."

She said, "Yes, I should very much like to see my father again," and went thither, accompanied by the Lions.

There was great joy when she arrived, for they had all believed that she had been torn in pieces by the Lion, and had long ceased to live. But she told them what a handsome husband she had, and how well off she was. She remained with them while the wedding-feast lasted, and then went back again to the forest.

When the second daughter was about to be married, and she was again invited to the wedding, she said to the Lion, "This time, I will not go alone. You must come with me."

The Lion, however, said that it was too dangerous for him, for if a ray from a burning candle should fall on him, he would be changed into a Dove, and for seven years long would have to fly about with the Doves.

She said, "Ah, but do come with me, I will take great care of you and guard you from all light."

So they went away together, and took with them their little child as well. She had a chamber built, so strong and thick that no ray could pierce through it. In this he was to shut himself up when the candles were lit for the wedding-feast. But the door was made of green wood which warped and left a little crack which no one noticed.

The wedding was celebrated with magnificence; but when the procession with all its candles and torches came back from church and passed by this apartment, a ray about the breadth of a hair fell on the King's Son. When this ray touched him, he was transformed in an instant. And when she came in, and looked for him, she did not see him, but a white Dove was sitting there.

The Dove said to her, "For seven years must I fly about the world, but at every seventh step that you take I will let fall a drop of red blood and a white feather. These will show you the way. If you follow the trace you can release me."

Thereupon the Dove flew out at the door, and she followed him. At every seventh step a red drop of blood and a little white feather fell down, and showed her the way.

So she went continually farther and farther, in the wide world, never looking about her nor resting, and the seven years were almost past. Then she rejoiced and thought that they would soon be delivered, and yet they were so far from it!

Once when they were thus moving onwards, no little feather and no drop of red blood fell, and when she raised her eyes the Dove had disappeared. And as she thought to herself, "In this no man can help me," she climbed up to the Sun, and said to him, "You shine into every crevice, and over every peak, have you not seen a white Dove flying?"

"No," said the Sun, "I have seen none, but I present you with a casket. Open it when you are in sorest need."

Then she thanked the Sun, and went on until evening came and the Moon appeared. She then asked her, "You shine the whole night through, and on every field and forest, have you not seen a white Dove flying?"

"No," said the Moon, "I have seen no Dove, but here I give you an egg. Break it when you are in great need."

She thanked the Moon, and went on until the Night Wind came up and blew on her, then she said to it, "You blow over every tree and under every leaf, have you not seen a white Dove flying?"

"No," said the Night Wind, "I have seen none, but I will ask the three other Winds; perhaps they have seen it."

The East Wind and the West Wind came, and had seen nothing, but the South Wind said, "I have seen the white Dove, it has flown to the Red Sea, there it has become a Lion again, for the seven years are over. The Lion is there fighting with a Dragon. The Dragon, however, is an enchanted Princess."

The Night Wind then said to her, "I will advise you. Go to the Red Sea, on the right bank are some tall reeds, count them, break off the eleventh, and strike the Dragon with it. Then the Lion will be able to subdue it, and both then will regain their human form. After that, look round and you will see the Griffin which is by the Red Sea. Swing yourself with your beloved, on to his back, and the bird will carry you over the sea to your own home.

"Here is a nut for you, when you are above the centre of the sea, let the nut fall. It will immediately shoot up, and a tall nut-tree will grow out of the water on which the Griffin may rest; for if he cannot rest, he will not be strong enough to carry you across. If you forget to throw down the nut, he will let you fall into the sea."

Then she went thither, and found everything as the Night Wind had said. She counted the reeds by the sea, and cut off the eleventh, struck the Dragon with it, whereupon the Lion overcame it. Immediately both of them regained their human shapes. But when the Princess, who had been the Dragon, was delivered from enchantment, she took the youth by the arm, seated herself on the Griffin, and carried him off with her.

There stood the poor maiden, who had wandered so far and was again forsaken! She sat down and cried, but at last she took courage and said, "Still I will go as far as the Wind blows and as long as the cock crows, until I find him."

She went forth by long, long roads, until at last she came to the castle, where both of them were living together. There she heard that a feast was to be held, in which they would celebrate their wedding, but she said, "God still helps me," and opened the casket that the Sun had given her. A dress lay therein as brilliant as the sun itself.

So she took it out and put it on, and went up into the castle, and every one, even the Bride, looked at her with astonishment. The dress pleased the Bride so well that she thought it might do for her wedding-dress, and asked if it was for sale?

"Not for money or land," answered she, "but for flesh and blood."

The Bride asked her what she meant by that, then she said, "Let me sleep a night in the chamber where the Bridegroom sleeps."

The Bride would not, yet wanted very much to have the dress. At last she consented, but the page was to give the Prince a sleeping-draught.

When it was night, and the youth was already asleep, she was led into the chamber. She seated herself on the bed and said, "I have followed you for seven years. I have been to the Sun and the Moon, and the Four Winds, and have inquired for you and have helped you against the Dragon. Will you, then, forget me?"

But the Prince slept so soundly that it only seemed to him as if the wind were whistling outside in the fir-trees. When therefore day broke, she was led out again, and had to give up the golden dress. And as that had been of no avail, she was sad, went out into a meadow, sat down there, and wept.

While she was sitting there, she thought of the egg which the Moon had given her. She opened it, and there came out a clucking hen with twelve chickens all of gold. They ran about chirping, and crept again under the old hen's wings. Nothing more beautiful was ever seen in the world!

She arose, and drove them through the meadow. The Bride looked out of the window, and the little chickens pleased her so that she came down and asked if they were for sale.

"Not for money or land, but for flesh and blood. Let me sleep again in the chamber where the Bridegroom sleeps."

The Bride said, "Yes," intending to cheat her as on the former evening. But when the Prince went to bed he asked the page what the murmuring and rustling in the night had been. On this the page told all; that he had been forced to give him a sleeping-draught, because a poor girl had slept secretly in the chamber, and that he was to give him another that night.

The Prince said, "Pour out the draught by the bedside."

At night, she was again led in, and when she began to relate how ill all had fared with her, he immediately recognized his beloved wife by her voice, sprang up and cried, "Now I really am released! I have been as it were in a dream, for the strange Princess has bewitched me so that I have been compelled to forget you! But God has delivered me from the spell at the right time."

Then they both left the castle secretly in the night, for they feared the father of the Princess, who was a sorcerer. They seated themselves on the Griffin which bore them across the Red Sea. When they were in the midst of it, she let fall the nut. Immediately a tall nut-tree grew up, whereon the bird rested, and then carried them home, where they found their child, who had grown tall and beautiful.

And they lived thenceforth happily until their death.

DOCTOR KNOWALL

There was once on a time, a poor peasant called Crab, who drove two oxen with a load of wood to town, and sold it to a doctor for two dollars.

When the money was being counted out to him, it so happened that the doctor was sitting at table, and when the peasant saw how daintily he ate and drank, his heart desired what he saw, and he would willingly have been a doctor. So he remained standing a while, and at length inquired if he, too, could not be a doctor.

"Oh, yes," said the doctor, "that is soon managed."

"What must I do?" asked the peasant.

"In the first place, buy yourself an A B C book of the kind which has a cock on the frontispiece. In the second, turn your cart and your two oxen into money, and get yourself some clothes, and whatsoever else pertains to medicine. Thirdly, have a sign painted with the words, 'I am Doctor Knowall,' and have that nailed up above your house-door."

The peasant did everything that he had been told to do. When he had doctored people a while, but not long, a rich and great lord had some money stolen. Then he was told about Doctor Knowall who lived in such and such a village, and must know what had become of the money. So the lord had the horses put in his carriage, drove out to the village, and asked Crab if he were Doctor Knowall?

Yes, he was, he said.

Then he was to go with him and bring back the stolen money.

"Oh, yes, but Grethe, my wife, must go too."

The lord was willing, and let both of them have a seat in the carriage. They all drove away together. When they came to the nobleman's castle, the table was spread, and Crab was told to sit down and eat.

"Yes, but my wife, Grethe, too," said he, and he seated himself with her at the table.

And when the first servant came with a dish of delicate fare, the peasant nudged his wife, and said, "Grethe, that was the first," meaning that was the servant who brought the first dish.

The servant, however, thought he intended by that to say, "That is the first thief," and as he actually was so, he was terrified, and said to his comrade outside, "The doctor knows all! we shall fare badly; he said I was the first."

The second did not want to go in at all, but was obliged to. So when he went in, the peasant nudged his wife, and said, "Grethe, that is the second." This servant was so frightened, that he got out.

With the third, it did not fare any better, for the peasant said again, "Grethe, that is the third."

The fourth had to carry in a covered dish. In it were crabs.

The lord told the doctor that he must show his skill by guessing what was under the cover. The doctor looked at the dish, had no idea what was in it, and cried out, "Alas! poor Crab!"

When the lord heard that, he cried, "There! he knows who has the money!"

At this, the servants were terribly anxious. They winked at the doctor to come out to them. When he went out, they all four confessed that they had stolen the money, and that they were willing to restore it. They led him to the spot where it was hidden.

Thus the lord got back his wealth, and Doctor Knowall received a large reward and became a famous man.

THE FIRST SERVANT CAME WITH A DISH OF DELICATE FARE

THE BLUE LIGHT

There was once on a time, a soldier who for many years had served the King faithfully. But when the war came to an end he could serve no longer because of the many wounds which he had received.

The King said to him, "You may return to your home, I need you no longer. You will not receive any more money, for only he receives wages who renders me service for them."

Then the soldier did not know how to earn a living, went away greatly troubled, and walked the whole day, until in the evening he entered a forest. When darkness came on, he saw a light, which he went toward, and came to a house wherein lived a Witch.

"Do give me one night's lodging, and a little to eat and drink," said he to her, "or I shall starve."

"Oho!" she answered, "who gives anything to a runaway soldier? Yet will I be compassionate, and take you in, if you will do what I wish."

"What do you wish?" said the soldier.

"That you should dig all round my garden for me, to-morrow."

The soldier consented, and next day labored with all his strength, but could not finish it by the evening.

"I see well enough," said the Witch, "that you can do no more to-day. But I will keep you yet another night, in payment for which you must to-morrow chop me a load of wood, and make it small."

The soldier spent the whole day in doing it, and in the evening the Witch proposed that he should stay one night more. "To-morrow, you shall do me a very trifling piece of work. Behind my house, there is an old, dry well, into which my light has fallen. It burns blue, and never goes out, and you shall bring it up again for me."

Next day, the Old Woman took him to the well, and let him down in a basket. He found the Blue Light, and made her a signal to draw him up again. She did draw him up, but when he came near the edge, she stretched down her hand and wanted to take the Blue Light away from him.

"No," said he, perceiving her evil intention, "I will not give you the light, until I am standing with both feet upon the ground."

The Witch fell into a passion, let him down again into the well, and went away.

The poor soldier fell without injury on the moist ground, and the Blue Light went on burning. But of what use was that to him? He saw very well that he could not escape death. He sat for a while very sorrowfully, then suddenly he felt in his pocket and found his pipe, which was still half full of tobacco.

"This shall be my last pleasure," thought he, pulled it out, lit it at the Blue Light and began to smoke.

When the smoke had circled about the cavern, suddenly a little Black Man stood before him, and said, "Master, what are your commands?"

"What commands have I to give you?" replied the soldier, quite astonished.

"I must do everything you bid me," said the Little Man.

"Good," said the soldier; "then in the first place help me out of this well."

The Little Man took him by the hand, and led him through an underground passage, but the soldier did not forget to take the Blue Light with him. On the way the Little Man showed him treasures hidden there, and the soldier took as much gold as he could carry.

When he was above, he said to the Little Man, "Now go and bind the old Witch, and carry her before the judge."

In a short time she, with frightful cries, came riding by, as swift as the wind, on a wild tom-cat, nor was it long after that before the Little Man reappeared. "It is all done," said he, "and the Witch is already hanging on the gallows. What further commands has my lord?" inquired the Little Man.

"At this moment, none," answered the soldier; "you may return home. Only be at hand immediately, if I summon you."

"Nothing more is needed than that you should light your pipe at the Blue Light, and I will appear before you at once." Thereupon he vanished from sight.

The soldier returned to the town from which he had come. He went to the best inn, ordered himself handsome clothes, and then bade the landlord furnish him a room as magnificent as possible.

When it was ready and the soldier had taken possession of it, he summoned the Little Black Man and said, "I have served the King faithfully, but he has dismissed me, and left me to hunger, and now I want to punish him."

"What am I to do?" asked the Little Man.

"Late at night, when the King's Daughter is in bed, bring her here in her sleep; she shall do servant's work for me."

The Little Man said, "That is an easy thing for me to do, but a very dangerous thing for you, for if it is discovered, you will fare ill."

When twelve o'clock had struck, the door sprang open, and the Little Man carried in the Princess.

"Aha! are you there?" cried the soldier, "get to your work at once! Fetch the broom and sweep the chamber."

When she had done this, he ordered her to come to his chair. Then he stretched out his feet and said, "Pull off my boots for me," and made her pick them up again, and clean and brighten them.

She, however, did everything he bade her, without opposition, silently and with half-shut eyes. When the first cock crowed, the Little Man carried her back to the royal Palace, and laid her in her bed.

Next morning, when the Princess arose, she went to her father, and told him that she had had a very strange dream. "I was carried through the streets with the rapidity of lightning," said she, "and taken into a soldier's room, and I had to wait upon him like a servant, sweep his room, clean his boots, and do all kinds of menial work. It was only a dream, and yet I am just as tired as if I really had done everything."

"The dream may have been true," said the King. "I will give you a piece of advice. Fill your pocket full of peas, and make a small hole in it, and then if you are carried away again, they will fall out and leave a track in the streets."

But unseen by the King, the Little Man was standing beside him when he said that, and heard all. At night, when the sleeping Princess was again carried through the streets, some peas certainly did fall out of her pocket, but they made no track, for the crafty Little Man had just before scattered peas in every other street. And again the Princess was compelled to do servant's work until cock-crow.

Next morning, the King sent his people out to seek the track, but it was all in vain, for in every street poor children were sitting, picking up peas, and saying, "It must have rained peas, last night."

"We must think of something else," said the King; "keep your shoes on when you go to bed, and before you come back from the place where you are taken, hide one of them there. I will soon find it."

The Little Black Man heard this plot, and at night when the soldier again ordered him to bring the Princess, revealed it to him, and told him that he knew of no way to overcome this stratagem, and that if the shoe were found in the soldier's house it would go badly with him.

"Do what I bid you," replied the soldier. And again this third night, the Princess was obliged to work like a servant, but before she went away, she hid her shoe under the bed.

Next morning, the King had the entire town searched for his daughter's shoe. It was found at the soldier's, and the soldier himself, who at the entreaty of the Little Man, had gone outside the city-gate, was soon brought back, and thrown into prison.

In his flight he had forgotten the most valuable things he had, the Blue Light and the gold, and had only one ducat in his pocket. And now loaded with chains, he was standing at the window of his dungeon, when he chanced to see one of his comrades passing by.

The soldier tapped at the pane of glass, and when this man came up, said to him, "Be so kind as to fetch me the small bundle I have left lying in the inn, and I will give you a ducat for doing it."

His comrade ran thither and brought him what he wanted. As soon as the soldier was alone again, he lighted his pipe and summoned the Little Black Man.

"Have no fear," said the latter to his master. "Go wheresoever they take you, and let them do what they will, only take the Blue Light with you."

Next day the soldier was tried, and though he had done nothing wicked, the judge condemned him to death. When he was led forth to die, he begged a last favor of the King.

"What is it?" asked the King.

"That I may smoke one more pipe on my way."

"You may smoke three," answered the King, "but do not imagine that I will spare your life."

Then the soldier pulled out his pipe and lighted it at the Blue Light. And as soon as a few wreaths of smoke had ascended the

Little Man was there with a small cudgel in his hand, and said, "What does my lord command?"

"Strike down to earth that false judge there, and his constable, and spare not the King who has treated me so ill."

Then the Little Man fell on them like lightning, darting this way and that, and whosoever was so much as touched by his cudgel fell to earth, and did not venture to stir again. The King was terrified; he threw himself on the soldier's mercy, and begged merely to be allowed to live. He gave him his kingdom for his own, and the Princess to wife.

THE SPINDLE, THE SHUTTLE, AND THE NEEDLE

There was once a girl whose father and mother died while she was still a little child. All alone, in a small house at the end of the village, dwelt her godmother, who supported herself by spinning, weaving, and sewing. The old woman took the forlorn child to live with her, kept her to her work, and educated her in all that is good.

When the girl was fifteen, the old woman became ill, called the child to her bedside, and said, "Dear Daughter, I feel my end drawing near. I leave you the little house, which will protect you from wind and weather, and my spindle, shuttle, and needle, with which you can earn your bread."

Then she laid her hands on the girl's head, blessed her, and said, "Only preserve the love of God in your heart, and all will go well with you."

Thereupon she closed her eyes, and when she was laid in the earth, the maiden followed the coffin, weeping bitterly, and paid her the last mark of respect.

And now the maiden lived quite alone in the little house, and was industrious, and span, wove, and sewed, and the blessing of the good old woman was on all that she did. It seemed as if the flax in the room increased of its own accord, and whenever she wove a piece of cloth or carpet, or had made a shirt, she at once found a buyer who paid her amply for it. So that she was in want of nothing, and even had something to share with others.

About this time, the Son of the King was traveling about the country looking for a Bride. He was not to choose a poor one, and did not want to have a rich one. So he said, "She shall be my wife who is the poorest, and at the same time the richest."

When he came to the village where the maiden dwelt, he inquired, as he did wherever he went, who was the richest and also the poorest girl in the place? They first named the richest; the poorest, they said, was the girl who lived in the small house quite at the end of the village.

The rich girl was sitting in all her splendor before the door of her house, and when the Prince approached her, she got up, went to meet him, and made him a low curtsey. He looked at her, said nothing, and rode on.

When he came to the house of the poor girl, she was not standing at the door, but sitting in her little room. He stopped his horse, and saw, through the window on which the bright sun was shining, the girl sitting at her spinning-wheel, busily spinning. She looked up, and when she saw that the Prince was gazing in, blushed all over her face, let her eyes fall, and went on spinning. I do not know whether, just at that moment, the thread was quite even; but she went on spinning until the King's Son had ridden away again.

Then she stepped to the window, opened it, and said, "It is so warm in this room!" but she still looked after him as long as she could see the white feathers in his hat. Then she sat down to work again in her own room and went on with her spinning. And a saying which the old woman had often repeated when she was sitting at her work, came into her mind, and she sang these words to herself:

"Spindle, my Spindle, haste, haste thee away,
Here to my house bring the wooer, I pray."

And what do you think happened? The spindle sprang out of her hand in an instant, and out of the door. And when, in her astonishment, she got up and looked after it, she saw that it was dancing out merrily into the open country, and drawing a shining golden thread after it. Before long, it had entirely vanished from her sight.

As she had now no spindle, the girl took the weaver's shuttle in her hand, sat down to her loom, and began to weave.

The spindle, however, danced continually onward, and just as the thread came to an end, reached the Prince.

"What do I see?" he cried; "the spindle certainly wants to show me the way!" He turned his horse about, and rode back with the golden thread. The girl was, however, sitting at her work singing:

"*Shuttle, my Shuttle, weave well this day,*
And guide the wooer to me, I pray."

Immediately the shuttle sprang out of her hand and out by the door. Before the threshold, however, it began to weave a carpet which was more beautiful than the eyes of man had ever yet beheld. Lilies and roses blossomed on both sides of it. And on a golden ground in the centre green branches ascended, under which bounded hares and rabbits. Stags and deer stretched their heads in between them. Brightly-colored birds were sitting in the branches above. They lacked nothing but the gift of song. The shuttle leapt hither and thither, and everything seemed to grow of its own accord.

As the shuttle had run away, the girl sat down to sew. She held the needle in her hand and sang:

"*Needle, my Needle, sharp-pointed and fine,*
Prepare for a wooer this house of mine."

Then the needle leapt out of her fingers, and flew everywhere about the room as quick as lightning. It was just as if invisible spirits were working. They covered tables and benches with green cloth in an instant, and the chairs with velvet, and hung the windows with silken curtains.

Hardly had the needle put in the last stitch, than the maiden saw through the window the white feathers of the Prince, whom the spindle had brought thither by the golden thread. He alighted, stepped over the carpet into the house, and when he entered the room, there stood the maiden in her poor garments, but she shone out from them like a rose surrounded by leaves.

"You are the poorest and also the richest," said he to her. "Come with me, you shall be my Bride."

She did not speak, but she gave him her hand. Then he kissed her, and led her forth, lifted her on to his horse, and took her to the royal castle, where the wedding was solemnized with great rejoicings.

The spindle, shuttle, and needle were preserved in the treasure-chamber, and held in great honor.

THE THREE LUCK-CHILDREN

A father once called his three sons before him. He gave to the first a cock, to the second a scythe, and to the third a cat.

"I am old," said he, "my death is nigh, and I have wished to take thought for you before my end. Money I have not, and what I now give you seems of little worth. But all depends on your making a sensible use of it. Only seek out a country where such things are still unknown, and your fortune is made."

After the father's death, the eldest went away with his cock. But wherever he came the cock was already known. In the towns, he saw him from a long distance, sitting upon the steeples and turning round with the wind; and in the villages he heard more than one crowing. No one would show any wonder at the creature, so that it did not look as if he would make his fortune by it.

At last, however, it happened that he came to an island where the people knew nothing about cocks, and did not even understand how to tell time. They certainly knew when it was morning or evening. But at night, if they did not sleep through it, not one of them knew how to find out the time.

WHEN THE CORN WAS RIPE, THEY SHOT IT DOWN

"Look!" said he, "what a proud creature! It has a ruby-red crown upon its head, and wears spurs like a knight. It calls you three times during the night, at fixed hours; and when it calls for the last time, the sun soon after rises. But if it crows by broad daylight, then take notice, for there will certainly be a change of weather."

The people were well pleased. For a whole night they did not sleep, and listened with great delight as the cock at two, four, and six o'clock, loudly and clearly proclaimed the time. They asked if the creature were for sale, and how much he wanted for it.

"About as much gold as an ass can carry," answered he.

"A ridiculously small price for such a precious creature!" they cried all together, and willingly gave him what he had asked.

When he came home with his wealth, his brothers were astonished, and the second said, "Well, I will go forth and see whether I cannot get rid of my scythe as profitably." But it did not look as if he would, for laborers met him everywhere, and they had scythes upon their shoulders as well as he.

At last, however, he chanced upon an island where the people knew nothing of scythes. When the corn was ripe, they took cannon out to the fields and shot it down. Now this was rather an uncertain affair. Many shot right over it, others hit the ears instead of the stems and shot them away, whereby much was lost; and besides all this it made a terrible noise.

So the man set to work and mowed it down so quietly and quickly that the people opened their mouths with astonishment. They agreed to give him what he wanted for the scythe, and he received a horse laden with as much gold as it could carry.

And now the third brother wanted to take his cat to the right man. He fared just like the others. So long as he stayed on the mainland, there was nothing to be done. Every place had cats, and there were so many of them that most new-born kittens were drowned in the ponds.

At last, he sailed to an island, and it luckily happened that no cats had ever yet been seen there, and that the mice had got the upper hand so much, that they danced upon the tables and benches whether the master were at home or not. The people complained bitterly of the plague. The King himself, in his palace, did not know how to secure himself against them. Mice squeaked in every corner, and gnawed whatever they could lay hold of with their teeth.

But now the cat began her chase, and soon cleared a couple of rooms, and the people begged the King to buy the wonderful beast for the country. The King willingly gave what was asked, which was a mule laden with gold; and the third brother came home with the greatest treasure of all.

The cat made merry with the mice in the royal palace, and killed so many that they could not be counted. At last she grew warm with the work and thirsty, so she stood still, lifted up her head and cried, "Mew! mew!"

When they heard this strange cry, the King and all his people were frightened, and in their terror ran out of the palace.

Then the King took counsel what was best to be done. At last, it was decided to send a herald to the cat, and command her to leave the palace; if not, she was to expect that force would be used against her.

The councilors said, "We would rather be plagued with mice to which misfortune we are accustomed, than give up our lives to such a monster as this."

A noble youth, therefore, was sent to ask the cat whether she "would peaceably quit the palace." But the cat, whose thirst had become still greater, answered again, "Mew! Mew!"

The youth thought that she said, "Most certainly not! Most certainly not!" and took this answer to the King.

"Then," said the councilors, "she must yield to force."

Cannon were brought out, and the palace was soon in flames. When the fire reached the room where the cat was sitting, she sprang safely out of the window. But the besiegers did not leave off, until the whole palace was shot down to the ground.

THE DONKEY CABBAGES

There was once a young huntsman, who went into the forest to lie in wait. He had a fresh and joyous heart, and as he was going thither, whistling upon a leaf, an ugly old crone came up, who spoke to him and said, "Good-day, dear huntsman, truly you are merry and contented, but I am suffering from hunger and thirst, do give me an alms."

The huntsman had compassion on the poor old creature, felt in his pocket, and gave her what he could afford.

He was then about to go further, but the old woman stopped him and said, "Listen, dear Huntsman, to what I tell you. I will make you a present in return for your kindness. Go on your way now, but in a little while you will come to a tree, whereon nine birds are sitting which have a cloak in their claws, and are plucking at it. Take your gun and shoot into the midst of them. They will let the cloak fall down to you, but one of the birds will be hurt, and will drop dead.

"Carry away the cloak, it is a Wishing-Cloak. When you throw it over your shoulders, you only have to wish to be in a certain place, and you will be there in the twinkling of an eye.

Take out the heart of the dead bird, swallow it whole, and every morning early, when you get up, you will find a gold piece under your pillow."

The huntsman thanked the Wise Woman, and thought to himself, "Those are fine things that she has promised me, if all does but come true!"

And verily when he had walked about a hundred paces, he heard in the branches above him a screaming and twittering. He looked up and saw a crowd of birds, who were tearing a piece of cloth with their beaks and claws, and tugging and fighting as if each wanted to have it all to himself.

"Well," said the huntsman, "this is wonderful. It has come to pass just as the old wife foretold!" and he took the gun from his shoulder, aimed and fired right into the midst of them, so that the feathers flew about.

The birds instantly took to flight with loud outcries, but one dropped down dead, and the cloak fell at the same time. Then the huntsman did as the old woman had directed him, cut open the bird, sought the heart, swallowed it down, and took the cloak home with him.

Next morning, when he awoke, the promise occurred to him. He wished to see if it also had been fulfilled. When he lifted up the pillow, the gold piece shone in his eyes. The next day, he found another, and so it went on, every time he got up. He gathered together a heap of gold, but at last he thought, "Of what use is all my gold to me if I stay at home? I will go forth and see the world."

He then took leave of his parents, buckled on his huntsman's pouch and gun, and went out into the world.

It came to pass, that one day he traveled through a dense forest, and when he came to the end of it, in the plain before him was a fine castle. An Old Woman was standing with a wonderfully beautiful maiden, looking out of one of the windows.

The Old Woman, however, was a Witch and said to the maiden, "There comes a man out of the forest, who has a wonderful treasure in his body. We must filch it from him, my dear Daughter. It is more suitable for us than for him. He has a bird's heart about him, by means of which every morning, a gold piece lies under his pillow." She told her what she was to do to get it, and what part she had to play, and finally threatened her, and said with angry eyes, "And if you do not attend to what I say, it will be the worse for you."

Now when the huntsman came nearer he descried the maiden, and said to himself, "I have traveled about for such a long time, I will take a rest for once, and enter that beautiful castle. I have certainly money enough." Nevertheless, the real reason was that he had caught sight of the pretty maiden.

He entered the house, and was well received and courteously entertained. Before long, he was so much in love with the young Witch that he no longer thought of anything else, and saw things as she saw them, and did what she desired.

The Old Woman then said, "Now we must have the bird's heart, he will never miss it." She prepared a drink, and when it was ready, poured it into a cup and gave it to the maiden, who was to present it to the huntsman.

She did so, saying, "Now, my Dearest, drink to me."

So he took the cup, and when he had swallowed the draught, he brought up the heart of the bird. The girl had to take it away secretly and swallow it herself, for the Old Woman would have it so. Thenceforward he found no more gold under his pillow. But it lay instead under that of the maiden, from whence the Old Woman fetched it away every morning. But he was so much in love and so befooled, that he thought of nothing else but of passing his time with the maiden.

Then the old Witch said, "We have the bird's heart, but we must also take the Wishing-Cloak away from him."

The maiden answered, "We will leave him that; he has lost his wealth."

The Old Woman was angry and said, "Such a mantle is a wonderful thing, and is seldom to be found in this world. I must and will have it!" She gave the maiden several blows, and said that if she did not obey, it should fare ill with her.

So she did the Old Woman's bidding, placed herself at the window and looked on the distant country, as if she were very sorrowful.

The huntsman asked, "Why do you stand there so sorrowfully?"

"Ah, my Beloved," was her answer, "over yonder lies the Garnet Mountain, where the precious stones grow. I long for them so much that when I think of them, I feel quite sad, but who can get them? Only the birds; they fly and can reach them, but a man never."

"Have you nothing else to complain of?" said the huntsman. "I will soon remove that burden from your heart."

With that he drew her under his mantle, wished himself on the Garnet Mountain. In the twinkling of an eye they were sitting on it together. Precious stones were glistening on every side, so that it was a joy to see them. Together they gathered the finest and costliest of them.

Now, the Old Woman had, through her sorceries, contrived that the eyes of the huntsman should become heavy. He said to the maiden, "We will sit down and rest a while. I am so tired, that I can no longer stand on my feet."

Then they sat down, and he laid his head in her lap, and fell asleep. When he was asleep, she unfastened the mantle from his shoulders, and wrapped herself in it, picked up the garnets and stones, and wished herself back at home with them.

But when the huntsman had had his sleep out, he awoke, and perceived that his sweetheart had betrayed him, and left him alone on the wild mountain. Then he said, "Oh, what treachery there is in the world!" and sat there in care and sorrow, not knowing what to do.

But the mountain belonged to some wild and monstrous Giants, who dwelt thereon and lived their lives there, and he had not sat long, before he saw three of them coming toward him. The Giants came up, and the first kicked him with his foot and said, "What sort of an earthworm is lying curled up here?"

The second said, "Step upon him and kill him."

But the third said, "Would that be worth your while? Let him live, he cannot remain here. When he climbs higher, toward the summit of the mountain, the clouds will lay hold of him and bear him away." So saying they passed by.

But the Huntsman had paid heed to their words, and as soon as they were gone, he rose and climbed up to the summit of the mountain. And when he had sat there a while, a cloud floated toward him, caught him up, carried him away, and traveled about for a long time in the heavens. Then it sank lower, and let itself down on a great cabbage-garden, girt round by walls, so that he came softly to the ground on cabbages and vegetables.

Then the huntsman looked about him, and said, "If I only had something to eat! I am so hungry, and my hunger will grow greater. But I see here neither apples nor pears, nor any other sort of fruit, everywhere there is nothing but cabbages." At length he thought, "At a pinch I can eat some of the leaves. They do not taste particularly good, but they will refresh me."

With that he picked himself out a fine head of cabbage, and ate it. But scarcely had he swallowed a couple of mouthfuls, when wonderful! he felt quite changed.

Four legs grew on him, a large head and two thick ears; and he saw with horror that he was changed into a Donkey. Still as his hunger became greater every minute, and as the juicy leaves were suitable to his present nature, he went on eating with great zest. At last he arrived at a different kind of cabbage, but as soon as he had swallowed it, he again felt a change, and resumed his human shape.

Then the huntsman lay down, and slept off his fatigue. When he awoke next morning, he broke off one head of the bad cabbages and another of the good ones, and thought to himself, "This shall help me to get my own again and punish treachery."

Then he took the cabbages with him, climbed over the wall, and went forth to seek for the castle of his sweetheart.

After wandering about for a couple of days, he was lucky enough to find it again. He dyed his face brown, so that his own mother would not have known him; and begged for shelter. "I am so tired," said he, "that I can go no further."

The Witch asked, "Who are you, Countryman, and what is your business?"

Said he, "I have been so fortunate as to find the most wonderful salad which grows under the sun, and am carrying it about with me."

When the Old Woman heard of the exquisite salad, she was greedy, and said, "Dear Countryman, let me just taste this wonderful salad."

"Why not?" answered he, "I have brought two heads with me, and will give you one of them," and he opened his pouch and handed her the bad cabbage.

The Witch suspected nothing amiss, and her mouth watered so for this new dish, that she herself went into the kitchen and prepared it. When it was ready she could not wait until it was set on the table, but took a couple of leaves at once, and put them in her mouth. Hardly had she swallowed them, than she was deprived of her human shape, and she ran out into the courtyard in the form of a Donkey.

Presently the maid-servant entered the kitchen, saw the salad standing there ready prepared, and was about to carry it up. But on the way, according to habit, she was seized by the desire to taste, and she ate a couple of leaves. Instantly the magic power showed itself, and she likewise became a Donkey, and ran out to the Old Woman. And the dish of salad fell to the ground.

Meantime the huntsman sat beside the beautiful maiden, and as no one came with the salad and she also was longing for it, she said, "I don't know what has become of the salad."

The huntsman thought, "The salad must have already taken effect," and said, "I will go to the kitchen and inquire about it."

As he went down he saw the two Donkeys running about in the courtyard. The salad, however, was lying on the ground. "All right," said he, "the two have taken their portion," and he picked up the other leaves, laid them on the dish, and carried them to the maiden. "I bring you the delicate food myself," said he, "in order that you may not have to wait longer."

Then she ate of it, and was, like the others, immediately deprived of her human form, and ran out into the courtyard in the shape of a Donkey.

After the huntsman had washed his face, so that the transformed ones could recognize him, he went down into the courtyard, and said, "Now you shall receive the wages of your treachery," and bound them together, all three with one rope, and drove them along until he came to a mill.

He knocked at the window, the miller put out his head, and asked what he wanted. "I have three unmanageable beasts," answered he, "which I don't want to keep any longer. Will you take them in, and give them food and stable room, and manage them as I tell you? Then I will pay you what you ask."

The miller said, "Why not? But how am I to manage them?"

The huntsman then said that he was to give three beatings and one meal daily to the old Donkey, and that was the Witch; one beating and three meals to the younger one, which was the servant-girl; and to the youngest, which was the maiden, no beatings and three meals, for he could not bring himself to have the maiden beaten. After that he went back into the castle, and found therein everything he needed.

After a couple of days, the miller came and said he must inform him that the old Donkey which had received three beatings and only one meal daily, was dead; "the two others," he continued, "are certainly not dead, and are fed three times daily, but they are so sad that they cannot last much longer."

The huntsman was moved to pity, put away his anger, and told the miller to drive them back again to him. And when they came, he gave them some of the good salad, so that they became human again.

The beautiful maiden fell on her knees before him, and said, "Ah, my Beloved, forgive me for the evil I have done you. My mother drove me to it. It was done against my will, for I love you dearly. Your Wishing-Cloak hangs in a cupboard, and as for the Bird's-Heart I will take a potion and bring it up again."

But he thought otherwise, and said, "Keep it. It is all the same, for I will take you for my true wife."

So the wedding was celebrated, and they lived happily together until their death.

CLEVER HANS

I

The mother of Hans said, "Whither away, Hans?"

Hans answered, "To Grethel."

"Behave well, Hans."

"Oh, I'll behave well. Good-bye, Mother."

"Good-bye, Hans."

Hans comes to Grethel. "Good day, Grethel."

"Good day, Hans. What do you bring that is good?"

"I bring nothing, I want to have something given me."

Grethel presents Hans with a needle.

Hans says, "Good-bye, Grethel."

"Good-bye, Hans."

Hans takes the needle, sticks it into a hay-cart, and follows the cart home. "Good evening, Mother."

"Good evening, Hans. Where have you been?"

"With Grethel."

"What did you take her?"

"Took nothing; had something given me."

"What did Grethel give you?"

"Gave me a needle."

"Where is the needle, Hans?"

"Stuck in the hay-cart."

"That was ill done, Hans. You should have stuck the needle in your sleeve."

"Never mind, I'll do better next time."

II

"Whither away, Hans?"

"To Grethel, Mother."

"Behave well, Hans."

"Oh, I'll behave well. Good-bye, Mother."

"Good-bye, Hans."

Hans comes to Grethel. "Good day, Grethel."

"Good day, Hans. What do you bring that is good?"

"I bring nothing, I want to have something given me."

Grethel presents Hans with a knife.

"Good-bye, Grethel."

"Good-bye, Hans."

Hans takes the knife, sticks it in his sleeve, and goes home.

"Good evening, Mother."

"Good evening, Hans. Where have you been?"

"With Grethel."

"What did you take her?"

"Took her nothing, she gave me something."

"What did Grethel give you?"

"Gave me a knife."

"Where is the knife, Hans?"

"Stuck it in my sleeve."

"That's ill done, Hans, you should have put the knife in your pocket."

"Never mind, will do better next time."

III

"Whither away, Hans?"

"To Grethel, Mother."

"Behave well, Hans."

"Oh, I'll behave well. Good-bye, Mother."

"Good-bye, Hans."

Hans comes to Grethel. "Good day, Grethel."

"Good day, Hans. What good thing do you bring?"

"I bring nothing. I want something given me."

Grethel presents Hans with a young goat.

"Good-bye, Grethel."

"Good-bye, Hans."

Hans takes the goat, ties its legs, and puts it in his pocket. When he gets home it is suffocated.

"Good evening, Mother."

"Good evening, Hans. Where have you been?"

"With Grethel."

"What did you take her?"

"Took nothing, she gave me something."

"What did Grethel give you?"

"She gave me a goat."

"Where is the goat, Hans?"

"Put it in my pocket."

"That was ill done, Hans, you should have put a rope round the goat's neck."

"Never mind, will do better next time."

IV

"Whither away, Hans?"

"To Grethel, Mother."

"Behave well, Hans."

"Oh, I'll behave well. Good-bye, Mother."

"Good-bye, Hans."

Hans comes to Grethel. "Good day, Grethel."

"Good day, Hans. What good thing do you bring?"

"I bring nothing, I want something given me."

Grethel presents Hans with a piece of bacon.

"Good-bye, Grethel."

"Good-bye, Hans."

Hans takes the bacon, ties it to a rope, and drags it away behind him. The dogs come and devour the bacon. When he gets home, he has the rope in his hand, and there is no longer anything hanging to it.

"Good evening, Mother."

"Good evening, Hans. Where have you been?"

"With Grethel."

"What did you take her?"

"I took her nothing, she gave me something."

"What did Grethel give you?"

"Gave me a bit of bacon."

"Where is the bacon, Hans?"

"I tied it to a rope, brought it home, dogs took it."

"That was ill done, Hans, you should have carried the bacon on your head."

"Never mind, will do better next time."

V

"Whither away, Hans?"

"To Grethel, Mother."

"Behave well, Hans."

"I'll behave well. Good-bye, Mother."

"Good-bye, Hans."

Hans comes to Grethel. "Good day, Grethel."

"Good day, Hans. What good thing do you bring?"

"I bring nothing, but would have something given me."

Grethel presents Hans with a calf.

"Good-bye, Grethel."

"Good-bye, Hans."

Hans takes the calf, puts it on his head, and the calf kicks his face.

"Good evening, Mother."

"Good evening, Hans. Where have you been?"

"With Grethel."

"What did you take her?"

"I took nothing, but had something given me."

"What did Grethel give you?"

"A calf."

"Where have you the calf, Hans?"

"I set it on my head and it kicked my face."

"That was ill done, Hans, you should have led the calf, and put it in the stall."

"Never mind, will do better next time."

VI

"Whither away, Hans?"

"To Grethel, Mother."

"Behave well, Hans."

"I'll behave well. Good-bye, Mother."

"Good-bye, Hans."

Hans comes to Grethel. "Good day, Grethel."

"Good day, Hans. What good thing do you bring?"

"I bring nothing, but would have something given me."

Grethel says to Hans, "I will go with you."

Hans takes Grethel, ties her to a rope, leads her to the rack, and binds her fast. Then Hans goes to his mother.

"Good evening, Mother."

"Good evening, Hans. Where have you been?"

"With Grethel."

"What did you take her?"

"I took her nothing."

"What did Grethel give you?"

"She gave me nothing, she came with me."

"Where have you left Grethel?"

"I led her by the rope, tied her to the rack, and scattered some grass for her."

"That was ill done, Hans, you should have cast friendly eyes on her."

"Never mind, will do better."

Hans went into the stable, cut out all the calves' and sheep's eyes, and threw them in Grethel's face. Then Grethel became angry, tore herself lose and ran away, and became the Bride of Hans.

THE IRON STOVE

In the days when wishing was having, a King's Son was enchanted by an old Witch, and shut up in an Iron Stove in a forest. There he passed many years, and no one could deliver him.

Then a King's Daughter came into the forest, who had lost herself and could not find her father's kingdom again. After she had wandered about for nine days, she at length came to the Iron Stove. Then a voice issued from it, and asked her, "Whence come you, and whither go you?"

She answered, "I have lost my father's kingdom, and cannot get home again."

Then a voice inside the Iron Stove said, "I will help you to get home, and that indeed most swiftly, if you will promise to do what I desire of you. I am the son of a far greater King than your father, and I will marry you."

Then was she afraid, and thought, "Alas! What use could I have with an Iron Stove?" But as she much wished to get home to her father, she promised to do as he desired.

He said, "You shall return here, and bring a knife with you, and scrape a hole in the iron."

Then he gave her a companion who walked near her, but did not speak. In two hours he took her home. There was great joy in the castle when the King's Daughter came back, and the old King fell on her neck, and kissed her.

She, however, was sorely troubled, and said, "Dear Father, what I have suffered! I should never have got home again from the great wild forest, if I had not come to an Iron Stove. But I have been forced to give my word that I will go back to it, set it free, and marry it."

Then the old King was so terrified that he all but fainted, for he had only this one daughter. They, therefore, resolved they would send, in her place, the miller's daughter, who was very beautiful. They took her there, gave her a knife, and said she was to scrape at the Iron Stove. So she scraped at it for four-and-twenty hours, but could not bring off the least morsel of it.

When day dawned, a voice in the stove said, "It seems to me it is day outside."

Then she answered, "It seems so to me too. I fancy I hear the noise of my father's mill."

"So you are a miller's daughter! Then go your way at once. Let the King's Daughter come here."

She went away at once, and told the old King that the man outside there would have none of her—he wanted the King's Daughter.

They, however, still had a swineherd's daughter, who was even prettier than the miller's daughter, and they determined to give her a piece of gold to go to the Iron Stove, instead of the King's Daughter. So she was taken thither, and she also had to scrape for four-and-twenty hours. She, likewise, made nothing of it.

When day broke, a voice inside the stove cried, "It seems to me it is day outside!"

Then answered she, "So it seems to me. I fancy I hear my father's horn blowing."

"Then you are a swineherd's daughter! Go away at once. Tell the King's Daughter to come, and tell her all must be done as was promised. And if she does not come, everything in the kingdom shall be ruined, and destroyed, and not one stone be left standing on another."

When the King's Daughter heard that, she began to weep. But now there was nothing for it but to keep her promise. So she took leave of her father, put a knife in her pocket, and went forth to the Iron Stove in the forest.

When she got there, she began to scrape, and the iron gave way, and when two hours were over, she had already scraped a small hole. Then she peeped in, and saw a youth so handsome, and so brilliant with gold and with precious jewels, that her very soul was delighted. Therefore, she went on scraping, and made the hole so large that he was able to get out.

Then said he, "You are mine, and I am yours. You are my Bride, and have released me."

He wanted to take her away with him to his kingdom, but she entreated him to let her go once again to her father. The King's Son allowed her to do so, but she was not to say more to her father than three words, and then she was to come back again.

So she went home, but she spoke more than three words, and instantly the Iron Stove disappeared, and was taken far away over glass mountains and piercing swords. But the King's Son was set free, and no longer shut up in it.

After this, she bade good-bye to her father, took some money with her, but not much, and went back to the great forest, and looked for the Iron Stove, but it was nowhere to be found. For nine days she sought it. Then her hunger grew so great that she did not know what to do, for she could no longer live.

When it was evening, she seated herself in a small tree, and made up her mind to spend the night there, as she was afraid of wild beasts. When midnight drew near, she saw in the distance a small light, and thought, "Ah, there I may be saved!" She got down from the tree, and went toward the light, and on the way she prayed. Then she came to a little old house, and much grass had grown all about it, and a small heap of wood lay in front of it.

She thought, "Ah, whither have I come!" and peeped in through the window. But she saw nothing inside but Toads, big and little, except a table covered with wine and roast meat, while the plates and glasses were of silver. Then she took courage, and knocked at the door. The fat Toad cried:

"Little green Waiting-Maid,
Waiting-Maid with the limping leg,
Little Dog of the limping leg,
Hop hither and thither,
And quickly see who is without!"

and a small Toad came along and opened the door to her.

When she entered, they all bade her welcome, and she was forced to sit down. They asked, "Where have you come from, and whither are you going?"

Then she related all that had befallen her, and how because she had disobeyed the order which had been given her not to say more than three words, the stove, and the King's Son also, had disappeared, and now she was seeking him over hill and dale until she found him. At that, the old fat one said:

"Little green Waiting-Maid,
Waiting-Maid with the limping leg,
Little Dog of the limping leg,
Hop hither and thither,
And bring me the great box."

Then the little one went and brought the box. After this they gave her meat and drink, and took her to a well-made bed, which felt like silk and velvet. She laid herself therein, in God's name, and slept.

THEN THE KING'S DAUGHTER CAME TO A LITTLE HOUSE

When morning came she arose, and the old Toad gave her three needles out of the great box, which she was to take with her; they would be needed by her, for she had to cross a high Glass Mountain, and go over three piercing swords and a great lake. If she did all this, she would get her lover back again. Then she gave her three things, which she was to take the greatest care of, namely, three large needles, a plough-wheel, and three nuts.

With these she traveled onwards, and when she came to the Glass Mountain, which was so slippery, she stuck the three needles first behind her feet and then before them, and so got over it. And when she was over it, she hid them in a place which she marked carefully. After this she came to the three piercing swords, and then she seated herself on her plough-wheel, and rolled over them. At last she arrived in front of a great lake, and when she had crossed it, she came to a large and beautiful castle.

She went in and asked for a place. She knew, however, that the King's Son whom she had released from the Iron Stove in the great forest, was in the castle. Then she was taken as a scullery-maid at low wages. But, already the King's Son had another maiden by his side, whom he wanted to marry, for he thought that she had long been dead.

In the evening, when she had washed up and was done, she felt in her pocket and found the three nuts which the old Toad had given her. She cracked one with her teeth, and was going to eat the kernel, when, lo and behold, there was a stately royal garment in it! But when the Bride heard of this she came and asked for the dress, and wanted to buy it, and said, "It is not a dress for a servant-girl."

She said, no, she would not sell it, but if the Bride would grant her one thing she should have it, and that was, leave to sleep one night in her Bridegroom's chamber. The Bride gave her permission because the dress was so pretty, and she had never had one like it.

When it was evening, she said to her Bridegroom, "That silly girl will sleep in your room."

"If you are willing so am I," said he.

She, however, gave him a glass of wine in which she had poured a sleeping-draught. So the Bridegroom and the scullery-maid went to sleep in the room, and he slept so soundly that she could not waken him.

She wept the whole night and cried, "I set you free when you were in an Iron Stove in the wild forest. I sought you, and walked over a Glass Mountain, and three sharp swords, and a great lake before I found you, and yet you will not hear me!"

The servants sat by the chamber-door, and heard how she thus wept the whole night through, and in the morning they told it to their lord.

And the next evening, when she had washed up, she opened the second nut, and a far more beautiful dress was within it. When the Bride beheld it, she wished to buy that also. But the girl would not take money, and begged that she might once again sleep in the Bridegroom's chamber. The Bride, however, gave him a sleeping-drink, and he slept so soundly that he could hear nothing.

But the scullery-maid wept the whole night long, and cried, "I set you free when you were in an Iron Stove in the wild forest. I sought you, and walked over a Glass Mountain, and over three sharp swords and a great lake before I found you, and yet you will not hear me!"

The servants sat by the chamber-door and heard her weeping the whole night through, and in the morning informed their lord of it.

And on the third evening, when she had washed up, she opened the third nut, and within it was a still more beautiful dress which was stiff with pure gold.

When the Bride saw that, she wanted to have it, but the maiden gave it up only on condition that she might for the third time sleep in the Bridegroom's apartment. The King's Son was, However, on his guard, and threw the sleeping-draught away.

Now, therefore, when she began to weep and to cry, "Dearest Love, I set you free when you were in the Iron Stove in the terrible wild forest," the King's Son leapt up and said, "You are the true one, you are mine, and I am yours."

Thereupon, while it was still night, he got into a carriage with her, and they took away the false Bride's clothes so that she could not get up. When they came to the great lake, they sailed across it, and when they reached the three sharp-cutting swords they seated themselves on the plough-wheel, and when they got to the Glass Mountain they thrust the three needles in it. And so at length they reached the little old house. But when they went inside that, it was a great castle, and the Toads were all disenchanted, and were King's children, and full of happiness.

Then the wedding was celebrated, and the King's Son and the Princess remained in the castle, which was much larger than the castles of their fathers. But, as the old King grieved at being left alone, they fetched him away, and brought him to live with them. And they had two Kingdoms, and lived together happily ever afterward.

A Mouse did run,
The story's done!

SWEET PORRIDGE

There was a poor, good little girl, who lived alone with her mother, and they had nothing more to eat.

So the child went into the forest, and an Old Woman met her, who knew of her sorrow, and gave her a Little Pot, which, when she said:

"Boil, Little Pot, boil!"

would cook good sweet Porridge. And when she said:

"Stop, Little Pot, stop!"

it ceased to cook.

The little girl took the Pot home to her mother. And now they were freed from their poverty and hunger, and ate sweet Porridge as often as they liked.

Once on a time, when the little girl had gone out, the mother said:

"Boil, Little Pot, boil!"

And it began to cook, and she ate till she was satisfied. Then she wanted the Pot to stop cooking, but did not know the word.

So it went on cooking, and the Porridge rose over the edge.

And still it cooked on till the kitchen, and the whole house was full, and then the next house, and then the whole street, just as if it wanted to satisfy the hunger of the whole world. And there was the greatest trouble, and no one knew how to stop it. At last, when only a single house was left, the child came home and just said:

"*Stop, Little Pot, stop!*"

and it stopped cooking.

And whosoever wished to return to the town, had to eat his way back.

SNOW-WHITE AND ROSE-RED

There was once a poor widow who lived in a lonely cottage. In front of the cottage was a garden wherein stood two rose-trees, one of which bore white and the other red roses. She had two children who were like the two rose-trees. One was called Snow-White, and the other Rose-Red.

They were as good and happy, as busy and cheerful as ever two children in the world were, only Snow-White was more quiet and gentle than Rose-Red. Rose-Red liked better to run about in the meadows and fields seeking flowers and catching butterflies. But Snow-White sat at home with her mother, and helped her with the housework, or read to her when there was nothing to do.

The two children were so fond of each other, that they always held each other by the hand when they went out together. When Snow-White said, "We will not leave each other," Rose-Red answered, "Never so long as we live." And their mother would add, "What one has, she must share with the other."

They often ran about the forest alone and gathered red berries. Beasts never did them any harm, but came close to them trustfully. The little hare would eat a cabbage-leaf out of their hands, the roe grazed by their side, the stag leapt merrily by them, and the birds sat still upon the boughs, and sang whatever they knew.

No mishap overtook them. If they stayed too late in the forest, and night came on, they laid themselves down near one another upon the moss, and slept until morning. Their mother knew this, and had no worry on their account.

One day, when they had spent the night in the wood and the dawn had roused them, they saw a beautiful Child in a shining white dress sitting near their bed. He got up and looked quite kindly at them, but said nothing and went away into the forest. And when they looked round, they found that they had been sleeping quite close to a precipice, and would certainly have fallen into it in the darkness, if they had gone only a few paces farther. And their mother told them that it must have been the Angel who watches over good children.

Snow-White and Rose-Red kept their mother's little cottage so neat, that it was a pleasure to look inside it. In the summer, Rose-Red took care of the house, and every morning laid a wreath of flowers by her mother's bed before she awoke, in which was a rose from each tree. In the winter, Snow-White lit the fire and hung the kettle on the hook. The kettle was of copper and shone like gold, so brightly was it polished.

In the evening, when the snowflakes fell, the mother said, "Go, Snow-White, and bolt the door," and then they sat round the hearth, and the mother took her spectacles and read aloud out of a large book. The two girls listened as they sat and span. And close by them lay a lamb upon the floor, and behind them upon a perch sat a white dove with its head hidden beneath its wings.

One evening, as they were thus sitting comfortably together, some one knocked at the door as if he wished to be let in. The mother said, "Quick, Rose-Red, open the door, it must be a traveler who is seeking shelter."

Rose-Red went and pushed back the bolt, thinking that it was a poor man, but it was not. It was a Bear that stretched his broad, black head within the door.

Rose-Red screamed and sprang back, the lamb bleated, the dove fluttered, and Snow-White hid herself behind her mother's bed.

But the Bear began to speak and said, "Do not be afraid. I will do you no harm! I am half-frozen, and only want to warm myself a little beside you."

"Poor Bear," said the mother, "lie down by the fire. Only take care that you do not burn your coat." Then she cried, "Snow-White, Rose-Red, come out, the Bear will do you no harm, he means well."

So they both came out, and by-and-by the lamb and dove came nearer, and were not afraid of him.

The Bear said, "Here, Children, knock the snow out of my coat a little;" so they brought the broom and swept the Bear's hide clean. And he stretched himself by the fire and growled contentedly and comfortably.

It was not long before they grew quite at home, and played tricks with their clumsy guest. They tugged at his hair with their hands, put their feet upon his back and rolled him about, or they took a hazel-switch and beat him, and, when he growled, they laughed. But the Bear took it all in good part, only when they were too rough he called out, "Leave me alive, Children:

"Snowy-white, Rosy-red,
Will you beat your lover dead?"

When it was bedtime, and the others went to sleep, the mother said to the Bear, "You may lie there by the hearth, and then you will be safe from the cold and the bad weather."

As soon as day dawned the two children let him out, and he trotted across the snow into the forest.

Henceforth the Bear came every evening at the same time, laid himself down by the hearth, and let the children amuse themselves with him as much as they liked. They got so used to him, that the doors were never fastened until their black friend had arrived.

When spring was come and all outside was green, the Bear said one morning to Snow-White, "Now I must go away, and cannot come back for the whole summer."

"Where are you going, then, dear Bear?" asked Snow-White.

"I must go into the forest and guard my treasures from the wicked Dwarfs. In the winter, when the earth is frozen hard, they are obliged to stay below and cannot work their way through. But now, when the sun has thawed and warmed the earth, they break through it, and come out to pry and steal. And what once gets into their hands and in their caves, does not easily see daylight again."

Snow-White was very sorry for his going away. And as she unbolted the door for him, and the Bear was hurrying out, he caught against the bolt and a piece of his hairy coat was torn off. It seemed to Snow-White as if she saw gold shining through it, but she was not sure about it. The Bear ran away quickly, and was soon out of sight behind the trees.

A short time afterward, the mother sent her children into the forest to get fire-wood. There they found a big tree which lay felled on the ground, and close by the trunk something was jumping backward and forward in the grass. But they could not make out what it was.

When they came nearer they saw a Dwarf with an old withered face and a snow-white beard a yard long. The end of the beard was caught in a crevice of the tree, and the little fellow was jumping backward and forward like a dog tied to a rope, and did not know what to do.

He glared at the girls with his fiery red eyes and cried, "Why do you stand there? Can you not come here and help me?"

"What are you about there, Little Man?" asked Rose-Red.

"You stupid, prying goose!" answered the Dwarf; "I was going to split the tree to get a little wood for cooking. The little bit of food that one of us wants gets burnt up directly with thick logs. We do not swallow so much as you coarse, greedy folk. I had just driven the wedge safely in, and everything was going as I wished; but the wretched wood was too smooth and suddenly sprang asunder, and the tree closed so quickly that I could not pull out my beautiful white beard. So now it is tight in, and I cannot get away. And you silly, sleek, milk-faced things laugh! Ugh! how odious you are!"

The children tried very hard, but they could not pull the beard out, it was caught too fast.

"I will run and fetch some one," said Rose-Red.

"You senseless goose!" snarled the Dwarf. "Why should you fetch some one? You are already two too many for me. Can you not think of something better?"

"Don't be impatient," said Snow-White, "I will help you," and she pulled her scissors out of her pocket, and cut off the end of the beard.

As soon as the Dwarf felt himself free, he grabbed a bag which lay amongst the roots of the tree, and which was full of gold, and lifted it up, grumbling to himself, "Rude people, to cut off a piece of my fine beard! Bad luck to you!" and then he swung the bag upon his back, and went off without even once looking at the children.

Some time after that Snow-White and Rose-Red went to catch a dish of fish. As they came near the brook, they saw something like a large grasshopper jumping toward the water, as if it were going to leap in. They ran to it and found it was the Dwarf.

"Where are you going?" said Rose-Red; "you surely don't want to go into the water?"

"I am not such a fool!" cried the Dwarf; "don't you see that the accursed fish wants to pull me in?" The Little Man had been sitting there fishing, and unluckily the wind had twisted his beard with the fishing-line. Just then a big fish bit, and the feeble creature had not strength to pull it out. The fish kept the upper hand and was pulling the Dwarf toward him. He held on to all the reeds and rushes, but it was of little good, he was forced to follow the fish, and was in great danger of being dragged into the water.

The girls came just in time. They held him fast and tried to free his beard from the line. But all in vain, beard and line were entangled fast together. Nothing was left but to bring out the scissors and cut the beard, whereby a small part of it was lost.

"DON'T BE IMPATIENT," SAID SNOW-WHITE, "I WILL HELP YOU"

When the Dwarf saw that, he screamed out, "Is that civil, you toadstool, to disfigure one's face? Was it not enough to clip off the end of my beard? Now you have cut off the best part of it. I cannot let myself be seen by my people. I wish you had been made to run the soles off your shoes!" Then he took out a sack of pearls which lay in the rushes, and, without saying a word more, he dragged it away and disappeared behind a stone.

It happened that soon afterward the mother sent the two children to the town to buy needles and thread, and laces and ribbons. The road led them across a heath upon which huge pieces of rock lay strewn about. They now noticed a large bird hovering in the air, flying slowly round and round above them. It sank lower and lower, and at last settled near a rock not far off. Directly afterward they heard a loud, piteous cry. They ran up and saw, with horror, that the eagle had seized their old acquaintance the Dwarf, and was going to carry him off.

The children, full of pity, at once took tight hold of the Little Man, and pulled against the eagle so long that at last he let his booty go.

As soon as the Dwarf had recovered from his first fright, he cried with his shrill voice, "Could you not have done it more carefully! You dragged at my brown coat, so that it is all torn and full of holes. You helpless, clumsy creatures!" Then he took up a sack full of precious stones, and slipped away again under the rock into his hole.

The girls, who by this time were used to his thanklessness, went on their way and did their business in the town.

As they crossed the heath again on their way home they surprised the Dwarf, who had emptied out his bag of precious stones in a clean spot, and had not thought that any one would come there at such a late hour. The evening sun shone upon the brilliant stones. They glittered and sparkled with all colors so beautifully, that the children stood still and looked at them.

"Why do you stand gaping there?" cried the Dwarf, and his ashen-gray face became copper-red with rage. He was going on with his bad words, when a loud growling was heard, and a black

Bear came trotting toward them out of the forest. The Dwarf sprang up in a fright, but he could not get to his cave, for the Bear was already close.

Then in the fear of his heart he cried, "Dear Mr. Bear, spare me! I will give you all my treasures! Look, the beautiful jewels lying there! Grant me my life. What do you want with such a slender little fellow as I? You would not feel me between your teeth. Come, take these two wicked girls, they are tender morsels for you, fat as young quails. For mercy's sake eat them!"

The Bear took no heed of his words, but gave the wicked creature a single blow with his paw, and he did not move again.

The girls had run away, but the Bear called to them, "Snow-White and Rose-Red, do not be afraid. Wait, I will come with you."

Then they knew his voice and waited. And when he came up to them, suddenly his bear-skin fell off, and he stood there a handsome man, clothed all in gold.

"I am a King's Son," he said, "and I was bewitched by that wicked Dwarf, who had stolen my treasures. I have had to run about the forest as a savage bear until I was freed by his death. Now he has got his well-deserved punishment."

Snow-White was married to him, and Rose-Red to his brother. They divided between them the great treasure which the Dwarf had gathered together in his cave. The old mother lived peacefully and happily with her children for many years. She took the two rose-trees with her, and they stood before her window, and every year bore the most beautiful roses, white and red.

THE HEDGE-KING

In former days, every sound had its meaning, the birds also had their own language which every one understood. Now it only sounds like chirping, screeching, and whistling, and to some, like music without words.

It came into the birds' mind, however, that they would no longer be without a ruler, and would choose one of themselves to be King.

One alone amongst them, the green plover, was opposed to this. He had lived free and would die free, and anxiously flying hither and thither, he cried, "Where shall I go? where shall I go?" He retired into a lonely and unfrequented marsh, and showed himself no more among his fellows.

The birds now wished to discuss the matter, and on a fine May morning they all gathered together from the woods and fields: eagles and chaffinches, owls and crows, larks and sparrows, how can I name them all? Even the cuckoo came, and the hoopoe, his clerk, who is so called because he is always heard a few days before him, and a very small bird which as yet had no name, mingled with the band.

The hen, which by some accident had heard nothing of the whole matter, was astonished at the great assemblage. "What, what, what is going to be done?" she cackled. But the cock calmed his beloved hen, and said, "Only rich people," and told her what they had on hand.

It was decided, however, that the one who could fly the highest should be King. A tree-frog which was sitting among the bushes, when he heard that, cried a warning, "No, no, no! no!" because he thought that many tears would be shed because of this. But the crow said, "Caw, caw," and that all would pass off peaceably.

It was now determined that, on this fine morning, they should at once begin to ascend, so that hereafter no one should be able to say, "I could easily have flown much higher, but the evening came on, and I could do no more."

On a given signal, therefore, the whole troop rose up in the air. The dust ascended from the land, and there was tremendous fluttering and whirring and beating of wings. It looked as if a black cloud was rising up. The little birds were, however, soon left behind. They could go no farther, and fell back to the ground.

The larger birds held out longer, but none could equal the eagle, who mounted so high that he could have picked the eyes out of the sun. And when he saw that the others could not get up to him, he thought, "Why should I fly any higher, I am the King?" and began to let himself down again.

The birds beneath him at once cried to him, "You must be our King, no one has flown so high as you."

"Except me," screamed the little fellow without a name, who had crept into the breast-feathers of the eagle. And as he was not at all tired, he rose up and mounted so high that he reached heaven itself. When, however, he had gone as far as this, he folded his wings together, and called down with clear and penetrating voice:

"*I am King! I am King!*"

"You, our King?" cried the birds angrily. "You have done this by trick and cunning!"

So they made another condition. He should be King who could go down lowest in the ground. How the goose did flap about with its broad breast when it was once more on the land! How quickly the cock scratched a hole! The duck came off the worst of all, for she leapt into a ditch, but sprained her legs, and waddled away to a neighboring pond, crying, "Cheating, cheating!"

The little bird without a name, however, sought out a mouse-hole, slipped down into it, and cried out of it, with his small voice:

"I am King! I am King!"

"You our King!" cried the birds still more angrily. "Do you think your cunning shall prevail?"

They determined to keep him a prisoner in the hole and starve him out. The owl was placed as sentinel in front of it, and was not to let the rascal out if she had any value for her life. When evening was come all the birds were feeling very tired after exerting their wings so much that they went to bed with their wives and children.

The owl alone remained standing by the mouse-hole, gazing steadfastly into it with her great eyes. In the meantime she, too, had grown tired and thought to herself, "You might certainly shut one eye, you will still watch with the other, and the little miscreant shall not come out of his hole." So she shut one eye, and with the other looked straight at the mouse-hole.

The little fellow put his head out and peeped, and wanted to slip away, but the owl came forward, and he drew his head back. Then the owl opened the one eye again, and shut the other, intending to shut them in turn all through the night.

But when she next shut the one eye, she forgot to open the other. And as soon as both her eyes were shut, she fell asleep. The little fellow soon saw that, and slipped away.

From that day forth, the owl has never dared to show herself by daylight, for if she does the other birds chase her and pluck her feathers out. She only flies out by night, but hates and pursues mice because they make such ugly holes.

The little bird, too, is very unwilling to let himself be seen, because he is afraid it will cost him his life if he is caught. He steals about in the hedges, and when he is quite safe, he sometimes cries, "I am King," and for this reason, the other birds call him in mockery, "Hedge-King."

No one, however, was so happy as the lark at not having to obey the little King. As soon as the sun appears, she ascends high in the air and cries, "Ah, how beautiful that is! beautiful that is! beautiful, beautiful! ah, how beautiful that is!"

ONE-EYE, TWO-EYES, AND THREE-EYES

There was once a woman who had three daughters, the eldest of whom was called One-Eye, because she had only one eye in the middle of her forehead, and the second, Two-Eyes, because she had two eyes like other folks, and the youngest, Three-Eyes, because she had three eyes; and her third eye was in the centre of her forehead.

Now, as Two-Eyes saw just as other human beings did, her sisters and her mother could not endure her. They said to her, "You, with your two eyes, are no better than common folk. You do not belong to us!"

They pushed her about, and threw old clothes to her, and gave her nothing to eat but what they left, and did everything that they could to make her unhappy.

It came to pass that Two-Eyes had to go out into the fields and tend the goat, but she was still very hungry, because her sisters had given her so little to eat. She sat down on a ridge and began to weep, and so bitterly that two streams ran down from her eyes.

And one day, when she looked up in her grief, a woman was standing beside her, who said, "Why are you weeping, little Two-Eyes?"

Two-Eyes answered, "Have I not reason to weep, when I have two eyes like other people, and my sisters and mother hate me for it, and push me from one corner to another, throw old clothes at me, and give me nothing to eat but the scraps they leave? To-day, they have given me so little that I am still very hungry."

Then the Wise Woman said, "Wipe away your tears, Two-Eyes, and I will tell you something to stop your ever suffering from hunger again; just say to your goat:

"'*Bleat, bleat, my little Goat, bleat,*
Cover the table with something to eat!'

and then a clean well-spread little table will stand before you, with the most delicious food upon it, of which you may eat as much as you are inclined. And when you have had enough, and have no more need of the little table, just say:

"'*Bleat, bleat, my little Goat, I pray,*
And take the table quite away!'

and then it will vanish again from your sight."

Hereupon the Wise Woman departed.

But Two-Eyes thought, "I must instantly make a trial, and see if what she said is true, for I am far too hungry," and she said:

"*Bleat, bleat, my little Goat, bleat,*
Cover the table with something to eat!"

and scarcely had she spoken the words than a little table, covered with a white cloth, was standing there, and on it was a plate with a knife and fork, and a silver spoon; and the most delicious food was there also, warm and smoking as if it had just come out of the kitchen.

Then Two-Eyes said a little prayer she knew, "Lord God, be with us always, Amen," and helped herself to some food, and enjoyed it. And when she was satisfied, she said, as the Wise Woman had taught her:

"Bleat, bleat, my little Goat, I pray,
And take the table quite away!"

and immediately the little table and everything on it was gone again.

"That is a delightful way of keeping house!" thought Two-Eyes, and was quite glad and happy.

In the evening, when she went home with her goat, she found a small earthenware dish with some food, which her sisters had set ready for her, but she did not touch it. Next day, she again went out with her goat, and left the few bits of broken bread which had been handed to her, lying untouched.

The first and second time that she did this, her sisters did not notice it, but as it happened every time, they did observe it, and said, "There is something wrong about Two-Eyes, she always leaves her food untasted. She used to eat up everything that was given her. She must have discovered other ways of getting food."

In order that they might learn the truth, they resolved to send One-Eye with Two-Eyes, when she went to drive her goat to the pasture, to watch what Two-Eyes did while she was there, and whether any one brought her things to eat and drink.

So when Two-Eyes set out the next time, One-Eye went to her and said, "I will go with you to the pasture, and see that the goat is well taken care of, and driven where there is food."

But Two-Eyes knew what was in One-Eye's mind, and drove the goat into high grass and said, "Come, One-Eye, we will sit down, and I will sing something to you."

One-Eye sat down, and was tired with the unaccustomed walk and the heat of the sun, and Two-Eyes sang constantly:

"One-Eye, wakest thou?
One-Eye, sleepest thou?"

until One-Eye shut her one eye, and fell asleep. As soon as Two-Eyes saw that One-Eye was fast asleep, and could discover nothing, she said:

"Bleat, bleat, my little Goat, bleat,
Cover the table with something to eat!"

and seated herself at her table, and ate and drank until she was satisfied. Then she again cried:

"Bleat, bleat, my little Goat, I pray,
And take the table quite away!"

and in an instant all was gone.

Two-Eyes now awakened One-Eye, and said, "One-Eye, you want to take care of the goat, and yet go to sleep while you are doing it! In the meantime, the goat might run all over the world. Come, let us go home again."

So they went home, and again Two-Eyes let her little dish stand untouched, and One-Eye could not tell her mother why she would not eat it, and to excuse herself said, "I fell asleep when I was out."

Next day, the mother said to Three-Eyes, "This time you shall go and watch if Two-Eyes eats anything when she is out, and if any one fetches her food and drink, for she must eat and drink in secret."

So Three-Eyes went to Two-Eyes, and said, "I will go with you and see if the goat is taken proper care of, and driven where there is food."

But Two-Eyes knew what was in Three-Eyes' mind, and drove the goat into high grass and said, "We will sit down, and I will sing something to you, Three-Eyes."

Three-Eyes sat down and was tired with the walk and with the heat of the sun, and Two-Eyes began the same song as before, and sang:

"Three-Eyes, are you waking?"
but then, instead of singing,
"Three-Eyes, are you sleeping?"
as she ought to have done, she thoughtlessly sang:
"Two-Eyes, are you sleeping?"
and sang all the time,
"Three-Eyes, are you waking?
Two-Eyes, are you sleeping?"

Then two of the eyes which Three-Eyes had, shut and fell asleep, but the third, as it had not been named in the song, did not sleep. It is true that Three-Eyes shut it, but only in her cunning, to pretend it was asleep too. But it blinked, and could see everything very well. And when Two-Eyes thought that Three-eyes was fast asleep, she used her little charm:

"Bleat, bleat, my little Goat, bleat,
Cover the table with something to eat!"

and ate and drank as much as her heart desired, and then ordered the table to go away again:

"Bleat, bleat, my little Goat, I pray,
And take the table quite away!"

and Three-Eyes had seen everything.

Then Two-Eyes came to her, waked her and said, "Have you been asleep, Three-Eyes? You are a good caretaker! Come, we will go home."

And when they got home, Two-Eyes again did not eat, and Three-Eyes said to the mother, "Now, I know why that proud thing there does not eat. When she is out, she says to the goat:

"'Bleat, bleat, my little Goat, bleat,
Cover the table with something to eat!'

and then a little table appears before her covered with the best of food, much better than any we have here. When she has eaten all she wants, she says:

"'Bleat, bleat, my little Goat, I pray,
And take the table quite away!'

and all disappears. I watched everything closely. She put two of my eyes to sleep by using a charm, but luckily the one in my forehead kept awake."

Then the envious mother cried, "Do you want to fare better than we do? The desire shall pass away!" and she fetched a butcher's knife, and thrust it into the heart of the goat, which fell down dead.

When Two-Eyes saw that, full of sorrow, she went outside, and seated herself on the ridge of grass at the edge of the field, and wept bitter tears.

Suddenly the Wise Woman once more stood by her side, and said, "Two-Eyes, why are you weeping?"

"Have I not reason to weep?" she answered. "The goat, which covered the table for me every day when I spoke your charm, has been killed by my mother, and now I shall again have to bear hunger and want."

The Wise Woman said, "Two-Eyes, I will give you a piece of good advice. Ask your sisters to give you the entrails of the slaughtered goat, and bury them in the ground in front of the house, and your fortune will be made."

Then she vanished, and Two-Eyes went home and said to her sisters, "Dear Sisters, do give me some part of my goat. I don't wish for what is good, but give me the entrails."

Then they laughed and said, "If that's all you want, you may have it."

So Two-Eyes took the entrails and buried them quietly, at evening, in front of the house-door, as the Wise Woman had counseled her to do.

Next morning, when they all awoke, and went to the house-door, there stood a wonderful, magnificent tree with leaves of silver, and fruit of gold hanging among them, so that in all the wide world there was nothing more beautiful or precious. They did not know how the tree could have come there during the night, but Two-Eyes saw that it had grown up out of the entrails of the goat, for it was standing on the exact spot where she had buried them.

Then the mother said to One-Eye, "Climb up, my Child, and gather some of the fruit of the tree for us."

One-Eye climbed up, but when she was about to lay hold of one of the golden apples, the branch escaped from her hands. And that happened each time, so that she could not pluck a single apple, let her do what she might.

Then said the mother, "Three-Eyes, do you climb up. You with your three eyes can look about you better than One-Eye."

One-Eye slipped down, and Three-Eyes climbed up. Three-Eyes was not more skillful, and might search as she liked, but the golden apples always escaped her.

At length, the mother grew impatient, and climbed up herself, but could grasp the fruit no better than One-Eye and Three-Eyes, for she always clutched empty air.

Then said Two-Eyes, "I will go up, perhaps I may succeed better."

The sisters cried, "You, indeed, with your two eyes! What can you do?"

But Two-Eyes climbed up, and the golden apples did not get out of her way, but came into her hand of their own accord, so that she could pluck them one after the other. And she brought a whole apronful down with her. The mother took them away from her, and instead of treating poor Two-Eyes any better for this, she and One-Eye and Three-Eyes were only envious, because Two-Eyes alone had been able to get the fruit. They treated her still more cruelly.

It so befell that once, when they were all standing together by the tree, a young Knight came up. "Quick, Two-Eyes," cried the two sisters, "creep under this and don't disgrace us!" and with all speed they turned an empty barrel, which was standing close by the tree, over poor Two-Eyes, and they pushed the golden apples which she had been gathering, under it too.

When the Knight came nearer he was a handsome lord, who stopped and admired the magnificent gold and silver tree, and said to the two sisters, "To whom does this fine tree belong? Any one who will bestow one branch of it on me may, in return for it, ask whatsoever he desires."

Then One-Eye and Three-Eyes replied that the tree belonged to them, and that they would give him a branch. They both tried very hard, but they were not able to do it, for every time the branches and fruit moved away from them.

Then said the Knight, "It is very strange that the tree should belong to you, and yet you should still not be able to break a piece off."

They again insisted that the tree was their property. Whilst they were saying so, Two-Eyes rolled a couple of golden apples from under the barrel to the feet of the Knight, for she was vexed with One-Eye and Three-Eyes, for not speaking the truth.

When the Knight saw the apples he was astonished, and asked from whence they came. One-Eye and Three-Eyes answered that they had another sister, who was not allowed to show herself, for she had only two eyes like any common person.

The Knight, however, desired to see her, and cried, "Two-Eyes, come hither!"

Then Two-Eyes, quite cheered, came from beneath the barrel, and the Knight was surprised at her great beauty, and said, "You, Two-Eyes, can certainly break off a branch from the tree for me."

"Yes," replied Two-Eyes, "that I certainly shall be able to do, for the tree belongs to me." And she climbed up, and with the greatest ease broke off a branch with beautiful silver leaves and golden fruit, and gave it to the Knight.

Then said the Knight, "Two-Eyes, what shall I give you for it?"

"Alas!" answered Two-Eyes, "I suffer from hunger and thirst, grief and want, from early morning till late night. If you would take me with you, and deliver me from these things, I should be happy."

So the Knight lifted Two-Eyes on his horse, and took her home with him to his father's castle. There he gave her beautiful clothes and meat and drink to her heart's content. And as he loved her so much he married her, and the wedding was solemnized with great rejoicing.

When Two-Eyes was thus carried away by the handsome Knight, her two sisters grudged her good fortune in downright earnest. "The wonderful tree, however, remains with us," thought they, "and even if we can gather no fruit from it, every one will stand still and look at it, and come to us and admire it. Who knows what good things may be in store for us?"

But next morning, the tree had vanished, and all their hopes were at an end. And when Two-Eyes looked out of the window of her own little room, to her great delight it was standing in front of it. And so it had followed her.

Two-Eyes lived a long time in happiness. One day, two poor women came to her castle, and begged for alms. She looked in their faces, and recognized her sisters, One-Eye, and Three-Eyes, who had fallen into such poverty that they had to wander about and beg their bread from door to door. Two-Eyes made them welcome, and was kind to them, and took care of them, so that they both, with all their hearts, repented of the evil that they had done in their youth to their sister.

THE GOOSE-GIRL AT THE WELL

The Old Witch

There was once upon a time, a very old woman, who lived with her flock of geese in a waste place among the mountains, and there had a little house. The waste was surrounded by a large forest, and every morning the Old Woman took her crutch and hobbled into it.

There, however, the dame was quite active, more so than any one would have thought, considering her age, and collected grass for her geese, picked all the wild fruit she could reach, and carried everything home on her back. Any one would have thought that the heavy load would have weighed her to the ground, but she always brought it safely home.

If any one met her, she greeted him quite courteously. "Good day, dear Countryman, it is a fine day. Ah! you wonder that I should drag grass about, but every one must take his burthen on his back."

Nevertheless, people did not like to meet her if they could help it, and took by preference a roundabout way. And when a father with his boys passed her, he whispered to them, "Beware of the Old Woman. She has claws beneath her gloves. She is a Witch."

One morning, a handsome young man was going through the forest. The sun shone bright, the birds sang, a cool breeze crept through the leaves, and he was full of joy and gladness. He had as yet met no one, when he suddenly perceived the old Witch kneeling on the ground cutting grass with a sickle. She had already thrust a whole load into her cloth, and near it stood two baskets, which were filled with wild apples and pears.

"But, good little Mother," said he, "how can you carry all that away?"

"I must carry it, dear Sir," answered she; "rich folk's children have no need to do such things, but with the peasant folk the saying goes, 'Don't look behind you, you will only see how crooked your back is!'

"Will you help me?" she said, as he remained standing by her. "You have still a straight back and young legs, it would be a trifle to you. Besides, my house is not so very far from here. It stands there on the heath behind the hill. How soon you would bound up thither!"

The young man took compassion on the Old Woman. "My father is certainly no peasant," replied he, "but a rich Count. Nevertheless, that you may see it is not only peasants who can carry things, I will take your bundle."

"If you will try it," said she, "I shall be very glad. You will certainly have to walk for an hour, but what will that signify to you? Only you must carry the apples and pears as well."

It now seemed to the young man just a little serious, when he heard of an hour's walk, but the Old Woman would not let him off, packed the bundle on his back, and hung the two baskets on his arm. "See, it is quite light," said she.

"No, it is not light," answered the Count, and pulled a rueful face. "Verily, the bundle weighs as heavily as if it were full of cobblestones, and the apples and pears are as heavy as lead! I can scarcely breathe."

He had a mind to put everything down again, but the Old Woman would not allow it. "Just look," said she mockingly, "the young gentleman will not carry what I, an old woman, have so often dragged along! You are ready with fine words, but when it comes to being in earnest, you want to take to your heels. Why are you standing loitering there?" she continued. "Step out. No one will take the bundle off again."

As long as he walked on level ground, it was still bearable, but when they came to the hill and had to climb, and the stones rolled down under his feet as if they were alive, it was beyond his strength. The drops of perspiration stood on his forehead, and ran, hot and cold, down his back.

"Dame," said he, "I can go no farther. I want to rest a little."

"Not here," answered the Old Woman, "when we have arrived at our journey's end, you can rest. But now you must go forward. Who knows what good it may do you?"

"Old woman, you are shameless!" said the Count, and tried to throw off the bundle, but he labored in vain. It stuck as fast to his back, as if it grew there. He turned and twisted, but he could not get rid of it.

The Old Woman laughed at this, and sprang about quite delighted on her crutch. "Don't get angry, dear Sir," said she, "you are growing as red in the face as a turkey-cock! Carry your bundle patiently. I will give you a good present when we get home."

What could he do? He was obliged to submit to his fate, and crawl along patiently behind the Old Woman. She seemed to grow more and more nimble, and his burden still heavier. All at once, she made a spring, jumped on to the bundle and seated herself on the top of it. And however withered she might be, she was yet heavier than the stoutest country lass.

The youth's knees trembled, but when he did not go on, the Old Woman hit him about the legs with a switch and with stinging-nettles. Groaning continually, he climbed the mountain, and at length reached the Old Woman's house, when he was just about to drop.

When the geese perceived the Old Woman, they flapped their wings, stretched out their necks, ran to meet her, cackling all the while. Behind the flock walked, stick in hand, an old wench, strong and big, but ugly as night. "Good Mother," said she to the Old Woman, "has anything happened to you, you have stayed away so long?"

"By no means, my dear Daughter," answered she, "I have met with nothing bad, but, on the contrary, with this kind gentleman, who has carried my burthen for me. Only think, he even took me on his back when I was tired. The way, too, has not seemed long to us. We have been merry, and have been cracking jokes with each other all the time."

At last the Old Woman slid down, took the bundle off the young man's back, and the baskets from his arm, looked at him quite kindly, and said, "Now seat yourself on the bench before the door, and rest. You have fairly earned your wages, and they shall not be wanting."

Then she said to the goose-girl, "Go into the house, my little Daughter, it is not becoming for you to be alone with a young gentleman. One must not pour oil on to the fire, he might fall in love with you."

The Count knew not whether to laugh or to cry. "Such a sweetheart as that," thought he, "could not touch my heart, even if she were thirty years younger."

In the meantime, the Old Woman stroked and fondled her geese as if they were children, and then went into the house with her daughter. The youth lay down on the bench, under a wild apple-tree. The air was warm and mild. On all sides stretched a green meadow, which was set with cowslips, wild thyme, and a thousand other flowers. Through the midst of it rippled a clear brook on which the sun sparkled, and the white geese went walking backward and forward, or paddled in the water.

"It is quite delightful here," said he, "but I am so tired that I cannot keep my eyes open. I will sleep a little. If only a gust of wind does not come and blow my legs off my body, for they are as brittle as tinder."

When he had slept a little while, the Old Woman came and shook him till he awoke. "Sit up," said she, "you cannot stay here. I have certainly treated you badly, still it has not cost you your life. Of money and land you have no need, here is something else for you."

Thereupon she thrust a little book into his hand, which was cut out of a single emerald. "Take great care of it," said she, "it will bring you good fortune."

The Count sprang up, and as he felt that he was quite fresh, and had recovered his vigor, he thanked the Old Woman for her present, and set off without even once looking back at the beautiful daughter. When he was already some way off, he still heard in the distance the noisy cry of the geese.

For three days, the Count had to wander in the wilderness before he could find his way out. He then reached a large town. As no one knew him, he was led into the royal palace, where the King and Queen were sitting on their throne. The Count fell on one knee, drew the emerald book out of his pocket, and laid it at the Queen's feet. She bade him rise and hand her the little book.

Hardly, however, had she opened it, and looked therein, than she fell as if dead to the ground. The Count was seized by the King's servants, and was being led to prison, when the Queen opened her eyes, and ordered them to release him, and every one was to go out, as she wished to speak with him in private.

When the Queen was alone, she began to weep bitterly, and said, "Of what use to me are the splendors and honors with which I am surrounded! Every morning I awake in pain and sorrow. I had three daughters, the youngest of whom was so beautiful, that the whole world looked on her as a wonder. She was as white as snow, as rosy as apple-blossoms, and her hair as radiant as sunbeams. When she cried, not tears fell from her eyes, but pearls and jewels only.

"When she was fifteen years old, the King summoned all three sisters to come before his throne. You should have seen how all the people gazed when the youngest entered. It was just as if the sun were rising! Then the King spoke, 'My Daughters, I know not when my last hour may arrive. I will to-day decide what each shall receive at my death. You all love me, but the one of you who loves me best, shall fare the best.'

"Each of them said she loved him best. 'Can you not express to me,' said the King, 'how much you do love me, and thus I shall see what you mean?'

"The eldest spoke. 'I love my Father as dearly as the sweetest sugar.' The second, 'I love my Father as dearly as my prettiest dress.' But the youngest was silent.

"Then the father said, 'And you, my dearest Child, how much do you love me?' 'I do not know, and can compare my love with nothing.' But her father insisted that she should name something. So she said at last, 'The best food does not please me without salt, therefore I love my Father like salt.'

"When the King heard that, he fell into a passion and said, 'If you love me like salt, your love shall also be repaid with salt.'

"Then he divided the kingdom between the two elder, but caused a sack of salt to be bound on the back of the youngest, and two servants had to lead her forth into the wild forest.

"We all begged and prayed for her," said the Queen, "but the King's anger was not to be appeased. How she cried when she had to leave us! The whole road was strewn with the pearls which flowed from her eyes.

"The King soon afterward repented of his great severity, and had the whole forest searched for the poor child, but no one could find her. When I think that the wild beasts have devoured her, I know not how to contain myself for sorrow. Many a time I console myself with the hope that she is still alive, and may have hidden herself in a cave, or has found shelter with compassionate people.

"But picture to yourself, when I opened your little emerald book, a pearl lay therein, of exactly the same kind as those which used to fall from my daughter's eyes. And then you can also imagine how the sight of it stirred my heart! You must tell me how you came by that pearl."

The Count told her that he had received it from the Old Woman in the forest, who had appeared very strange to him, and must be a Witch. But he had neither seen nor heard anything of the Queen's child. The King and the Queen resolved to seek out the Old Woman. They thought that there where the pearl had been, they would obtain news of their daughter.

The Gray Mask

The Old Woman was sitting in that lonely place at her spinning-wheel, spinning. It was already dusk, and a log which was burning on the hearth gave a scanty light. All at once, there was a noise outside, the geese were coming home from the pasture, and uttering their hoarse cries. Soon afterward the daughter entered. But the Old Woman scarcely thanked her, and only shook her head a little. The daughter sat down beside her, took her spinning-wheel, and twisted the threads as nimbly as a young girl. Thus they both sat for two hours, and exchanged never a word.

At last, something rustled at the window, and two fiery eyes peered in. It was an old night-owl, which cried, "*Uhu!*" three times.

The Old Woman looked up just a little, then she said, "Now, my little Daughter, it is time for you to go out and do your work."

She rose and went out, and where did she go? Over the meadows ever onward into the valley. At last, she came to a well, with three old oak-trees standing beside it. Meanwhile the moon had risen large and round over the mountain, and it was so light that one could have found a needle.

She removed a skin which covered her face, then bent down to the well, and began to wash herself. When she had finished, she dipped the skin also in the water, and laid it on the meadow, so that it should bleach in the moonlight, and dry again.

But how the maiden was changed! Such a change as that was never seen before! When the gray mask fell off, her golden hair broke forth like sunbeams, and spread about like a mantle over her whole form. Her eyes shone out as brightly as the stars in heaven, and her cheeks bloomed a soft red like apple-blossoms.

WHEN THE GRAY MASK FELL OFF, HER GOLDEN HAIR BROKE FORTH

But the fair maiden was sad. She sat down and wept bitterly. One tear after another forced itself out of her eyes, and rolled through her long hair to the ground. There she sat, and would have remained sitting a long time, if there had not been a rustling and cracking in the boughs of the neighboring tree. She sprang up like a roe which has been overtaken by the shot of the hunter.

Just then the moon was obscured by a dark cloud, and in an instant the maiden had slipped on the old skin and vanished, as does a light blown out by the wind.

She ran back home, trembling like an aspen-leaf. The Old Woman was standing on the threshold, and the maiden was about to relate what had befallen her, but the Old Woman laughed kindly, and said, "I already know it."

She led her into the room and lighted a new log. She did not, however, sit down to her spinning again, but fetched a broom and began to sweep and scour. "All must be clean and sweet," she said to the maiden.

"But, Mother," said the maiden, "why do you begin work at so late an hour? What do you expect?"

"Do you know then what time it is?" asked the Old Woman.

"Not yet midnight," answered the maiden, "but already past eleven o'clock."

"Do you not remember," continued the Old Woman, "that it is three years to-day since you came to me? Your time is up, we can no longer remain together."

The maiden was terrified, and said, "Alas! dear Mother, will you cast me off? Where shall I go? I have no friends, and no home to which I can go. I have always done as you bade me, and you have always been satisfied with me. Do not send me away."

The Old Woman would not tell the maiden what lay before her. "My stay here is over," she said to her, "but when I depart, house and parlor must be clean: therefore do not hinder me in my work. Have no care for yourself. You shall find a roof to shelter you, and the wages which I will give you shall also content you."

"But tell me what is about to happen," the maiden continued to entreat.

"I tell you again, do not hinder me in my work. Do not say a word more, go to your chamber, take the skin off your face, and put on the silken gown which you had on when you came to me, and then wait in your chamber until I call you."

But I must once more tell of the King and Queen, who had journeyed forth with the Count in order to seek out the Old Woman in the wilderness. The Count had strayed away from them in the wood by night, and had to walk onward alone.

Next day, it seemed to him that he was on the right track. He still went forward, until darkness came on, then he climbed a tree, intending to pass the night there, for he feared that he might lose his way. When the moon illumined the surrounding country he perceived a figure coming down the mountain. She had no stick in her hand, yet he could see that it was the goose-girl, whom he had seen before in the house of the Old Woman.

"Oho," cried he, "there she comes, and if I once get hold of one of the Witches, the other shall not escape me!"

But how astonished he was, when she went to the well, took off the skin and washed herself. Her golden hair fell down all about her, and she was more beautiful than any one whom he had ever seen in the whole world. He hardly dared to breathe, but stretched his head as far forward through the leaves as he dared, and stared at her. Either he bent over too far, or whatever the cause might be, the bough suddenly cracked, and that very moment the maiden slipped into the skin, sprang away like a roe, and as the moon was suddenly covered, disappeared from his eyes.

Hardly had she disappeared, before the Count descended from the tree, and hastened after her with nimble steps. He had not gone far before he saw, in the twilight, two figures coming over the meadow. It was the King and Queen, who had perceived from a distance the light shining in the Old Woman's little house, and were going to it.

The Count told them what wonderful thing he had seen by the well, and they did not doubt but that she was their lost daughter. They walked onward full of joy, and soon came to the little house. The geese were sitting all round it, and had thrust their heads under their wings and were sleeping, and not one of them moved.

The King and Queen looked in at the window. The Old Woman was sitting there quietly spinning, nodding her head and never looking round. The room was perfectly clean, as if the little Mist Men, who carry no dust on their feet, lived there. Their daughter, however, they did not see. They gazed at all this for a long time. At last they took heart, and knocked softly at the window.

The Old Woman appeared to have been expecting them. She rose, and called out quite kindly, "Come in,—I know you already."

When they had entered the room, the Old Woman said, "You might have spared yourself the long walk, if you had not three years ago unjustly driven away your child, who is so good and lovable. No harm has come to her. For three years she has had to tend the geese. With them she has learnt no evil, but has preserved her purity of heart. You, however, have been sufficiently punished by the misery in which you have lived."

Then she went to the chamber and called, "Come out, my little Daughter."

Thereupon the door opened, and the Princess stepped out in her silken garments, with her golden hair and her shining eyes, and it was as if an Angel from Heaven had entered.

She went up to her father and mother, fell on their necks and kissed them. There was no help for it, they all had to weep for joy. The young Count stood near them; and when she perceived him, she became as red in the face as a moss-rose, she herself did not know why.

The King said, "My dear Child, I have given away my kingdom, what shall I give thee?"

"She needs nothing," said the Old Woman. "I give her the tears that she has wept on your account. They are precious pearls, finer than those that are found in the sea, and worth more than your whole kingdom, and I give her my little house as payment for her services."

When the Old Woman had said that, she disappeared from their sight. The walls rattled a little, and when the King and

Queen looked round, the little house had changed into a splendid palace, a royal table had been spread, and the servants were running hither and thither.

THE SHOES THAT WERE DANCED TO PIECES

There was once upon a time, a King who had twelve daughters, each one more beautiful than the other. They all slept together in one chamber, in which their beds stood side by side.

Every night, when they were in them, the King locked the door, and bolted it. But in the morning, when he unlocked the door, he saw that their shoes were worn out with dancing, and no one could find out how that had happened.

Then the King caused it to be proclaimed that whosoever could discover where they danced at night, should choose one of them for his wife and be King after his death. But that whosoever came forward and had not discovered it within three days and nights, should forfeit his life.

It was not long before a King's Son presented himself, and offered to undertake the enterprise. He was well received, and in the evening was led into a room adjoining the Princesses' sleeping-chamber. His bed was placed there, and he was to watch where they went and danced. And in order that they might do nothing secretly or go away to some other place, the door of their room was left open.

But the eyelids of the Prince grew heavy as lead, and he fell asleep.

When he awoke in the morning, all twelve had been to the dance, for their shoes were standing there with holes in the soles.

On the second and third nights it fell out just the same, and then his head was struck off without mercy. Many others came after this and undertook the enterprise, but all forfeited their lives.

Now, it came to pass that a poor soldier, who had a wound, and could serve no longer, found himself on the road to the town where the King lived. There he met an Old Woman, who asked him where he was going.

"I hardly know myself," answered he, and added in jest, "I had half a mind to discover where the Princesses danced their shoes into holes, and thus become King."

"That is not so difficult," said the Old Woman, "you must not drink the wine which will be brought to you at night."

With that she gave him a little cloak, and said, "If you put on that, you will be invisible, and then you can steal after the twelve."

When the soldier had received this good advice, he took heart, went to the King, and announced himself as a suitor. He was as well received as the others, and royal garments were put upon him.

He was conducted that evening, at bedtime, into the outer-chamber, and as he was about to go to bed, the eldest came and brought him a cup of wine.

He lay down, but did not drink the wine.

The Twelve Princesses, in their chamber, laughed, and the eldest said, "He, too, might as well have saved his life."

With that they got up, opened wardrobes, presses, cupboards, and brought out pretty dresses; dressed themselves before the mirrors, sprang about, and rejoiced at the prospect of the dance.

Only the youngest said, "I know not how it is. You are very happy, but I feel strange. Some misfortune is certainly about to befall us."

"You are a goose, who are always frightened," said the eldest. "Have you forgotten how many King's Sons have already come here in vain? I had hardly any need to give the soldier a sleeping-draught. In any case, the clown would not have awakened."

When they were all ready, the eldest then went to her bed and tapped it.

It immediately sank into the earth; and one after the other they descended through the opening, the eldest going first.

The soldier, who had watched everything, tarried no longer, put on his little cloak, and went down last with the youngest. Half-way down the steps, he just trod a little on her dress.

She was terrified at that, and cried out, "What is that? who is pulling at my dress?"

"Don't be so silly!" said the eldest, "you have caught it on a nail."

Then they went all the way down, and when they were at the bottom, they were standing in a wonderfully pretty avenue of trees, all the leaves of which were of silver, and shone and glistened. The soldier thought, "I must carry a token away with me," and broke off a twig from one of them, on which the tree cracked with a loud report.

The youngest cried out again, "Something is wrong, did you hear the crack?"

But the eldest said, "It is a gun fired for joy, because we have got rid of our Prince so quickly."

After that they came into an avenue where all the leaves were of gold, and lastly into a third where they were of bright diamonds. He broke off a twig from each, which made such a crack each time that the youngest started back in terror, but the eldest still declared that they were salutes.

They went on and came to a great lake whereon stood twelve little boats, and in every boat sat a handsome Prince, all of whom were waiting for the Twelve Princesses. Each took one of them with him, but the soldier seated himself by the youngest.

Then her Prince said, "I can't tell why the boat is so much heavier to-day. I shall have to row with all my strength, if I am to get it across."

"What should cause that," said the youngest, "but the warm weather? I feel very warm too."

On the opposite side of the lake stood a splendid, brightly-lit castle, from whence resounded the joyous music of trumpets and kettle-drums. They rowed thither, entered, and each Prince danced with the maiden he loved, but the soldier danced with them unseen. And when one of them had a cup of wine in her hand he drank it up, so that the cup was empty when she carried it to her mouth. The youngest was alarmed at this, but the eldest always made her be silent.

They danced there till three o'clock in the morning, when all the shoes were danced into holes, and they were forced to leave off. The Princes rowed them back again over the lake, and this time the soldier seated himself by the eldest. On the shore they took leave of their Princes, and promised to return the following night.

When they reached the stairs, the soldier ran on in front and lay down in his bed, and when the Twelve Princesses had come up slowly and wearily, he was already snoring so loudly that they could all hear him, and they said, "So far as he is concerned, we are safe."

They took off their beautiful dresses, laid them away, put the worn-out shoes under the bed, and lay down. Next morning, the soldier was resolved not to speak, but to watch the wonderful goings on, and that night again went with them. Then everything was done just as it had been done the first time, and they danced until their shoes were worn to pieces. But the third time, he took a cup away with him as a token.

When the hour had arrived for him to give his answer, he took the three twigs and the cup, and went to the King, but the Twelve Princesses stood behind the door, and listened for what he was going to say.

When the King put the question, "Where have my Twelve Daughters danced their shoes to pieces in the night?" he answered, "In an underground castle with Twelve Princes," and related how it had come to pass, and brought out the tokens.

The King then summoned his daughters, and asked them if the soldier had told the truth, and when they saw that they were betrayed, and that falsehood would be of no avail, they were obliged to confess all.

Thereupon the King asked which of them he would have for his wife?

He answered, "I am no longer young, so give me the eldest."

Then the wedding was celebrated on the self-same day, and the kingdom was promised him after the King's death. But the Princes were bewitched for as many days more as they had danced nights with the Twelve.

THE NIX OF THE MILL-POND

There was once upon a time, a miller who lived with his wife in great contentment. They had money and land, and their prosperity increased year by year more and more. But ill-luck comes like a thief in the night, as their wealth had increased so did it again decrease, year by year.

At last the miller could hardly call the mill in which he lived his own. He was in great distress, and when he lay down after his day's work, found no rest, but full of care, tossed about in his bed.

One morning, he rose before daybreak and went out into the open air, thinking that perhaps there his heart might become lighter. As he was stepping over the mill-dam, the first sunbeam was just breaking forth, and he heard a rippling sound in the pond. He turned round and perceived a beautiful woman, rising slowly out of the water. Her long hair, which she was holding off her shoulders with her soft hands, fell down on both sides, and covered her white body.

He saw that she was the Nix of the Mill-pond, and in his fright did not know whether he should run away or stay where he was.

But the Nix made her sweet voice heard, called him by his name, and asked him why he was so sad? The miller was at first struck dumb, but when he heard her speak so kindly, he took heart, and told her how he had formerly lived in wealth and happiness, but that now he was so poor that he did not know what to do.

"Be easy," answered the Nix, "I will make you richer and happier than you have ever been before, only you must promise to give me the young thing which has just been born in your house."

"What else can that be," thought the miller, "but a young puppy or kitten?" and he promised her what she desired.

The Nix descended into the water again, and he hurried back to his mill, consoled and in good spirits. He had not yet reached it, when the maid-servant came out of the house, and cried to him to rejoice, for his wife had a little boy. The miller stood as if struck by lightning. He saw very well that the cunning Nix had been aware of it, and had cheated him.

Hanging his head, he went up to his wife's bedside and when she said, "Why do you not rejoice over the fine boy?" he told her what had befallen him, and what kind of a promise he had given to the Nix. "Of what use to me are riches and prosperity?" he added, "if I am to lose my child; but what can I do?"

Even the relations, who had come thither to wish them joy, did not know what to say. In the meantime prosperity again returned to the miller's house. All that he undertook succeeded; it was as if presses and coffers filled themselves of their own accord, and as if money multiplied nightly in the cupboards.

It was not long before his wealth was greater than it had ever been before. But he could not rejoice over it untroubled, the bargain which he had made with the Nix tormented his soul.

Whenever he passed the mill-pond, he feared she might ascend and remind him of his debt. He never let the boy himself go near the water. "Beware," he said to him, "if you do but touch the water, a hand will rise, seize you, and draw you down."

But as year after year went by, and the Nix did not show herself again, the miller began to feel at ease. The boy grew up to be a youth and was apprenticed to a huntsman. When he had learnt everything, and had become an excellent huntsman, the lord of the village took him into his service. In the village lived a beautiful and true-hearted maiden, who pleased the huntsman.

When his master perceived that, he gave him a little house, the two were married, lived peacefully and happily, and loved each other with all their hearts.

One day, the huntsman was chasing a roe. And when the animal turned aside from the forest into the open country, he pursued it and at last shot it. He did not notice that he was now in the neighborhood of the dangerous mill-pond, and went, after he had disembowelled the stag, to the water, in order to wash his blood-stained hands.

Scarcely, however, had he dipped them in than the Nix ascended, smilingly wound her dripping arms around him, and drew him quickly down under the waves, which closed over him.

When it was evening, and the huntsman did not return home, his wife grew alarmed. She went out to seek him, and as he had often told her that he had to be on his guard against the snares of the Nix, and dared not venture into the neighborhood of the mill-pond, she already suspected what had happened. She hastened to the water, and when she found his hunting-pouch lying on the shore, she could no longer have any doubt of the misfortune.

Lamenting her sorrow, and wringing her hands, she called on her beloved by name, but in vain. She hurried across to the other side of the pond, and called him anew. She reviled the Nix with harsh words, but no answer followed. The surface of the water remained calm, only the crescent moon stared steadily back at her. The poor woman did not leave the pond. With hasty steps, she paced round and round it, without resting a moment, sometimes in silence, sometimes uttering a loud cry, sometimes softly sobbing. At last her strength came to an end, she sank down to the ground and fell into a heavy sleep.

Presently a dream took possession of her. She was anxiously climbing upward between great masses of rock. Thorns and briars caught her feet, the rain beat in her face, and the wind tossed her long hair about. When she had reached the summit, quite a different sight presented itself to her. The sky was blue, the air soft, the ground sloped gently downward, and on a green meadow, gay with flowers of every color, stood a pretty cottage.

She went up to it and opened the door. There sat an Old Woman with white hair, who beckoned to her kindly.

At that very moment, the poor woman awoke, day had already dawned, and she at once resolved to act in accordance with her dream. She laboriously climbed the mountain. Everything was exactly as she had seen it in the night. The Old Woman received her kindly, and pointed out a chair on which she might sit. "You must have met with a misfortune," she said, "since you have sought out my lonely cottage."

With tears, the woman related what had befallen her.

"Be comforted," said the Old Woman, "I will help you. Here is a Golden Comb for you. Tarry till the full moon has risen, then go to the mill-pond, seat yourself on the shore, and comb your long black hair with this comb. When you have done, lay it down on the bank, and you will see what will happen."

The woman returned home, but the time till the full moon came, passed slowly. At last the shining disc appeared in the heavens, then she went out to the mill-pond, sat down and combed her long black hair with the Golden Comb. When she had finished, she laid it down at the water's edge.

It was not long before there was a movement in the depths, a wave rose, rolled to the shore, and bore the comb away with it.

In not more than the time necessary for the comb to sink to the bottom, the surface of the water parted, and the head of the huntsman arose. He did not speak, but looked at his wife with sorrowful glances. At the same instant, a second wave came rushing up, and covered the man's head. All had vanished, the mill-pond lay peaceful as before, and nothing but the face of the full moon shone on it.

Full of sorrow, the woman went back, but again the dream showed her the cottage of the Old Woman. Next morning, she again set out and complained of her woes to the Wise Woman.

SHE COMBED HER LONG BLACK HAIR

The Old Woman gave her a Golden Flute, and said, "Tarry till the full moon comes again, then take this flute. Play a beautiful air on it, and when you have finished, lay it on the sand. Then you will see what will happen."

The wife did as the old woman told her. No sooner was the flute lying on the sand, than there was a stirring in the depths, and a wave rushed up and bore the flute away with it.

Immediately afterward the water parted, and not only the head of the man, but half of his body also arose. He stretched out his arms longingly toward her. But a second wave came up, covered him, and drew him down again.

"Alas, what does it profit me?" said the unhappy woman, "that I should see my beloved, only to lose him again?"

Despair filled her heart anew, but the dream led her a third time to the house of the Old Woman. She sat out, and the Wise Woman gave her a Golden Spinning-Wheel, consoled her and said, "All is not yet fulfilled, tarry until the time of the full moon. Then take the spinning-wheel, seat yourself on the shore, and spin the spool full. When you have done that, place the spinning-wheel near the water, and you will see what will happen."

The woman obeyed all she said exactly. As soon as the full moon showed itself, she carried the Golden Spinning-Wheel to the shore, and spun industriously until the flax came to an end, and the spool was quite filled with the threads. No sooner was the wheel standing on the shore than there was a more violent movement than before in the depths of the pond, and a mighty wave rushed up, and bore the wheel away with it.

Immediately the head and the whole body of the man rose into the air, in a water-spout. He quickly sprang to the shore, caught his wife by the hand and fled.

But they had scarcely gone a very little distance, when the whole pond rose with a frightful roar, and streamed out over the open country. The fugitives already saw death before their eyes, when the woman in her terror implored the help of the Old Woman, and in an instant they were transformed, she into a Toad, he into a Frog.

The flood which had overtaken them could not destroy them, but it tore them apart and carried them far away.

When the water had dispersed and they both touched dry land again, they regained their human form, but neither knew where the other was. They found themselves among strange people, who did not know their native land. High mountains and deep valleys lay between them. In order to keep themselves alive, they were both obliged to tend sheep.

For many long years, they drove their flocks through field and forest and were full of sorrow and longing. When spring had once more broken forth on the earth, one day they both went out with their flocks, and as chance would have it, they drew near each other. They met in a valley, but did not recognize each other. Yet they rejoiced that they were no longer so lonely. Henceforth they every day drove their flocks to the same place. They did not speak much, but they felt comforted.

One evening when the full moon was shining in the sky, and the sheep were already at rest, the shepherd pulled the flute out of his pocket, and played on it a beautiful but sorrowful air. When he had finished, he saw that the shepherdess was weeping bitterly.

"Why are you weeping?" he asked.

"Alas," answered she, "thus shone the full moon when I played this air on the flute for the last time, and the head of my beloved rose out of the water."

He looked at her, and it seemed as if a veil fell from his eyes, and he recognized his dear wife. And when she looked at him, and the moon shone in his face she knew him also. They embraced and kissed each other, and no one need ask if they were happy.

THE LITTLE HOUSE IN THE WOOD

A poor woodcutter lived with his wife and three daughters in a little hut on the edge of a lonely wood. One morning as he was about to go to his work, he said to his wife, "Let my dinner be brought into the wood to me by my eldest daughter, or I shall never get my work done. And in order that she may not miss her way," he added, "I will take a bag of millet with me and strew the seeds on the path."

When, therefore, the sun was just above the centre of the wood, the girl set out on her way with a bowl of soup. But the field-sparrows, and wood-sparrows, larks and finches, blackbirds and siskins had picked up the millet long before, and the girl could not find the track. Then trusting to chance, she went on and on, until the sun sank and night began to fall. The trees rustled in the darkness, the owls hooted, and she began to be afraid.

Then in the distance she perceived a light which glimmered between the trees. "There ought to be some people living there, who can take me in for the night," thought she, and went up to the light. It was not long before she came to a house the windows of which were all lighted up.

She knocked, and a rough voice from the inside cried, "Come in."

The girl stepped into the dark entrance, and knocked at the door of the room. "Just come in," cried the voice.

And when she opened the door, an old gray-haired man was sitting at the table, supporting his face with both hands, and his white beard fell down over the table almost as far as the ground. By the stove lay three animals, a hen, a cock, and a brindled cow.

The girl told her story to the Old Man, and begged for shelter for the night. The man said:

"Pretty little Hen,
Pretty little Cock,
And pretty brindled Cow,
What say ye all now?"

"*Duks,*" answered the animals, and that must have meant, "We are willing," for the Old Man said, "Here you shall have shelter and food. Go to the fire, and cook us our supper."

The girl found in the kitchen abundance of everything and cooked a good supper, but had no thought of the animals. She carried the full dishes to the table, seated herself by the gray-haired man, ate and satisfied her hunger.

When she had had enough, she said, "But now I am tired. Where is there a bed in which I can lie down, and sleep?" The animals replied:

"Thou hast eaten with him,
Thou hast drunk with him,
Thou hast had no thought for us,
So find out for thyself where thou canst pass the night."

Then said the Old Man, "Just go up-stairs, and you will find a room with two beds. Shake them up, and put white linen on them, and then I, too, will come and lie down to sleep."

The girl went up, and when she had shaken the beds and put clean sheets on, she lay down in one of them without waiting any longer for the Old Man.

After some time, however, the gray-haired man came, took his candle, looked at the girl and shook his head. When he saw that she had fallen into a sound sleep, he opened a trap-door, and let her down into the cellar.

Late at night, the woodcutter came home, and reproached his wife for leaving him to hunger all day. "It is not my fault," she replied, "the girl went out with your dinner, and must have lost herself, but she is sure to come back to-morrow."

The woodcutter, however, arose before dawn to go into the wood, and requested that the second daughter should take him his dinner that day. "I will take a bag with lentils," said he; "the seeds are larger than millet. The girl will see them better, and can't lose her way."

At dinner-time, therefore, the girl took out the food, but the lentils had disappeared. The birds of the wood had picked them up as they had done the day before, and had left none.

The girl wandered about in the wood until night, and then she too reached the house of the Old Man, was told to go in, and begged for food and a bed. The man with the white beard again asked the animals:

"Pretty little Hen,
Pretty little Cock,
And pretty brindled Cow,
What say ye all now?"

The animals again replied "*Duks*." And everything happened just as it had happened the day before. The girl cooked a good meal, ate and drank with the Old Man, and did not concern herself about the animals, and when she inquired about her bed, they answered:

"Thou hast eaten with him,
Thou hast drunk with him,
Thou hast had, no thought for us,
So find out for thyself where thou canst pass the night."

When she was asleep the Old Man came, looked at her, shook his head, and let her down into the cellar.

On the third morning, the woodcutter said to his wife, "Send our youngest child out with my dinner to-day, she has always been good and obedient, and will stay in the right path, and not run about after every wild bumblebee, as her sisters did."

The mother did not want to do it, and said, "Am I to lose my dearest child, as well?"

"Have no fear," he replied, "the girl will not go astray; she is too prudent and sensible. Besides, I will take some peas with me, and strew them about. They are still larger than lentils, and will show her the way."

But when the girl went out with her basket on her arm, the wood-pigeons had already got all the peas in their crops, and she did not know which way to turn. She was full of sorrow and never ceased to think how hungry her father would be, and how her good mother would grieve, if she did not return home.

At length, when it grew dark, she saw the light and came to the house in the wood. She begged quite prettily to be allowed to spend the night there. And the man with the white beard once more asked his animals:

"Pretty little Hen,
Pretty little Cock,
And pretty brindled Cow,
What say ye all now?"

"*Duks*," said they. Then the girl went to the stove where the animals were lying, and petted the cock and hen, and stroked their smooth feathers with her hand, and caressed the brindled cow between her horns.

And when, in obedience to the Old Man's orders, she had made ready some good soup, and the bowl was placed upon the table, she said, "Am I to eat as much as I want, and the good animals to have nothing? Outside is food in plenty, I will look after them first."

So she went and brought some barley and strewed it for the cock and hen, and a whole armful of sweet-smelling hay for the cow. "I hope you will like it, dear Animals," said she, "and you shall have a refreshing draught in case you are thirsty."

Then she fetched in a bucketful of water, and the cock and hen jumped on to the edge of it and dipped their beaks in. Then held up their heads as the birds do when they drink, and the brindled cow also took a hearty draught.

When the animals were fed, the girl seated herself at the table by the Old Man, and ate what he had left. It was not long before the cock and the hen began to thrust their heads beneath their wings, and the eyes of the cow likewise began to blink. Then said the girl, "Ought we not to go to bed?"

"Pretty little Hen,
Pretty little Cock,
And pretty brindled Cow,
What say ye all now?"

The animals answered "*Duks*."

"Thou hast eaten with us,
Thou hast drunk with us,
Thou hast had kind thought for all of us,

We wish thee good-night."

Then the girl went up-stairs, shook the feather-beds, and laid clean sheets on them. And when she had done it the Old Man came and lay down on one of the beds, and his white beard reached down to his feet. The girl lay down on the other, said her prayers, and fell asleep.

She slept quietly till midnight, and then there was such a noise in the house that she awoke. There was a sound of cracking and splitting in every corner. The doors sprang open, and beat against the walls. The beams groaned as if they were being torn out of their joints. It seemed as if the staircase were falling down. And at length there was a crash as if the entire roof had fallen in.

As, however, all grew quiet once more, and the girl was not hurt, she stayed quietly lying where she was, and fell asleep again. But when she woke up in the morning with the brilliancy of the sunshine, what did her eyes behold?

She was lying in a vast hall, and everything around her shone with royal splendor. On the walls, golden flowers grew up on a ground of green silk. The bed was of ivory, and the canopy of red velvet, and on a chair close by, was a pair of shoes embroidered with pearls.

The girl believed that she was in a dream, but three richly clad attendants came in, and asked what orders she would like to give?

"If you will go," she replied, "I will get up at once and make ready some soup for the Old Man, and then I will feed the pretty little hen, and the cock, and the beautiful brindled cow."

She thought the Old Man was up already, and looked round at his bed. He, however, was not lying in it, but a stranger.

And while she was looking at him, and becoming aware that he was young and handsome, he awoke, sat up in bed, and said, "I am a King's Son, and was enchanted by a wicked Witch, and made to live in this wood, as an old gray-haired man. No one was allowed to be with me but my three attendants in the form of a cock, a hen, and a brindled cow. The spell was not to be broken until a girl came to us, whose heart was so good that she showed herself full of love, not only toward mankind, but toward animals —and that you have done, and by you, at midnight, we were set free, and the old house in the wood was changed back again into my royal palace."

And when they had arisen, the King's Son ordered the three attendants to set out and fetch the father and mother of the girl to the marriage feast.

"But where are my two sisters?" inquired the girl.

"I have locked them in the cellar, and to-morrow they shall be led into the wood, and shall live as servants to a charcoal-burner, until they have grown kinder, and do not leave poor animals to suffer hunger."

MAID MALEEN

There was once a King who had a son who asked in marriage the daughter of a mighty King. She was called Maid Maleen, and was very beautiful. As her father wished to give her to another, the Prince was rejected.

But since they both loved each other with all their hearts, they would not give each other up, and Maid Maleen said to her father, "I can and will take no other for my husband."

Then the King flew into a passion, and ordered a dark tower to be built, into which no ray of sunlight or moonlight should enter. When it was finished, he said, "Therein shall you be imprisoned for seven years, and then I will come and see if your perverse spirit is broken."

Meat and drink for the seven years were carried into the tower; and then she and her waiting-woman were led into it and walled up, and thus cut off from the sky and from the earth. There they sat in the darkness, and knew not when day or night began. The King's Son often went round and round the tower, and called their names, but no sound from without pierced through the thick walls. What else could they do but lament and complain?

Meanwhile, the time passed, and by the small amount of food and drink left they knew that the seven years were coming to an end. They thought the moment of their deliverance was come. But no stroke of the hammer was heard, no stone fell out of the wall, and it seemed to Maid Maleen that her father had forgotten her. As they had food for only a short time longer, and saw a miserable death awaiting them, Maid Maleen said, "We must try our last chance, and see if we can break through the wall."

She took the bread-knife, and picked and bored at the mortar of a stone, and when she was tired, the waiting-maid took her turn. With great labor they succeeded in getting out one stone, then a second, and third. And when three days were over, the first ray of light fell on their darkness, and at last the opening was so large that they could look out.

The sky was blue, and a fresh breeze played on their faces; but how melancholy everything looked all around! Her father's castle lay in ruins, the town and the villages were, so far as could be seen, destroyed by fire, the fields far and wide laid to waste, and no human being was visible.

When the opening in the wall was large enough for them to slip through, the waiting-maid sprang down first, and then Maid Maleen followed. But where were they to go? The enemy had ravaged the whole kingdom, driven away the King, and slain all the inhabitants. They wandered forth to seek another country, but nowhere did they find a shelter, or a human being to give them a mouthful of bread. Their need was so great that they were forced to appease their hunger with nettle-plants.

When, after long journeying, they came into another country, they tried to get work everywhere. But wherever they knocked they were turned away, and no one would have pity on them.

At last they arrived in a large city and went to the royal palace. There also they were ordered to go away, but at last the cook said that they might stay in the kitchen and be scullions.

The King's Son in whose kingdom they were, was, however, the very man who had been betrothed to Maid Maleen. His father had chosen another Bride for him, whose face was as ugly as her heart was wicked. The wedding was fixed, and the girl had already arrived. Because of her great ugliness, however, she shut herself in her room, and allowed no one to see her, and Maid Maleen had to take her her meals from the kitchen.

When the day came for the Bride and the Bridegroom to go to church, she was ashamed of her ugliness, and afraid that if she showed herself in the streets, she would be mocked and laughed at by the people. Then said she to Maid Maleen, "A great piece of luck has befallen you. I have sprained my foot, and cannot walk through the streets. You shall put on my wedding-clothes and take my place. A greater honor than that you cannot have!"

Maid Maleen, however, refused it, and said, "I wish for no honor which is not suitable for me."

It was in vain, too, that the Bride offered her gold. At last she said angrily, "If you do not obey me, it shall cost you your life. I have but to speak the word, and your head will lie at your feet."

Then she was forced to obey, and put on the Bride's magnificent clothes and all her jewels. When she entered the royal hall, every one was amazed at her great beauty, and the King said to his son, "This is the Bride whom I have chosen for you, and whom you must lead to church."

The Bridegroom was astonished, and thought, "She is like my Maid Maleen, and I should believe that it was she herself, but she has long been shut up in the tower or dead."

He took her by the hand and led her to church. On the way was a nettle-plant, and she said:

"Nettle-plant, Nettle-plant,
Nettle-plant so small!
What are you doing here,
Alone by the wall?
I have the time known,
When unroasted, unboiled,
I ate thee alone!"

THE PRINCE TOOK HER BY THE HAND AND LED HER TO CHURCH

"What are you saying?" asked the King's Son.

"Nothing," she replied, "I was only thinking of Maid Maleen."

He was surprised that she knew about her, but kept silence. When they came to the foot-plank into the churchyard, she said:

"Foot-bridge, break not,
I am not the true Bride."

"What are you saying there?" asked the King's Son.

"Nothing," she replied, "I was only thinking of Maid Maleen."

When they came to the church-door, she said once more:

"Church-door, break not,
I am not the true Bride."

"What are you saying there?" asked he.

"Ah," she answered, "I was only thinking of Maid Maleen."

Then he took out a precious chain, put it round her neck, and fastened the clasp. Thereupon they entered the church, and the priest joined their hands together before the altar, and married them. He led her home but she did not speak a single word the whole way.

When they got back to the royal palace, she hurried into the Bride's chamber, put off the magnificent clothes and the jewels, dressed herself in her gray gown, and kept nothing but the jewel on her neck, which she had received from the Bridegroom.

When the night came, and the Bride was to be led into the apartment of the King's Son, she let her veil fall over her face, that he might not observe the deception.

As soon as every one had gone away, he said to her, "What did you say to the nettle-plant which was growing by the wayside?"

"To which nettle-plant?" asked she; "I don't talk to nettle-plants."

"If you did not do it, then you are not the true Bride," said he.

So she bethought herself, and said:

"I must go my maid to see,
Who keeps my secret thoughts for me."

She went out and sought Maid Maleen. "Girl, what have you been saying to the nettle?"

"I said nothing but:

"Nettle-plant, Nettle-plant,
Nettle-plant so small!
What are you doing here,
Alone by the wall?
I have the time known,
When unroasted, unboiled,
I ate thee alone!"

The Bride ran back into the chamber, and said, "I know now what I said to the nettle," and she repeated the words which she had just heard.

"But what did you say to the foot-bridge when we went over it?" asked the King's Son.

"To the foot-bridge?" she answered. "I don't talk to foot-bridges."

"Then you are not the true Bride."

She again said:

"I must go my maid to see,

Who keeps my secret thoughts for me,"

and ran out and found Maid Maleen. "Girl, what did you say to the foot-bridge?"

"I said nothing but:

"*Foot-bridge, break not,*
I am not the true Bride."

"That costs you your life!" cried the Bride, but she hurried into the room, and said, "I know now what I said to the foot-bridge," and she repeated the words.

"But what did you say to the church-door?"

"To the church-door?" she replied; "I don't talk to church-doors."

"Then you are not the true Bride."

She went out and found Maid Maleen, and said, "Girl, what did you say to the church-door?"

"I said nothing but:

"*Church-door, break not,*
I am not the true Bride."

"That will break your neck for you!" cried the Bride, and flew into a terrible passion, but she hastened back into the room, and said, "I know now what I said to the church-door," and she repeated the words.

"But where have you the jewel which I gave you at the church-door?"

"What jewel?" she answered; "you did not give me any jewel."

"I myself put it round your neck, and I myself fastened it. If you do not know that, you are not the true Bride."

He drew the veil from her face, and when he saw her ugliness, he sprang back terrified, and said, "How come you here? Who are you?"

"I am your betrothed Bride, but because I feared lest the people should mock me when they saw me out of doors, I commanded the scullery-maid to dress herself in my clothes, and to go to church instead of me."

"Where is the girl?" said he; "I want to see her, go and bring her here."

She went out and told the servants that the scullery-maid was an impostor, and that they must take her out into the courtyard and strike off her head.

The servants laid hold of Maid Maleen and wanted to drag her out, but she screamed so loudly for help, that the King's Son heard her voice, hurried out of his chamber and ordered them to set the maiden free.

Lights were brought, and then he saw on her neck the gold chain which he had given her at the church-door.

"You are the true Bride," said he, "who went with me to church. Come with me now to my room."

When they were both alone, he said, "On the way to the church you did name Maid Maleen, who was my betrothed Bride. If I could believe it possible, I should think she was standing before me—you are like her in every respect."

She answered, "I am Maid Maleen, who for your sake was imprisoned seven years in the darkness, who suffered hunger and thirst, and has lived so long in want and poverty. To-day, however, the sun is shining on me once more. I was married to you in the church, and I am your lawful wife."

Then they kissed each other, and were happy all the days of their lives.

The false Bride was rewarded for what she had done by having her head cut off.

The tower in which Maid Maleen had been imprisoned remained standing for a long time, and when the children passed by it, they sang:

"Kling, klang, gloria.
Who sits within this tower?
A King's Daughter, she sits within,
A sight of her I cannot win,
The wall it will not break,
The stone cannot be pierced.
Little Hans, with your coat so gay,
Follow me, follow me, fast as you may."

THE END

Transcriber's Notes

Punctuation, hyphenation, and spelling were made consistent when a predominant preference was found in this book; otherwise they were not changed.
Simple typographical errors were corrected; ambiguous hyphens at the ends of lines were retained.

Printed in Great Britain
by Amazon

22235963R00195